Brighton Beach

A Kurtz and Barent Mystery

Also by Robert I. Katz

Edward Maret: A Novel of the Future

The Cannibal's Feast

The Kurtz and Barent Mystery Series:
Surgical Risk
The Anatomy Lesson
Seizure
The Chairmen

The Chronicles of the Second Interstellar Empire of
Mankind:
The Game Players of Meridien
The City of Ashes
The Empire of Dust
The Empire of Ruin
The Well of Time (Forthcoming)

Brighton Beach

A Kurtz and Barent Mystery

By

Robert I. Katz

Brighton Beach

A Kurtz and Barent Mystery

Acknowledgements

Thanks as always to Lynn and Erica for their assistance in preparing this manuscript, and a special thanks to Philip M. Marshall, former prosecuting attorney, defense attorney and judge of the City Court of Buffalo, NY, for his critique regarding the accuracy of legal aspects and police procedures referred to in this book.

Cast of Characters (in order of appearance)

Arnaldo Figueroa: New York City detective, working undercover.

Three hoodlums trailed by Arnaldo Figueroa: Members of a Russian criminal organization.

Richard Kurtz: Surgeon, on the staff of Easton Medical Center and Staunton College of Medicine in New York City, also working part-time as a police surgeon for the NYPD. Kurtz is ex-army, has a black belt in taekwondo and can handle himself in a fight.

Drew Johnson: Fifth year surgery resident.

Linda Rodriguez: Surgical intern.

Lew Barent: New York City homicide detective, Kurtz' friend.

Harry Moran: New York City homicide detective, Barent's frequent partner.

Allen Wong: Neurosurgeon.

Iosif Kozlov: Former Colonel in the Intelligence Directorate of the Soviet Union, one of three Russian mob bosses in Brooklyn.

Grigory Mazlov: Iosif Kozlov's principal lieutenant.

Vinnie Steinberg: Anesthesiologist.

Jeffrey McDonald: Victim of a motor vehicle accident, Kurtz' patient.

Audrey Schaeffer: Jeffrey McDonald's girlfriend.

Christy McDonald: Jeffrey McDonald's ex-wife.

Mahendra Patel: Anesthesiologist.

Steve Ryan: Plastic surgeon.

Donna Ryan (née Petrovich): Steve Ryan's wife, an investment banker and a childhood friend of Lenore Kurtz.

Lydia James: Patient operated on by Steve Ryan, with Kurtz' assistance.

Lenore Kurtz (née Brinkman): Kurtz' wife, a graphic artist.

Juan Moreno: Colombian mob boss in New York.

Hector Montillo: Juan Moreno's first victim.

Betty Barent: Lew Barent's wife.

Mitchell Price: Stockbroker and murder victim.

Elias Levin and Walter Stockton: Surgeons.

Gerald Cox: Co-worker of Mitchell Price.

Javier Garcia: Mexican mob boss in New York.

Sergei Ostrovsky: Former Major in The Intelligence Directorate of the Soviet Union, one of three Russian mob bosses in Brooklyn.

Bill Werth: Psychiatrist and a friend of Kurtz.

Stephanie Myers, Brad Jenkins, Bert Armstrong: Sick or injured cops, all patients of Kurtz.

Cynthia Figueroa: Arnaldo Figueroa's wife.

The rabbi who marries Kurtz and Lenore.

Kurtz' father and Lisa, his guest, at Kurtz and Lenore's wedding.

David Chao: Surgeon, Kurtz' partner.

Carrie Owens: Emergency Room physician, David Chao's fiancée.

Jordan Chance: Martial artist.

Joe Ressler: Medical intensivist.

Steven Hayward, Howard Mather and Douglas Jefferson: Friends of Jeffrey McDonald.

Marilyn Hayward: Steven Hayward's wife.

Mrs. Velasquez: Steven Hayward's cleaning lady.

Jason Klein: Co-owner and Manager of Kingsford Household Supply, Steven Hayward's boss.

Sal Marino: Co-owner of Kingsford Household Supply, Steven Hayward's cousin.

Cindy Daniels: Assistant Manager of Kingsford Household Supply.

Esther Brinkman: Lenore's mother, a former housewife currently employed in a real estate agency.

Stanley Brinkman: Lenore's father.

Sylvia Hersch: Esther Brinkman's cousin, the owner of the real estate agency where Esther Brinkman is employed.

Milton Hersch: Husband of Sylvia Hersch.

Moishe and Natalie Hale, and their son: Guests of Esther and Stanley Brinkman.

Esteban Martinez: Friend and associate of Javier Garcia.

Croft: Pimp and police informant.

Regina: Croft's fiancée.

Christine Morales: Owner of an exclusive and upscale escort agency.

Joachim: Argentine businessman, client of Christine Morales.

Reginald Rinear: Wealthy commodities broker, client of Christine Morales.

Everett Johns: Reginald Rinear's lawyer.

An anonymous attempted murderer.

Father Robert Kamenov: Orthodox Catholic priest, well-known and highly respected in the Russian community in Brooklyn.

Alexei Rugov: Veteran of the Soviet Security Services, one of three Russian mob bosses in Brooklyn.

Gregory Samms, Gene Bauer and Albert Morelli: Sick or injured cops, all patients of Kurtz.

Vasily Lukin: Donna Ryan's cousin, a principal lieutenant of Alexei Rugov.

Ted Weiss: Senior Assistant District Attorney.

James: Reginald Rinear's butler.

Andrew Fox: Partner of Steven Hayward.

Ilya Sokolov: Sergei Ostrovsky's principal lieutenant.

Sean Brody: Chairman of the Department of Surgery at Staunton College of Medicine.

Arkady Lukin: Donna Ryan's cousin and Vasily Lukin's brother, a financial analyst.

Olga and Natasha Lukin: Vasily and Arkady Lukin's younger sisters.

Alan Saunders: Drug addict.

Alicia: Alan Saunder's girlfriend.

Reggie Johnson: Friend of Alan Saunders, host of parties where drugs are bought and sold.

A group of anonymous gunmen.

Joe Danowski: Cop on the Narcotics Squad of the NYPD.

Alejandro Gonzales: Member of Javier Garcia's criminal organization.

Mrs. Schapiro: Kurtz' secretary.

Abner Goodell: Lawyer.

Abby Blake: Junior assistant District Attorney.

Ilya and Dimitri Fedorov: Brothers who work in a bakery specializing in Russian pastries, owned by Masha Fedorov, their aunt, petty criminals.

Celia Bauman: Gerald Cox' secretary.

Stephanie Rogers: School acquaintance of Celia Bauman.

James Reilly: Lawyer.

Dimitri Petrovich: Donna Ryan's father, owner of an expensive and highly regarded restaurant that specializes in Russian cuisine.

Jason Blair: Internal Affairs investigator with the NYPD.

Rodrigo Diaz: Member of a Southwest gang with ties to Javier Garcia's organization.

Sebastian: Colleague of Rodrigo Diaz.

Anonymous Gang Member: kidnapped, tortured and murdered by Rodrigo Diaz and his colleague, Sebastian.

Anita Lopez: Waitress.

Irina Zharkov and Natasha Baranov: Alexei Rugov's two favorite mistresses.

Timur Beshimov: Russian assassin.

Jerry Conlon: Cop, Bert Armstrong's partner.

Alice Boyer: Cop, Union Representative.

Eric Cantrell: Lawyer.

Jeremiah Phelps: Investment banker and Senior Partner in the firm of Hotchkiss and Phelps, Donna Ryan's employer.

Ken Fischel, Dave Mahoney and Beverly Levinson: Junior partners in the firm of Hotchkiss and Phelps.

Nika Fedorov: Ilya and Dimitri Fedorov's mother.

Olga Lukin: Arkady and Vasily Lukin's mother.

Chapter 1

During the course of a long and successful career as an undercover cop, Arnaldo Figueroa had developed a talent for passing unnoticed. He was average height, with an average face, thin but not unusually so. He looked nothing like an athlete, though he was, in fact, endowed with superior eye-hand coordination and excellent reflexes and had wrestled in high school and then in college.

He had trailed the three men through the neighborhood at night. The three walked as if they owned the place, looking neither to the left nor the right. Though they were not on their own turf, they seemed afraid of nothing. The three passed four small groups of pedestrians, all of whom stepped to the side and hurried by without looking at their faces.

Wise, Arnaldo Figueroa thought. These were not men whose attention you wanted to attract. Not at all.

The three were big, white and probably Russian. Figueroa regarded the three men as an anomaly. They had no business here...unless, of course, they did have business here, which would be bad news for the denizens of New York City.

Figueroa, whose business it was to keep track of other peoples' business, was curious. He wasn't crazy, though. He followed the three at a discreet distance, flitting from the cover of a tree to a parked van to a screen of bushes, from corner to corner, staying far back. Unnoticed. Hopefully.

The three men stopped in front of a brownstone that was undergoing renovation. Scaffolding covered the sides and a sign reading, "Construction Zone: Keep Out" was displayed in front. The door was boarded up, the building dark and seemingly empty.

One of the three knocked on the door. The door opened. A short, thin man looked at them, puffed up his cheeks and gave an abrupt nod. The three men walked inside. None of them had said a word.

Expected, then. Arnaldo Figueroa shook his head and sighed. This was bad. Nobody scheduled legitimate meetings in an abandoned building.

Turning on his heel, he scurried away. The blare of a car horn a block or so over saved his life. He jerked his head up at the sudden sound and neither heard nor felt the bullet that was intended to scramble his brain.

The car horn was the last thing he would remember for a long, long time.

Richard Kurtz held out his hand. "Sponge," he said.

The nurse handed him a pair of forceps with a folded four-by-four held in the tip. He dabbed at the abdominal wall, decided that the oozing was insufficient to cause any problems, and proceeded to run the bowel. Ten centimeters above the cecum, he found what he was looking for: a hard, solid mass.

Kurtz' fingers moved almost without thinking. He had performed this operation a hundred times before. The mass was isolated and the patient had been adequately prepped, having had an asymptomatic tumor found on routine colonoscopy a couple of weeks prior. The colonoscopist had taken multiple specimens and so far as could be determined by biopsy, the tumor had not spread.

Unfortunately, however, the tumor had spread. Once the abdomen was opened, it could be seen that the liver was infested with multiple, tiny nodules. It was a surprise, since the patient's liver functions were normal and MRI showed nothing suspicious. Kurtz sighed.

The patient was forty-seven years old, young for colon cancer, but it ran in his family, which was why he had elected to have the colonoscopy at such a relatively young age. Not young enough, as it turned out.

"Fuck," Kurtz muttered.

Drew Johnson, the fifth-year assisting on the case, nodded but didn't say a word. There was nothing to say.

Linda Rodriguez, the intern, too inexperienced to know better, said, "How about RFA?"

Drew Johnson rolled his eyes. Radiofrequency ablation was the hot new thing. Like most hot new things, its benefits over the tried and true were hazy and still unproven.

"Too many of them," Kurtz said. "His liver is riddled." He shook his head. "Fuck," he said again.

Might as well do the bowel resection, Kurtz reflected. No reason not to. Chemotherapy, mostly 5-fluorouracil and leucovorin, would probably give him another year or so, and at least he would die without a drainage tube. They took half a dozen punch biopsies of the liver nodules and sent them off to pathology, then Kurtz watched as Johnson clamped the colon above and below the tumor and cut out the offending piece of bowel. Then they waited. Twenty minutes later, pathology called to confirm that the frozen sections of the margins were clear and that the nodules from the liver were indeed the same type of poorly differentiated adenocarcinoma as the mass from the bowel. Once assured that this was the case, Johnson proceeded to stitch the two segments of bowel back together.

Forty minutes later, the patient, awake but sedated, was resting comfortably in the recovery room. Kurtz had already given the family the bad news, a job that he always hated, and was changing in the locker room when the police beeper went off.

He stared at it for a moment, then pushed the small button on the top and scanned the number. It was one that he knew well. He sighed and picked up his phone.

New York City Health and Hospitals/Bellevue, formerly known simply as Bellevue Hospital, was the oldest such public institution in the United States, dating back to 1736. Bellevue had a long and storied history, having been responsible for numerous innovations such as the first city-wide sanitary code in the United States, the first cadaver kidney transplant in the world, the first mitral valve replacement, the first resection of a femoral aneurysm and the establishment of the first nursing school for men. Despite this illustrious history, Bellevue, as a city hospital devoted primarily to the care of those who cannot afford to pay, is today looked down upon by the more elite institutions in the city.

Kurtz, who had unfortunately come to know the place well, did not share this opinion. The care provided by Bellevue, so far as Kurtz' experience went, was generally excellent. Tonight, was no exception.

Lew Barent and Harry Moran met him in the ER. "It's Arnie," Barent said. "Arnie Figueroa."

Kurtz winced. He knew Arnie Figueroa well. "Shit," he said.

"He's been working undercover. We don't know who shot him. It was a residential neighborhood in Williamsburg."

Kurtz by now knew the drill. As a police surgeon with the august rank of "Inspector," his principal job was to oversee the care of injured cops, particularly those injured in the line of duty. In most cases, however, and this case was not an exception, the injured cop was already under the care of perfectly competent physicians who resented having an outsider looking over their shoulder, potentially criticizing the quality of care that they provided and gathering evidence for any professional liability suits that might result from a less than stellar outcome.

Kurtz didn't blame them. His real job, in his own opinion, was to provide a little hand holding, give some reassurance to the other cops and the patient's family that New York City's best was on the case, making certain that everything was being done to the highest standards. Which it was.

As a police surgeon, Kurtz was entitled to come into the OR and observe, which he did as gingerly and unobtrusively as possible. The surgeon, a tall, skinny guy named Allen Wong, didn't even glance at him, his attention focused on the patient's exposed brain. Kurtz couldn't see much of the actual operation, since the surgical field in a neurosurgery case was small and almost entirely obscured by the drapes and the bodies of the surgical team clustered around the field. That was alright. He listened for a half hour or so, gathered enough information to know that the patient was stable and the operation proceeding in as normal a fashion as possible, and made his way back out to the waiting room.

As he entered, the patient's wife, mother-in-law and three kids all looked at him, their eyes filled with desperate hope. They were surrounded by about ten cops, who looked at him with flat, level gazes, clearly expecting the worst.

"It's going well," Kurtz said. "Probably another hour or so until he's out of surgery. He's stable."

Figueroa's wife gave a little sigh and bowed her head over a string of rosary beads. The cops sat back. Kurtz glanced at Barent and Harry Moran, then gave a nod toward the door. The two cops rose to their feet and followed him out.

16

"No way for me to tell how much of his brain is going to be left after this," Kurtz said. "You know that, right?"

Moran winced. Barent looked away. "Yeah," he said.

"The surgeon is Allen Wong. He's good."

Barent grimaced. "We'll see," he said.

"Yeah," Kurtz said. "We'll see."

Iosif Kozlov was angry. He was angry at the three idiots who had allowed themselves to be tailed to the meeting place of his recently acquired associates. He was angry at the supposedly competent sniper who had shot the undercover cop in the head without, somehow or other, killing him. Not that they had known he was a cop, of course. He had been dressed like a bum, which was what his idiotic henchmen had assumed him to be. It wasn't until the news hit the internet in the morning that any of them had put two and two together and realized that they had shot a cop in the head.

Yes, Iosif Kozlov was angry. In the normal course of things, the still breathing cop would have been swiftly carried away and never seen again, his dead body buried in a landfill or ground down into dogfood. In this case, however, a group of six young men passing by had immediately stumbled upon the bleeding cop and called the police. The Colombians had decided that killing an additional six men, some of whom might have been armed for all any of them knew, just to dispose of some random vagrant, would be an inappropriate escalation. The meeting had been abruptly ended, the building evacuated of both their personnel.

He took a deep breath. Calm, he told himself. His primary enforcer and personal bodyguard, Grigory Mazlov, stood to the side. The three idiots stood in front of his desk, their faces blank.

"Why?" Kozlov asked.

One of the men frowned. The two others remained outwardly impassive. The first man cleared his throat. "We didn't see him."

"Did you see anything? Did you look?"

"We did." The first man gave the two others an uncertain glance. "He was good."

The cop probably had been good, Iosif Kozlov conceded. It didn't matter. He and his men were operating in a foreign country, surrounded by enemies. You stayed alert. You were better than the opposition. You had to be. Or you died.

"Hold up your left hand," Iosif Kozlov said. "All of you."

All of them did so, their faces grim. They were sweating. One of them drew a deep breath.

"It remains to be seen if you can redeem yourselves from this failure," Kozlov said. He opened the middle drawer of his desk and pulled out a bolt cutter. He waved it lazily in front of his face, then put it down on the desk and slid it across. All three men stared at it. "Pick it up," Kozlov said.

Slowly, the first man, the one who had spoken, reached out. He picked up the bolt cutter with his right hand.

"Before we go any further," Kozlov said, "I wish you to understand a few things. First, we must be strong." He stopped, leaned back and stared for a moment into space. "I have reason to know that all of you are strong. Second, we must be brave." He smiled. "And I also know that you are brave, but strength and courage are the most basic, the most common attributes that we must possess. We must also be dedicated, to ourselves and to our cause. We must be obedient to those who have been placed above us and we must be loyal to the organization of which we are privileged to be a part. All of these qualities, you are about to demonstrate. In addition, however, there are other qualities that are not only useful, but vital to the work that we are called upon to do. We must be intelligent. We must understand our environment and our world and the requirements of success, and perhaps most of all, we must know ourselves. We must know of what we are capable and we must know our limitations, as soldiers and as men." Iosif Kozlof's lips quirked upward. "You underestimated the enemy. You are allowed to make such a mistake only once. Do you understand?"

Grigory Mazlov remained impassive, watching all three men with hooded eyes. All three nodded their heads. "This is good," Kozlov said gently. "Now go ahead."

Slowly, the first man put the little finger of his left hand between the jaws of the bolt cutter and squeezed the handle.

Iosif Kozlov smiled.

Chapter 2

"Strange," Vinnie Steinberg said.

Kurtz looked up. "What is?"

Steinberg frowned. "This guy's not taking any anesthesia at all."

The comment rolled around the back of Kurtz' brain but at the moment, a small artery in the abdominal wound began to spurt. "Clamp," Kurtz said.

The nurse handed him a clamp and he clicked it tight around the artery. The spurting stopped. Kurtz looked up at Steinberg. "What do you mean?" he said.

"I mean the guy's anesthetized. His vital signs are stable. The BIS monitor is in the teens, but I've got the gas turned down almost to zero."

Kurtz wrinkled his brow. The patient was a middle-aged male named Jeffrey McDonald, who had come into the ER with a ruptured spleen, courtesy of being hit by a car while crossing a street in midtown. A much younger girlfriend had accompanied him but the girlfriend couldn't tell them much about the guy's medical history.

"Maybe you should call his ex-wife," she had reluctantly said.

A good idea. Kurtz had spoken to Christy McDonald on the phone while the ER staff cut off the guy's clothes, started IV's and did the preliminary workup. The patient had stopped breathing at the scene and was already intubated on arrival, the ventilator next to his head pumping a steady stream of oxygen into his lungs.

"He's forty-seven years old," Christy McDonald had said. "He had what I believe they refer to as a 'mid-life crisis.'" Her voice was flat. "You know what that means? Mid-life crisis?"

"I do," Kurtz said.

She went on as if Kurtz had not spoken. "It means that he's not making as much money as he thinks he deserves. It means that his hair is thinning, his waistline is expanding, and he's desperately trying to recapture the triumphs of his lost, lamented youth, not that he was ever such hot stuff back in what he sometimes nostalgically referred to as the 'glory days.'" Christy McDonald sniffed. "It means that he wants a pretty young thing that will look up to him and think he's wonderful because he's so experienced and so worldly and so sophisticated, not that he was *ever* very experienced, worldly or sophisticated. Let's see how long that lasts. Jackass."

This was not exactly what Kurtz had been hoping to hear. "Does he have any medical problems?" he asked.

"Mitral valve prolapse," Christy McDonald said. "He's supposed to take antibiotics if he has any medical procedures. Also, his cholesterol is high."

"Good to know," Kurtz said. "Anything else?"

"No."

"Alright then. Thank you."

Christy McDonald sniffed again and hung up.

The case, all-in-all, was going smoothly, more smoothly than most such cases, at any rate, since a multiple trauma patient often had injuries that were not immediately apparent and the apparent injuries were often immediately life threatening. "The CAT scan of the brain was normal," Kurtz said.

"Yeah," Steinberg said, "but despite a normal CAT scan, he was unconscious at the scene. He wasn't breathing, and now his anesthetic requirement is nil."

Kurtz frowned. "How low is the BIS?"

'BIS' stood for 'bi-spectral index,' a computerized version of an EEG. The BIS monitor recorded brain waves, ran them through an algorithm and produced a number that supposedly correlated to depth of anesthesia. Anything below sixty was supposed to mean adequately anesthetized.

"At the moment, seventeen," Steinberg said. "He doesn't have any head trauma but he was unconscious at the scene and he's not requiring any anesthesia at all. You know what that means…"

Kurtz sighed. "The tox screen will be interesting." The tox screen would be back in an hour or so. The results wouldn't affect the surgery but might help guide the post-op care.

"I imagine it will," Steinberg said. "He's high on something."

And maybe by then the pretty young girlfriend would have a little more to say. Or maybe not.

"It's unusual," Kurtz said.

"But not unheard of," Moran said.

Barent gave a small nod of his head, meant to convey agreement with Moran's declaration and poured his glass full from the pitcher of beer sitting on the table. Both Barent and Moran were off duty and so felt free to enjoy a cold one after work. The bar was an upscale place that served excellent pub style food and an assortment of craft beers on tap. At the moment, they were drinking Captain Lawrence Imperial Stout, at a cool 12% alcohol by weight, not a beer for the faint of heart.

"No," Kurtz conceded. "Certainly not unheard of."

They took a moment to enjoy their food, a blue cheese burger for Kurtz, pastrami on rye for Barent and Moran.

"Any other middle-aged executive types OD'ing that you know of?" Kurtz asked.

Barent glanced at Moran. "Not at the moment," he said.

Moran sighed. "No. Not at the moment," he echoed.

"The tox screen showed low levels of Xanax, for which he has a prescription. Also, trace doses of heroin—nowhere near enough to explain his symptoms, but he's definitely been using. Nothing else has shown up. He slept for a lot longer than would have been expected. He looked and acted like he overdosed on an opioid but the tests don't show it. Aside from that, he admits nothing." Kurtz grimaced. "The girlfriend looked concerned but if she knows anything at all, she's not saying."

Barent squinted at Kurtz. "Isn't telling us this a HIPAA violation?"

"No," Kurtz said. "Reporting of substance abuse is an allowable exception where there is a presumption of an imminent danger, either to the individual involved or the public. Unknown but presumably potent narcotics floating around is certainly an imminent danger."

Barent, who had known this but who occasionally enjoyed pulling Kurtz' leg, merely smiled and sipped his beer. "So why are we here?" Barent asked.

Kurtz shrugged. Truthfully, he wasn't sure why they were here, except that Jeffrey McDonald gave him a bad feeling. "There are a lot of drugs that don't show up on tox screens. There are specialized tests for almost all of them but they're expensive and they aren't run unless there are suspicions." He shrugged again. "The normal tox screen picks up morphine, meperidine and heroin, the most commonly abused narcotics. If he had OD'd on something, it was something else."

"We'll keep an eye out," Barent said.

"Okay," Kurtz said. "Thanks."

Arnaldo Figueroa was doing as well as could be expected, which was not, at this point, saying very much. He was still on the ventilator and still in a barbiturate coma. Barbiturates reduce intracranial pressure, which is almost always elevated after an injury to the brain. Barbiturate coma also reduces brain activity to essentially zero, and in doing so reduces the metabolic demand on the brain by approximately fifty percent. Barbiturate coma, among other therapeutic modalities such as reducing body temperature, has been shown on numerous studies to improve outcome after trauma to the brain.

Arnaldo Figueroa was a cop, and since he was assumed to have suffered his near fatal injury in the line of duty, two other cops in uniform stood guard at the entrance to the ICU at all times.

"How's he doing?" Kurtz asked.

"No change," Allen Wong said. "We'll keep him under for a week. Then we'll see."

Hopefully, with a lot of luck, Arnaldo Figueroa would then wake up. With even more luck, he would recover. Whether he would ever recover enough to return to work, or even be able to walk, talk or go to the bathroom without assistance, was doubtful, but not beyond the realm of possibility.

"Alright," Kurtz said. "Keep us informed if anything changes."

"Will do," Allen Wong said.

"Thanks."

Kurtz' first three cases the next morning were routine: two gallbladders followed by an inguinal hernia. He was finishing up the hernia, letting Linda Rodriguez suture the skin under Drew Johnson's watchful eye, when Mahendra Patel poked his nose into the OR. He gingerly walked up to the table, being careful not to touch the field. Kurtz glanced at him. "What's up, Manny?"

"Can you scrub out?" Patel asked.

Mahendra Patel was the Site Director for the Department of Anesthesiology at Easton. He looked concerned.

"Don't worry about us," Johnson said.

The skin was almost closed, and Johnson and Rodriguez were perfectly capable of finishing the case. "Sure," Kurtz said. He pulled off his gown and gloves, dropped them in the wastebasket and followed Patel out into the hall. Once there, Patel seemed reluctant to speak. His eyes wandered around the scrub sink and the equipment carts lined up against the wall. Kurtz waited. Finally, Patel drew a sigh. "I'm not really supposed to get involved in this way, but could you wander into Room C?"

"Why? What's going on?"

"Steve Ryan is doing what was supposed to be a panniculectomy. It's turned out to be a little more complicated than he thought."

Steve Ryan...Inwardly, Kurtz winced. Steve Ryan was married to Donna Ryan, an old school friend of Lenore. The two couples occasionally socialized. "In what way?"

"The lady is morbidly obese. Turns out it's not exactly a pannus. It's an umbilical hernia. There are loops of bowel all around the thing. Steve seems a little out of his depth."

How delicately Patel put it. Steve Ryan, Kurtz thought, was almost always just a little out of his depth. Steve Ryan was a very unfortunate and all too common phenomenon in the surgical field: a smart, enthusiastic, hard-working, well-meaning guy who loved surgery but had no talent for it whatsoever. Steve Ryan might not be stupid but he was definitely self-deluded. He probably would have made a crackerjack internist but he was, very sad to say, a lousy surgeon. Pity he didn't seem to know it.

Luckily for all, Steve Ryan was a plastic surgeon, not a general surgeon, and as such, his procedures tended to be superficial and rarely invasive, which did not prevent his complication rate from bordering on the unacceptable, but even a good plastic surgeon would not be tackling an umbilical hernia on a morbidly obese patient without the assistance of a general surgeon, not unless it was a totally unexpected finding.

"And you want me to wander in there and just take over his case?"

"Yeah," Patel said.

"You know I can't do that."

"Oh, for Christ's sake." Patel raised both hands, dropped them to his sides. "You can go in and ask him if he needs any help. If he's not insane, he'll say 'Yes.'"

Kurtz sighed. "Okay. Sure. I suppose I can do that."

Some cases start out bad and some turn slowly to shit. This one had started out bad. The lady weighed 650 pounds. Nothing is easy or routine on a patient who weighs 650 pounds. Her abdomen rose from the OR table like a solid, quivering dome. Her head sat on the pillow like a pumpkin. Steve Ryan stood on a step stool with his arms literally buried up to the elbow in an enormous sheet of quivering fat.

It did look like a pannus, which is essentially nothing more than a solid mass of overhanging abdominal tissue. It probably was a pannus, with all of that adipose concealing an umbilical hernia. An easy diagnosis to miss, if you were just going by physical exam, except that a CAT scan or even just a simple abdominal x-ray should have shown loops of bowel inside the pannus…assuming that the x-rays were able to penetrate through all the fat.

"Crap," Kurtz muttered to himself. This case was just begging for a malpractice suit, and anybody unfortunate enough to have his name on the chart was going to get drowned in the oncoming legal tsunami.

"Richard," Steve Ryan said, his eyes lighting up, "could you lend a hand?"

"Sure," Kurtz said, and squared his shoulders. "That's why I'm here."

"Thanks."

"And then what?" Lenore said.

They were eating in a local Indian place that was both excellent and cheap, one of hundreds just like it throughout the five boroughs. Stolidly, Kurtz swallowed a mouthful of fiery shrimp vindaloo and followed it up with a gulp of ice cold beer. "Then we took her to the ICU and left her intubated. The idiot had gotten into the bowel at least twice before I arrived." Kurtz dolefully shook his head. "We carved at least eighty pounds of fat off her but that's not the problem. Fecal material was oozing out all over the abdomen. She's going to get septic. The wound is going to get infected. The anastomoses are probably going to break down. It's going to be a disaster." He shook his head again. "It's already a disaster."

Lenore looked down at her lamb korma and winced.

"Sorry," Kurtz said.

"Doctors have a different idea of dinner conversation." She smiled weakly. "I'm sure I'll get used to it, sooner or later."

"Anyway," Kurtz said. "Steve Ryan is one of those guys who looks good and sounds good but who's spent his whole career faking it. He means well but he doesn't know an ileum from an appendix. I just don't get it. How did he ever finish a residency?"

"Is he dyslexic?"

Kurtz spooned some dal and basmati rice onto his plate, paused for a moment, then added some raita and a little onion chutney. "That's a thought. Dyslexics have trouble telling left from right. The letters all look the same, supposedly, like meaningless squiggles. Would being dyslexic make somebody a lousy surgeon?" He shrugged. "I don't know. It's an interesting theory."

"How is the cop doing? Arnie Figueroa?"

"He's still alive. Will he wake up? Will his brain still be there? They're stopping the barbiturates tomorrow. We'll soon know."

Chapter 3

Juan Moreno had grown up in Cartagena at the height of the drug wars and had killed his first man at the age of eleven. He had been given a knife and a .22 caliber pistol and told to enter the victim's house, shoot him in the abdomen, tie him down and then cut off both of his hands. He had been ordered to leave one hand at the scene and bring the other hand back to the gang's headquarters, as proof that he had carried out his mission. He had waited until the man's wife was out shopping and then had done as he was told.

Juan Moreno was small, even for an eleven-year-old, but he was smart. He knew that, contrary to what is shown in the movies, a man shot in the abdomen does not immediately collapse, roll over and die—not unless he is shot with a bullet large enough to tear open a very large hole. No, a man shot in the abdomen will most likely bleed to death but he will bleed to death slowly. In the meantime, he can run and he can fight, and he can probably live long enough to strangle an eleven year old kid who has the audacity to shoot him in the abdomen.

Of course, Juan Moreno could have shot him in the chest; a bullet in the chest will generally kill the victim much more quickly than a bullet in the abdomen, but that was at least part of the point. Juan Moreno's putative victim was meant to be an object lesson. They didn't want him to die quickly. They wanted him to die slowly. Without his hands.

The victim was named Hector Montillo. He was the owner of a small shop who had very stupidly refused to pay protection money. Unlike most such small business owners, Hector Montillo thought he was immune because his cousin was the Chief of the local police.

So, Juan Moreno, being a smart little eleven-year-old, waited, holding the pistol behind his back, until Hector Montillo opened the door and then Juan Moreno shot him in both knees before shooting him twice in the abdomen. Hector Montillo collapsed, screaming.

Ignoring the screams, Juan Moreno walked past the victim into the foyer. There, he found a large ceramic vase standing next to the doorway. The vase, he thought, should do nicely. He picked it up and smacked Hector Montillo in the head with it, which rendered him momentarily unconscious, then Juan Moreno dragged Hector Montillo inside, shut the door and tied his victim up. He waited for Hector Montillo to regain consciousness before he used the knife (it was a very large knife, more of a machete than a knife) to chop off both his hands. Then, as instructed, he took one of the hands and left.

That was many years ago, but Juan Moreno thought often of that day and of that victim, the first of many. In a way, Juan Moreno was grateful to Hector Montillo, grateful for the sacrifice (as Juan Moreno thought of it) that Hector Montillo had made, the sacrifice that had proved to be the making of Juan Moreno, propelling him upward on his subsequent criminal career. Aware and grateful even then that something special had been accomplished, Juan Moreno had dressed in his finest shorts, tee shirt and sneakers and gone to Hector Montillo's funeral.

"You know what to do?" the Russian said, in English. The Russian did not speak Spanish and Juan Moreno did not speak Russian.

Juan Moreno noted that both Russians had bandages where the little finger of their left hand used to be. Juan Moreno blinked at him. "Eh?" he said. "*Porqué?*"

The Russian frowned. "Your instructions. You know what to do?"

Juan Moreno allowed a bewildered expression to pass across his face. "Si," he said doubtfully. "*Instructiones*. Si."

The Russian drew a deep breath. He seemed annoyed. He tapped his foot against the carpet in front of Juan Moreno's desk and glanced at the second Russian, who stood by his side without speaking. Juan Moreno smiled at the first Russian, his expression suddenly no longer bewildered. The Russian's face went blank. His foot stopped tapping.

"*Yesss…*" Juan Moreno hissed in unaccented English. "I do know what to do. Tell your boss that his *request* will be carried out. Now get out of here."

The Russian said not another word. Both of them turned and walked out.

Russians, Juan Moreno reflected, liked to give orders. Despite their ultimately disastrous seventy-year flirtation with Communism, the secular religion of the common man, Russians had this unconscious assumption that they, their culture and their society were superior to those of all other races and people, and that this superiority gave them the right to tell all others what to do. It was a delusion most common among the young and the dumb ones. These two, he thought, were particularly dumb. Inwardly, he shrugged. Dumb Russians were not his problem.

Still, doing their boss this little favor cost him very little, and it put the Russians in his debt. It was always useful, Juan Moreno reflected, for other people to owe him favors. One never knew when a favor could come in handy.

Lew Barent had just finished eating his dinner when the phone rang. He sighed and stared at it for a moment, then shook his head and picked it up. His wife, Betty, gave him a sad smile but said not a word. Betty had been a cop's wife for many years. She knew the score.

"Dead body reported in Apartment 3B, 1437 McCallister Street. The scene has been secured," the dispatcher said.

"Right," Barent said. "Has Detective Moran been notified?"

"Detective Moran is on his way."

Forty minutes later, Barent pulled his car up to the yellow barrier and parked. A uniform came over, disapproval plain on his face. His expression smoothed out when he recognized Barent. Silently, the uniform moved the sawhorse to the side and Barent stepped through.

The building was old but immaculate, small by modern standards, four floors, each floor divided into four large apartments. A small tiled lobby led to an elevator and a set of stairs. Two security cameras were suspended near the ceiling. He took the elevator up to the top floor, which opened up into another small lobby with two stout, wooden doors. One door, to the side of the elevator, led into the stairwell. The second, directly across from the elevator, opened into Apartment 3B. Two uniformed cops stood flanking the apartment door. Both nodded at Barent. The one on the left frowned and puffed up his cheeks.

Harry Moran was already inside. He grinned crookedly as Barent walked into the spacious living room, waited while Barent inspected the scene.

Cause of death was obvious: a slit throat. A lot of blood, Barent noted. None of the furniture appeared to have been disturbed. The victim was male, white and middle-aged, dressed in a business suit. Two expensive looking leather couches surrounded an oak coffee table, facing a large screen TV mounted on the wall. The victim was sitting on one of the couches, his legs crossed in front of him, his expression vacant. An open bottle of wine and two glasses sat on the coffee table. A brown leather briefcase lay on its side on a granite counter that demarcated the living room from the kitchen. The crime scene guys were carefully covering the room, taking photos and in some cases, samples of blood, dust and microscopic debris.

"What do we know?" Barent asked.

"His name is Mitchell Price, a stockbroker. He's divorced and currently lives alone. One ex-wife and three grown children, none of them in New York."

"Who called it in?"

Moran hesitated. "Anonymous. Female."

"Good old anonymous."

Moran nodded.

"ME already gone?"

"Ten minutes ago."

"He have anything to say, aside from the obvious?"

Moran shrugged. "I'm not sure what you consider obvious, aside from the slit throat."

"No signs of a struggle, that's obvious."

"The ME did note that the victim seemed to expire rather more peacefully than would have been expected. Most people try to fight back when somebody is slitting their throat."

"Any sign of the knife?"

"No. Presumably, our perpetrator took it with him." Moran shrugged. "Or her."

"The bottle of wine should prove interesting," Barent said.

"I expect so," Moran said. He mirthlessly grinned. "Also, the second wineglass. Hopefully we'll get some prints, or even DNA."

As Kurtz expected, the morbidly obese lady, whose name was Mrs. Lydia James, was not doing well. As a mere assistant on the case, Kurtz had no specific responsibilities for her ongoing care, but of course, he had an interest. Steve Ryan, Kurtz noted, seemed depressed. And why not? He had missed the principal diagnosis and had mishandled the operation. By the time Kurtz had arrived to help out, the damage had already been done.

Grand rounds on Friday morning, which doubled as the joint Staunton/Easton Quality Assurance Conference, proved interesting. Surgeons, Kurtz had often noted, were an unforgiving bunch, trained to regard themselves as both responsible for everything around them and in-charge at all times, each the Captain of his ship. With great power comes great responsibility, Kurtz thought. Not necessarily a realistic way of looking at things, but that's the way it was. Their judgments tended to be harsh.

In the old days, and those days were not so very long ago, it was just casually assumed that whenever something went wrong, it was because somebody had fucked up. The more modern way of thinking maintained that an adverse outcome was more likely to be the result of a "system error," this theory holding that almost all of the people, almost all of the time, were doing exactly what they were supposed to be doing and if something went wrong, it was because the system was poorly designed. Surgeons had been slower to adopt this attitude than most, and in times of trouble, tended to revert to type.

It was just so much *easier* to find somebody to blame, to point out the numerous ways in which the offending practitioner had screwed up, maybe give some poor resident or a junior attending a symbolic ten lashes or so, and in really bad cases, even fire the offending practitioner and then assume that the problem had been fixed.

In this case, however, Steve Ryan really had screwed up. Sometimes, it happened.

Quality Assurance proceedings, for some idiotic reason, were treated differently in New York than in any other state, where QA deliberations were confidential and could not be used in a court of law (unless a lawyer tried to introduce such deliberations and some self-important judge decreed that the outcome in this case was so heinous that, by God, he would allow it…in which event, he would probably—though not certainly—be reversed on appeal). Confidentiality in such proceedings was a concession to the generally recognized need to honestly evaluate an adverse outcome and then hopefully change things for the better. In New York, however, QA proceedings were confidential with the singular exception that any statements made by the principals in the case were discoverable. Anything that anybody else might have to say, remained confidential. Steve Ryan, therefore, plus Kurtz, plus any resident, any nurse and anybody else who might have had anything at all to do with the case and might therefore be subject to a future professional liability suit, were strongly advised to keep their mouths shut.

This did not prevent anybody else in the audience from crucifying poor Steve Ryan.

A senior resident, in this case Drew Johnson, presented the case. He outlined the lab results, the physical findings and the preliminary diagnosis, the first slides snapping from one to the next in the darkened auditorium. At this point, he paused. "Any questions?"

A few of the audience turned and surveyed Steve Ryan, sitting near the back. None of them said a word. Steve Ryan hunched down in his seat and did his best to turn invisible.

"No?" Drew Johnson smiled. "Let me go on."

Things got a bit testy as Drew Johnson described the surgery itself. The first question came from Elias Levin, an old timer who fancied himself a hernia specialist. "Why did you make a vertical incision?"

Drew Johnson smiled the happy smile of a man who had no axe to grind, no stake in the outcome and was not, despite superficial appearances, anywhere in the line of fire. "I didn't do the case," he reminded the audience.

Amazing, Kurtz thought. They went through this every week, and every week, the audience seemed to have trouble with the concept that the guy presenting the case was not the guy who did the case. Probably instinct, Kurtz thought. As it did with most predators, the scent of blood drove surgeons into a frenzy.

Elias Levin frowned. "Why was a vertical incision made? It should have been a transverse incision below the umbilicus."

"I believe that in this case, the volume of excess adipose was believed to require a vertical incision, as well. The plan was to use both a vertical incision and a transverse incision."

Elias Levin shook his head. He looked grim.

Walter Stockton, a wizened, crotchety little guy who should have retired ten years ago, called out, "What was your first clue that you were dealing with a hernia instead of a pannus?"

Drew Johnson smiled again. "I believe that the *surgeon's* first clue was when the first loop of bowel popped out of the wound."

Drew Johnson was being diplomatic, or maybe he just didn't know what had actually happened. The real first clue had come when Steve Ryan's scalpel opened a three-centimeter incision in the small intestine (leaking the contaminated remains of the patient's last meal into the abdomen), which was looping in and out of about a hundred pounds of fat.

And so it went, on and on and on, and as the hour dragged to its exhausted, merciless close, Steve Ryan slumped lower and lower in his chair.

Poor fucker, Kurtz thought. Not as poor as the poor patient, of course, but still…Steve Ryan was trapped in a job that he had no talent for. He wasn't a bad guy. He didn't want to fuck up. He tried not to, but it didn't matter. As a surgeon, Steve Ryan was, and would remain, a fuck-up.

Poor fucker, Kurtz thought again.

Chapter 4

The second wineglass yielded neither fingerprints nor DNA, nor did the bottle, nor did any polished surface anywhere in the apartment. The bottle of wine and the glasses had been washed out with water and detergent and then placed back on the coffee table, almost as if they were staged. Too much to say that the perp was a professional, but he or she (okay, probably *she*) certainly knew enough about crime scene analysis to remove any trace of her presence.

The traces of wine left in the bottle did yield a clue, however.

"Alpha-methylfentanyl," Moran said.

Barent, sitting at his desk and eating a ham and Swiss, blinked at him. "Really?"

"Take a look." He placed a sheet of paper down on Barent's desk, then sat in the opposite chair.

"Oh, crap," Barent muttered as he scanned the report. The tox screens employed by law enforcement covered a much larger number of illicit substances than the screens routinely used in an ER. Some traces of Naproxen, probably non-prescription, a little Viagra, some Minoxidil, probably for hair loss since the guy had no history of high blood pressure and at the age of fifty-three, he didn't have much left on top, and there it was, alpha-methylfentanyl, flagged in red on the report.

Fentanyl was a synthetic opioid originally developed by the Jannsen Corporation and widely used as an adjunct to anesthesia since the early 1970's. It was a hundred times more potent than morphine and fifty times more potent than heroin. It had a faster onset of action and a shorter duration than either drug. Unfortunately, it caused a similar high, was easy to make and was much cheaper. A kilo of the stuff, legitimately purchased, cost about ten thousand bucks and had a street value of over twenty million.

Fentanyl was rarely used on its own, however, since its potency made it difficult to judge the dosage. Drug dealers depend on the needs and desires of their clients to make money. Not much money to be made when your clients all stop breathing. It had become common, therefore, to cut heroin with just a bit of fentanyl.

Alpha-methylfentanyl was even worse, being considerably more potent and longer lasting than its parent drug. Most of it came from China, hence the street name: "China White."

"We haven't seen any of this stuff around," Barent said. "Not lately."

"Thank God," Moran said.

"Why this guy? Where did he get it?"

Moran shrugged. "You mean who slipped it into his wine glass?"

Barent frowned. "Yeah. That, too."

The questioning of the buildings' other occupants had revealed nothing. Not surprising, since there were only four apartments on each floor and each column of apartments above the ground floor had its own semi-private elevator, four elevators in total. The walls were thick and effectively sound-proof. Nobody in the building had more than a superficial acquaintance with their neighbors.

The ex-wife had remarried, lived in Oregon and expressed regret, but by the tone of her voice, couldn't have cared less. The three children spoke to their father every few weeks or so but hadn't seen him in months. One of them, the oldest daughter, said, "I think he had a new girlfriend."

"Do you have a name," Barent had asked.

"No. He never mentioned it."

"Can you tell me anything about her?"

"I wish I could, but he liked to keep his love life private." The daughter's voice seemed to hesitate over the phone. "This wasn't the first. He liked them young."

Most do, Barent thought, but no, that wasn't much of a help.

Mitchell Price had worked for a small brokerage firm called Adler and Bowen, Associates. His co-workers had been only a bit more helpful than the daughter and the ex-wife. One of them, a thin guy named Gerald Cox, who wore suspenders and a designer suit, very respectable in a stock-brokerish sort of way, said, "She was blonde. Mitchell liked blondes. His ex-wife was a brunette. He tended to go for women who wouldn't remind him of his past mistakes."

"Do you have a name?" Moran asked.

Gerald Cox shook his head. "Afraid not."

"Any idea what this blonde does for a living? Or where she works?"

"Sorry," Gerald Cox said. "No clue."

And that, so far, was that. No clue. Except for the knife wound in the neck, of course. That was definitely a clue, but so far, a clue that was leading them nowhere.

There was one other potential clue, of course. It was a long shot but since they had nothing else worth pursuing, they might as well pursue this one.

Jeffrey McDonald owned a car dealership in the Bronx. He was middling successful and resented it. With his talents, he should have been rich by now, or so Jeffrey McDonald thought. He was no dummy, however. When contacted by Barent, he had immediately clammed up. "Talk to my lawyer," he said, and hung up.

Barent frowned at the phone. *Win some, lose some*, he thought. The fact that McDonald refused to talk was suspicious but suspicions went only so far, these days. Barent had no basis to arrest the guy and nothing that would convince a judge to issue a search warrant. They could put him under surveillance but at this point, Barent's very hazy suspicions wouldn't justify the time and expense.

"Crap," he muttered. Then he smiled. There was one other possible way to get to Jeffrey McDonald.

The pretty young girlfriend, as McDonald's ex-wife had predicted, was already becoming disillusioned. Her name was Audrey Schaeffer. Jeffrey McDonald, it turned out, was not exactly the man of her dreams.

When Barent and Moran had knocked on her door, she had been more intrigued than suspicious. Audrey Schaeffer had been raised in a small town in Indiana. Her father was a veteran who owned a gas station. Her uncle was a cop. Audrey Schaeffer, unlike so many denizens of New York City, was inclined to look favorably upon the police.

"Jeffrey…" she said, and winced. "I'm afraid that Jeffrey was a mistake."

No surprise, there, Barent thought.

"In what way?" Moran said.

She shrugged. "I was flattered, at first. He's older, good-looking, successful…" She shrugged again.

Jeffrey McDonald was certainly older, Barent reflected, and not bad looking in a washed out sort of way, and successful by the standards of a small town girl far from the big city. He owned his own home, he drove a new car and he certainly wasn't starving.

Audrey Schaeffer smiled. "He's not a bad guy, you understand. It's just that he has a predictable routine and I barely fit into it at all. He gets up at the same time every day and goes to work. He plays golf on the weekends. He likes Ruby Tuesday and Uno's pizza. He watches TV after dinner." She raised an eyebrow.

Barent and Moran looked at each other. "So?" Barent said.

"So that's it," Audrey Schaeffer said. "He has this little, compartmentalized life and there isn't a lot of room in it for me, or for anything outside of the usual." She grinned. "Aside from the obvious, of course, and even there, he sticks to his routine."

This was not exactly what they wanted to know. "Tell us about the night of the accident," Barent said.

"Not much to tell. We saw a movie and then went to dinner. On the way out of the restaurant, he seemed pretty drunk but we had shared a bottle of wine, so I was a little drunk, too. We were walking down the street to the parking lot and he just keeled over. Luckily, we were near the corner and the cars were all going slow. The guy who hit him tried to swerve away but Jeffrey fell right in front of his car."

"He keeled over before the car hit him," Barent said.

"Yes."

"And you had one bottle of wine between you…"

"What sort of wine?" Moran said.

She blinked. "Why does that matter?"

"Most white wine," Barent said, "ranges from between eleven percent and thirteen percent alcohol, depending on the type of grape and where the wine comes from. Sweet wines are even lower, since some of the sugar is retained and doesn't ferment into alcohol. Most red wine ranges from thirteen percent and up. It makes a big difference to how drunk somebody can get from one bottle."

"Oh," she said. "I didn't know that." She frowned. "It was white. I don't like those big, heavy Chardonnays. It was a Riesling."

"Dry or sweet?"

"Off-dry. A little sweet."

Barent glanced at Moran. "More like eleven, then, maybe even less."

"He probably had more of it than I did," Audrey Schaeffer ventured.

"Still," Moran said, "it's not likely that half a bottle of relatively low alcohol wine would put a grown man down for the count."

"I suppose not." Audrey Schaeffer shrugged.

"And so far as you know," Barent asked, "he has no history of drug abuse?"

"No," Audrey Schaeffer said. "Not so far as I know."

"How about you?" Moran said. "Any history of drug abuse?"

She blinked at him, looking hurt. "No," she said.

Barent frowned at Moran. "Forgive my partner," he said. "Sometimes he just can't help himself."

She grimaced and looked away. "Is there anything else?"

"No," Barent said. He and Moran both rose to their feet. "Thank you for your cooperation." He handed her a card. "If you think of anything, anything at all that might shed some light on what happened, please give me a call."

She fingered the card, looking uncertain, then shrugged.

On the way out of the apartment, Barent turned to Moran and said, "Jerk."

Moran smiled. "You were right," he said. "I just couldn't help myself."

Steve Ryan was depressed. He was very depressed. He swirled the glass of 18-year old Macallan and peered through it at the light. Dark brown, smoky, in Steve Ryan's opinion, it was the best Scotch he had ever had. Certainly, the best for the price.

Steve Ryan was a plastic surgeon. Plastic surgeons make a lot of money. *With great power comes great responsibility*, Steve Ryan thought. He forgot who said that. Churchill, maybe...or maybe it was Voltaire.

Comparing himself to Churchill might have been just a tad egotistical but only just a tad. He was a surgeon, after all, and surgeons do have great responsibility.

Steve Ryan loved surgery. He always had.

What was that other saying? Oh, yes…*Stupid is as stupid does*. Steve Ryan had a high IQ. Steve Ryan had received A's in every course he had ever taken. Steve Ryan had goals, aspirations and direction. Steve Ryan had always known what he wanted and where he was going. Steve Ryan had never been plagued with the doubts common to lesser mortals…not until it had all come crashing down on top of him because he had been really, *really* stupid.

Know thyself and act accordingly. He forgot who said that. Socrates, maybe…or maybe Sun-Tzu. A much better saying, in the end, and one that Steve Ryan knew well and had chosen to ignore.

A lot of high IQ morons in this business. He sighed, sipped his Scotch and let the taste swirl around his tongue. The glass, he dimly noted, was almost empty. He carefully poured it full.

Always a thoughtful young man, Steve Ryan had long ago discovered that smart people did not always make smart decisions. Most mistakes, he had come to realize, were not caused by stupidity or even ignorance. No, most of the very worst mistakes were caused by flaws in one's character, and the most common such flaws were arrogance and self-delusion.

I'm smarter than all the rest. I'm so smart that I'm never wrong.

Except, sometimes he was.

Steve Ryan had wanted to be a surgeon and by God, Steve Ryan had managed to become one. He had gone to Princeton, then Medical School at Columbia, always succeeding, always being praised, then surgical training at MGH. It was there, early in his residency, that Steve Ryan dimly began to comprehend that he had made a fundamental mistake.

He lifted a hand and stared at it. Long, delicate fingers, narrow hands, hands that could slip easily into a wound, a *surgeon's* hands, or so he had always told himself.

He had always been just a little bit clumsy. He had graduated at the top of his class but had never been much of an athlete. The baseball was almost always in the catcher's mitt before he could manage to swing his bat. The football, somehow, would rarely stick in his hands.

That was okay. Steve Ryan was the cerebral sort. He didn't need to be an athlete. He was a genius, or so his parents and sometimes his teachers had told him. A genius was above such things.

Athletic ability, or the lack of it, should have been his first clue. Oh, a surgeon didn't need to be able to hit a baseball but he did need eye-hand coordination, and a really good surgeon needed more than most. He needed to be able to direct his instruments to the proper place, to make precise cuts, to sew a neat, tidy line, to be delicate, to be precise.

Steve Ryan, as was sometimes said among surgeons, had lousy hands. By the time he had come to realize this, it was too late. His mentors had known, of course. He hadn't graduated with the rest of his class. They had held him back, making him take his senior year of residency over again, which he had bitterly resented, and after that, they had gently suggested a year in the lab, which he had reluctantly agreed to. They had tried to steer him into a career in research, where his high IQ would be an asset and his lack of coordination would not be a hindrance.

Oh, well…

The second glass of Scotch was somehow, unaccountably, almost empty. He squared his shoulders and put down the glass. Decisions, he thought. It was time to face up to reality. It was time to get his life in order…

"Thanks for your help the other night," Steve Ryan said.

Kurtz looked up. Steve Ryan was standing next to the table, carrying a tray with what appeared to be a plate of chicken tenders and some coleslaw. Kurtz himself had nearly finished a second slice of the cafeteria's mediocre pizza.

Steve Ryan sat down opposite Kurtz, dipped a piece of chicken into some honey mustard and stolidly chewed it.

"How's it going?" Kurtz asked.

Steve Ryan shook his head, looking sorrowful. "I've decided that I need to specialize," he said.

"What do you mean?" Kurtz said. "You're a plastic surgeon. You're already specializing."

Steve Ryan, unfortunately for them all, had a sense of civic responsibility. The big money in plastic surgery was in cosmetics but the tough cases, the cases that actually meant something to the patient beyond mere vanity, lay in reconstructive plastic surgery, fixing the anomalies, usually either congenital or caused by trauma that made a victim truly hideous, that precluded a normal life.

Steve Ryan wanted to do good. It was just too bad that he couldn't do it.

Steve Ryan gave a tired grin. "It has been shown on numerous studies that surgeons who specialize on a limited number of procedures have a better outcome."

This was true. One of the prime causes of a poor outcome was what the statisticians sometimes called "excessive variation," which meant simply doing a lot of different things and generally doing them differently every time. Doing a few things and doing them the same way tended to produce much better results.

Steve Ryan, it occurred to Kurtz, whether consciously or not, had finally come to realize something very important about himself: he was a lousy surgeon.

"What are you going to specialize in?"

"Rhinoplasties."

Rhinoplasties…otherwise known as 'nose jobs.' Kurtz nodded. "A good choice," he said. Cosmetic, lucrative, and as surgery went, easy. Everybody wanted a perky, up-tilted little nose. A lot of girls in New York started out with noses that were neither up-tilted, little nor perky. In some sections of New York, a nose job was almost a rite-of-passage marking a teenager's entrance into womanhood.

"Yeah." Steve Ryan nodded. "I thought so."

"You can be the next Dr. Diamond." With offices in Beverly Hills, Dr. Jason Diamond was world famous as the go-to guy for Hollywood stars looking for a little nip or tuck.

Steve Ryan smiled wanly. "One step at a time, but yeah, a limited series of procedures in which I'll be the acknowledged expert: nose jobs, botox, lip augmentation, maybe blepharoplasties also."

All good choices. Botox eliminated superficial wrinkles. Lip augmentation usually involved little more than the injection of dermal fillers and blepharoplasties, sometimes referred to as "eye lifts," were a common procedure among middle-aged, well-to-do women about town. All of these had the advantage, like nose jobs, of being relatively low-risk and not particularly difficult.

"I do them all, anyway," Ryan said. "A little advertising and before long, I'll have a boutique practice. Less trouble, more money…why not?"

Lydia James, meanwhile, was septic, bacteria from her perforated bowel having spread from the surgical wound into the peritoneum and then into her blood stream. Her blood pressure at this point was supported by increasing doses of Levophed (derisively referred to by generations of residents as "Leave-'Em-Dead") but Levophed was a drug of last resort and could only do so much. Unless the antibiotics were able to clear the infection, which at this point seemed unlikely, Lydia James was going to die.

"That seems like a smart decision," Kurtz said. "Good luck with it."

Chapter 5

Though he had no formal education beyond the fifth grade, Javier Garcia was highly intelligent and had read widely. As a young man, he had always been careful to keep his literary preferences to himself. Being from a small village in Mexico and having been recruited by *La Familia* at the age of nine, first as a runner, then an enforcer, then an assassin-in-training, he knew how to impress his colleagues and competitors (they were the same) as well as his superiors in the organization. They would have been more suspicious than impressed if they had known of Javier Garcia's fondness for Thomas Aquinas, Octavio Paz, Miguel de Unamuno and Gabriel Garcia Marquez.

Sadly, Javier Garcia's extensive reading and wide experience had given him a jaundiced view of mankind.

Satisfaction verging on excitement filled him, however, as he waited for his guest this evening to arrive. The restaurant as usual was busy, as it should be, since the food it served was excellent. His bodyguards, eating at booths and tables scattered across the floor, did not stand out in any way.

Javier Garcia had never met Juan Moreno, but he knew of him. He was the leader of an organization much like his own, and Javier Garcia imagined that the two of them had much in common, both now middle-aged and seasoned, having survived the testosterone fueled machismo of their youth and risen through the ranks of their respective organizations, both having demonstrated over and over again that they were smart, tough, disciplined and ruthless.

The door to the restaurant opened. A small man with broad shoulders entered, followed by another and then two more. After them came another, a bit taller, a bit thinner, with a hint of gray at the temples. Juan Moreno. This one surveyed the restaurant, taking in the diners and the bustling waitstaff, letting his eyes linger for a moment on the booth where Javier Garcia sat in the shadows.

The hostess said something to him and he said something back. The hostess smiled and nodded her head. She turned. Juan Moreno's men fanned out and sat down with their backs to the wall. They were handed menus, which they barely glanced at. The taller man followed the hostess to Javier Garcia's booth. He slid inside, looking at Javier Garcia with interest.

"Your waiter will be with you shortly," the hostess said.

Juan Moreno nodded, his eyes fixed on Javier Garcia.

"So," Garcia said, "welcome to *Casa Lindo*." He pondered Juan Moreno's blandly smiling face. "Your request for a meeting came as a surprise," he said. "We both play similar roles in the life of this city, and yet we have never sat down together before this evening."

Juan Moreno's lips quirked upward. "I stick to my neighborhoods. You stick to yours." He shrugged. "The arrangement works. We have had peace for many years."

Javier Garcia frowned. Juan Moreno's words were true. "Is something about to change that?"

Juan Moreno drew a deep breath. "I hope not, but I tell you nothing that you do not already know when I say that things always change. The old pass away. The young take their place and wish to do things differently and then they, too, grow old and set in their ways." He shrugged.

Javier Garcia's eyes flicked to the side. A waiter stood there, holding a bottle and two glasses. He placed these on the table, bowed and walked away without a word. Javier Garcia picked up the bottle and poured each glass a quarter full. "Try it," he said.

Juan Moreno picked up his glass, swirled the brown liquid, sipped. He tilted his head to the side. "What is this?" he asked.

"Barbados Private Estate. I think it is the finest rum in the world. It is not the most expensive, merely the finest."

"You are hospitable," Juan Moreno said. "For that, I thank you." He sipped again. "I might have expected tequila."

Javier Garcia shrugged. "I prefer rum."

Juan Moreno sipped again and grimaced. "You wonder why I asked to meet with you." It was a statement, not a question.

Javier Garcia nodded.

"I have come to you, to one of your places, as a mark of my respect and also as a demonstration of my faith in your good sense. I am under no illusions that my four men are enough to protect me, should you wish to do me harm."

"I have no doubt," Javier Garcia said, "that the consequences of causing you harm would be wide-spread and severe."

"This is true." Juan Moreno smiled. "But in chaos, there is opportunity."

"I would be foolish to seek such opportunity. In chaos, there is also risk. I have no need to assume such a risk. As you say, we have had peace. I have no reason to change that."

Juan Moreno nodded. "You, your organization and your people, have lived in this city for many years, far longer than we have. You possess channels of distribution that my people lack. If possible, we wish to take advantage of these channels."

"Do you?" Javier Garcia frowned. "You never have before."

"We never needed to, before. Now we do."

"As you say, things change. Why this change? Why now?"

Juan Moreno leaned forward. "Do you know Sergei Ostrovsky?"

Javier Garcia blinked. He sipped his rum and pondered this question for a long moment, then he smiled. "Tell me more," he said.

"I don't get it," Kurtz said. "He was telling me just a week ago about his plans to start a new practice."

"That's not uncommon, actually," Bill Werth said. "People often come up with grandiose schemes before blowing their brains out." Bill Werth was a psychiatrist, and as such, eminently qualified to make pronouncements on what made a man blow his brains out.

Steve Ryan's dead body had been found in his office, along with a short note declaring his love and devotion to his wife and kids and a declaration that he had reached the end of his rope and just couldn't continue.

They were sitting in Kurtz' office, along with Lew Barent and Harry Moran. Barent looked grim. Moran had on his usual poker face.

Lydia James, after lingering for over a month, had died the night before. Steve Ryan followed her only a few hours later.

"He didn't blow his brains out," Barent said. "At this point, we're not even sure how he died."

"He left a note," Kurtz said. "The note seems pretty clear."

"Anybody can write a note."

Kurtz looked at him and frowned. "What are you suggesting?"

Barent shrugged. "Maybe I'm getting cynical in my old age."

Moran looked upward toward the ceiling and rolled his eyes.

"Are you seriously suggesting he was murdered?" Kurtz said.

"No," Barent said. He gave a half-hearted grin. "Not seriously, but I'm not ruling it out either, not until we know the cause of death."

"How long will that take?"

"The ME has the body. It should be soon."

"Why you?" Lenore said.

"Are you kidding?" Kurtz said.

She frowned. "Are you the official liaison for medically related crime? When did this happen?"

Kurtz barely smiled. "I guess it happened when Sharon Lee was strangled, or maybe when Rod Mahoney was torn to pieces."

Lenore winced. "So much for being a hard-working surgeon."

"Yeah, well...I work hard at a lot of things."

She made a rude noise. "Please pass the potatoes."

Kurtz was not a small man and he worked out at least three times a week. He kept an eye on his cholesterol but saw no need to watch what he ate. Lenore was a bit more restrained but also enjoyed her dinner. They ate out at least twice a week. Tonight, it was Italian, a little family style place near their apartment: veal marsala, a side dish of penne a la vodka, eggplant parmigiana and roasted potatoes with sea-salt and rosemary.

"Barent has been a cop for a long time. He has a sense for these things. He told me once that a lot of apparent suicides, particularly when the victim is elderly, are actually murders. The family gets tired of waiting for grandma to keel over, so they help her along a little."

"That's disgusting," Lenore said.

"Disgusting, but supposedly true."

"Also, very sad."

Kurtz shrugged.

"So why is he suspicious about Steve Ryan?"

"I don't know. He didn't say."

"And Bill? What does he think?"

"He thinks suicide is perfectly plausible. Steve had a lot of complications and he had just lost a patient who should never have died. Doctors aren't stupid. They study hard, get good grades and are usually right. They're not used to fucking things up. Some of us can't take it."

Lenore shrugged. "You'll know soon."

"I'm hoping it's suicide," Kurtz said. "I'm really not in the mood for another idiotic murder." Kurtz was angry and frustrated. The world, once again, had been knocked off its kilter. Should he have seen it, somehow? If he had said something different to the poor depressed schmuck, would Steve Ryan still be alive? He shook his head. What was even worse, if Kurtz was being honest with himself, and Kurtz tried to always be honest with himself, was the sense of closure that Steve Ryan's suicide had brought, not quite relief, but almost. Sadness, sure, also frustration, but somewhere mixed in with these, just a tiny bit of relief. Steve Ryan had been a good husband, a good father and a good guy, but he was a lousy surgeon, and the world was better off with one less lousy surgeon.

"Yeah," Lenore said. "Let's hope." She shook her head. "Poor Donna."

"Diazepam," the ME said.

"Oh," Barent said. "Okay." He frowned.

The ME was a small, skinny guy who never seemed to get depressed by the morbid nature of his work. Barent appreciated the fact that he was good at his job but found his attitude sometimes disturbing.

"What's the matter?" the ME said. "You're not happy with Diazepam?"

"Diazepam is Valium," Barent said. "He had a prescription for Valium."

The ME shrugged.

"Anything else?" Barent asked.

"High levels of alcohol. Diazepam plus alcohol is a pretty good way to go, if you're going to go."

"So," Barent said, "suicide…?"

"If it wasn't, I can't tell the difference." The ME raised his hands, let them fall to his side.

"Nothing else on the body?"

The ME shrugged again. "A couple of bruises on the upper left arm. Nothing to indicate foul play." The ME loved the term 'foul play.' He used it a lot, almost always with a creepy little smile.

"Okay," Barent said. "Suicide. Why not? It makes my job easier. I should be happy." For some reason that he couldn't figure out, he wasn't, but Barent's lack of happiness was a matter of concern to no one except himself, and maybe his wife. He sighed. "Good enough. Another case closed."

Chapter 6

In addition to overseeing the care of officers wounded in the line of duty, Kurtz' responsibilities as a police surgeon required him to spend a few days each month at the precinct, where a rotating roster of police surgeons occupied a somewhat dilapidated but basically functional series of exam rooms and small offices. Here, it was his responsibility to examine and certify all officers who had medical problems of all sorts.

Officers of the NYPD had as a benefit of their job an unlimited number of sick days, but those out-of-work for longer than forty-eight hours were required to report in and be certified by a police surgeon as unfit for duty. Most such officers were eager to get back to work. A very few tended to malinger.

Kurtz' first appointment of the day was Stephanie Myers, a small, very fit young woman who had sprained an ankle in hot pursuit of a pickpocket. "See," she said with a bright smile, "it's all better." She held the foot up and rotated it around.

The range of motion was good but the ankle still looked swollen. "Stand up on it," Kurtz said.

Stephanie Myers gave him an aggrieved look but seemed to have no trouble standing on her swollen ankle.

"Let me see you walk across the room."

She frowned. She walked to the wall and then back. Her limp was slight but noticeable.

Kurtz shook his head. "I admire your dedication, but you need a couple more days. I don't think you can chase suspects with this ankle."

"Oh, shit," she muttered. "I'm going nuts just sitting around."

Kurtz repressed a smile. "Two more days," he said. "Watch TV. Try reading a book."

She sighed. "I've been reading books until my head is ready to explode. "She sighed again. "Oh, well. It could have been worse," she said.

The next patient was named Brad Jenkins, fat, fiftyish and looking forward to retirement. Jenkins had been out for nearly a week with a wrist injury, the result of a physical altercation with a meth dealer in Fort Tryon Park. "What do you think, Doc?" he said.

"It's looking good. I think you're ready to return to work," Kurtz said.

"Yeah?" Jenkins rotated the wrist. "It still hurts."

"You've got full range of motion and you can lift with it. Take some Motrin. It'll be fine."

Reluctantly, Jenkins nodded. "Okay."

Kurtz had thirty minutes for lunch, which he ate at his desk. The first patient after lunch was Bert Armstrong, a little guy with pale skin, red hair and freckles. Armstrong had been out for over a month with an assortment of poorly defined complaints. He had shoulder pain. He had abdominal pain. He had headaches. Armstrong had fallen on some ice at the tail end of winter, hit his head on a fallen tree branch, been briefly rendered unconscious and been taken to St. Vincent's, where a diagnosis of a concussion had been made. A CAT scan two weeks later revealed no residual damage but the patient's symptoms had not improved.

The previous surgeon who had examined Armstrong had gone the easy, diplomatic route. He had taken the guy at his word and signed off on Armstrong's request for continued leave. Looking a patient in the eye, Kurtz reflected, and telling him he was full of shit, was never easy and few physicians wanted a confrontation with a hostile cop, but Bert Armstrong was clearly malingering.

"I think you're ready to go back to work," Kurtz said.

Armstrong glared. "That's bullshit."

"I don't think so," Kurtz said.

"Listen, you stupid fuck. Don't push me. You don't know what you're dealing with here."

Kurtz blinked. A slow smile spread across his face. "What I'm dealing with, here, is a malingering patient. Your symptoms are as phony as a three-dollar bill. I'm certifying you as fit for duty. You don't like it? Take it up with the Union."

Armstrong's nostrils flared. He took a slow, deep breath and drew himself up to his full, not impressive height. "You son-of-a bitch, I'll remember you," he said.

"Sure," Kurtz said. "And I'll remember you, too. So, what?"

Armstrong turned on his heel and walked out without another word. Kurtz released the breath he hadn't realized he'd been holding, sighed and made a notation on Armstrong's chart.

Arnaldo Figueroa had been weaned off the barbiturates and once it became apparent that he could breathe without assistance, the endotracheal tube was removed. He was transferred from the ICU to a room on the Neurosurgical Floor. He seemed unaware of this, however and over the next three days, he did little but sleep.

A day later, Arnaldo Figueroa opened his eyes and grinned at his wife, Cynthia, and the kids, before his eyelids fluttered and then closed. It was a start. The day after, his eyes followed the nurses and technicians around the room. He smiled. He frowned. He clenched his right hand into a fist and wriggled the toes on his right foot. His left hand twitched. The toes on his left foot barely trembled. This was expected. He had been shot in the right side of the head. The left side of his body, therefore, was affected more than the right. Allen Wong was encouraged. "Any activity at all this soon after a major head injury is a good sign. I expect he'll get better." How much better, he could not, at this point, say.

Mrs. Figueroa listened intently, compressed her lips in a thin line, nodded and prayed.

A day later, Barent and Moran dropped by. They nodded to the two guards still posted outside of Figueroa's room, and walked gingerly up to the bed. Figueroa was propped up against three pillows, spooning applesauce into his mouth with his right hand. His eyes flicked back and forth between Barent and Moran. He grinned.

"Arnie," Barent said. "How are you feeling?"

Arnaldo Figueroa's smile grew wider. "Considering the alternative? It could have been worse."

Moran nodded. "What happened?" he asked.

"I've been told I was shot in the head."

"Yeah, a residential neighborhood in Williamsburg."

Arnaldo Figueroa frowned. "Williamsburg..."

Barent glanced at Moran. "So, what happened?"

"I don't remember a lot of it. I was following some white guys. That's all I remember."

"What did they look like?"

Arnaldo Figueroa shrugged. "Big, tough. They wore suits and ties and they walked like they owned the sidewalk." He grinned. "Or they thought they did."

"Tough guys, huh?" Moran said. "A lot of wise guys start out tough."

"Yeah. The process winnows them down."

"So, who were they?" Barent asked.

"I don't really know. I couldn't hear them. I couldn't really see them that well. I was keeping my distance, trying to be inconspicuous."

"You should have tried harder," Moran said.

Arnaldo Figueroa shrugged. "I think they were Russian."

Barent sat back, pondering. "Makes sense. A lot of Russians in Williamsburg."

"So, where were they going?"

"That's what I don't remember," Arnaldo Figueroa said.

Barent sighed and glanced at Moran. "Well, keep trying. Maybe it'll come to you."

Chapter 7

The honeymoon was definitely not over.

Kurtz and Lenore Brinkman (Lenore *Kurtz*, he reminded himself with satisfaction) had been married for a little over two months. The wedding, despite Esther Brinkman's intermittent attempts to dictate the guest list, the venue, the menu, the rabbi and the exact wording of the ceremony, had gone just as Lenore had planned it. It was a small wedding, as such things went, a little over fifty people, most of them from Lenore's side.

Kurtz' father, not quite as silent and dour as he used to be, sat on Kurtz' side of the aisle, along with a woman named Lisa who Kurtz had never met before. Lisa was middle-aged but well preserved...*very* well preserved, black-haired, tall, with smooth skin, full lips, wide shoulders, a curving figure and warm blue eyes. Kurtz liked the way his father looked at her, as if wondering how he could have gotten so lucky. Kurtz wondered the same thing, both for his father and himself.

The rabbi, a small guy with a short black beard that hugged his face, had kept the ceremony mercifully short. After pledging their love and fealty to each other, Kurtz and Lenore had shared a few sips of sweet kosher wine. The rabbi had smiled and said, "When you marry a nice Jewish girl, you drink a nice Jewish wine."

The wine glass had been placed on the floor, covered with a white napkin and Kurtz had stamped on it, shattering it to pieces. The shattering of the glass had numerous interpretations. Supposedly, according to one story, it was a reminder of the destruction of the Temple, symbolizing the pain and suffering of the Jewish people even in the midst of a joyous occasion. Another interpretation stated that it was a reminder of the fragility of human relationships, a warning therefore, not to take the marriage vows for granted. A third held that the loud noise of a breaking glass would frighten away evil spirits who might otherwise be inclined to torment the happy couple.

Whatever, Kurtz got a kick out of stomping it, after which the crowd yelled, "Mazel tov!" and the celebration began.

A lot of food. A lot of dancing. Despite his years in New York, Kurtz had never been to a Jewish wedding before, though he had been told what to expect. It wasn't much like the weddings he had attended, growing up in West Virginia, which had been shorter and far more restrained, with a lot less food.

"Food is the way families show their love," Lenore had stated. "It's that way for the Jews, the Chinese, the Italians and pretty much every culture on Earth except for you cold Northern European types."

"Traditionally, the Northern Europeans," Kurtz had said, "didn't have much food to spare; because it was cold."

There was plenty of food to spare at Kurtz' and Lenore's wedding, though the raw clam bar and the shrimp cocktails seemed both ostentatious and just a little out of place. Lenore had fixed him with a gimlet eye. "We're not kosher. We can have a raw clam bar."

Kurtz, despite his pretensions toward being a gourmet, had a serious aversion toward raw seafood. As a physician, he knew too much about vibrio, hepatitis, tapeworms and fecal coliform bacteria. As a prospective bridegroom, however, he knew which battles were worth fighting. "Whatever you say, dear."

Lenore had smiled her wide, brilliant smile. "Just keep sucking up to me. We're going to have a great future."

"Yes, dear," Kurtz said.

They had gone back to Cancun, to the same resort where they had met, to spend an idyllic honeymoon and now here they were, two months later, enjoying a picnic lunch in Central Park on a Saturday afternoon. Spring was giving way to Summer. The breeze was mild. A few high clouds scudded by overhead. The sun was warm. They had spread a blanket on the lawn near Belvedere Castle.

Three young men threw a Frisbee on the lawn. A golden retriever ran in circles, chased by a small bulldog. Two kids on rollerblades glided along the path. Lenore wriggled out of her jeans and took off her shirt. She had on a white bikini underneath. One of the kids with the Frisbee blinked and stared. The Frisbee hit him in the head, which he barely noticed. Kurtz felt his palms begin to tingle. Lenore smirked at him. "I need to catch some sun," she said. Lenore liked having a tan. "Wake me when it's time to go." She lay down on her stomach.

"Sure," Kurtz said. "Enjoy."

Within a few minutes, Lenore's breathing grew even. Kurtz pulled out a book and began to read.

Officially, alcohol was not allowed in Central Park. Unofficially, putting some beer or wine in a thermos, where it might as well be tea or soda was every New Yorker's routine solution. Today's beverage of choice was Chardonnay. Kurtz occasionally took a swig from his bottle and soon felt pleasantly buzzed. Forty minutes later, he glanced at his watch and tugged one of Lenore's toes. She stirred and turned on her side. "Time to go?"

"Yup."

She yawned and pulled on her clothes. Twenty minutes later, they were seated in the dojo. David Chao, Kurtz' partner, and David's fiancée, Carie Owens, a small, blonde ER doc, walked in five minutes after and sat down next to them. David wore his gi.

The first bout was between two brown belts. They were evenly matched and both seemed more interested in defending than attacking but finally, one got through his opponent's guard with a snap kick. They bowed and exited the circle. The next bout was a little more interesting, two black belts, one a young guy, the other much smaller and older. The old guy didn't look like he had much chance but he moved around the ring like liquid. A roundhouse kick swept by his face. He stepped in and hit the younger guy with a palm strike to the chest.

"Point," the referee said.

The young guy gave the referee a peeved look, which the referee ignored.

The young guy won the next point with a left jab, after which he raised both arms above his head and bounced around the ring.

"Jerk," David muttered.

Kurtz agreed. Carrie and Lenore, chatting between the two men, ignored this byplay.

The referee held up his hand and dropped it. The young guy charged. The older man slid to the side and connected with a fist to the young guy's head.

"Bout," the referee said.

The young guy shook his head, a disbelieving expression on his face. "Shit," he muttered. The referee gave him a level look and cleared his throat. The young guy sighed and bowed to his opponent, who bowed back. They both exited the ring.

"I'm up," David said.

David was good. Kurtz and David sparred frequently. It's a truism that a good big man almost always beats a good little man. Kurtz was two inches taller than David and thirty pounds heavier. Kurtz almost always won but David knew what he was doing. His opponent was a middle-weight named Jordan Chance, who had ambitions of turning pro. Chance, like a lot of guys in this business, had an ego. He was barely twenty and thought he was hot stuff. As soon as the referee dropped his hand, he swept in, aiming a kick at David's ribs. David stepped inside his guard and tapped him on the cheek.

"Point," the referee said. Chance gave the referee a dirty look.

He was a little more wary after that. The two men circled, looking for an opening. David stepped in. They exchanged blows, each deflecting punches. Chance feinted to the side and David fell for it. Chance connected with a punch to the abdomen.

"Point," the referee said.

Two minutes later, David swept Chance's legs out from under him with a lateral sweep and the bout was over. Chance looked grim but he bowed when he was supposed to and exited the ring.

Forty minutes later, David had showered and changed and they were sipping a bottle of 2002 Rodney Strong Cabernet at Smith and Wollensky. "Excellent bout," Kurtz said.

"The guy's pretty good," David said. "Cocky but good."

"He'll get over it," Kurtz said, "or he'll get his head beat in."

David sipped his wine and solemnly nodded.

"Carrie was telling me that she has something you might be interested in," Lenore said.

"Oh?" Kurtz looked at Carrie.

"Yeah," Carrie said. "I admitted a guy the night before last, an apparent overdose." Carrie grinned and glanced at Lenore. "I won't mention names but I think you'll know who I mean. His chart was interesting. You operated on him and drug abuse had been suspected on his last admission. The 10-panel screen showed traces of heroin, but the amount seemed too small to account for his symptoms and he didn't wake up with naloxone, so this time, we sent the blood for forensics, which includes mass spec. We should know in about a week if he was on anything else."

Kurtz waited while their waiter placed the appetizers on the table, then he asked, "What happened to him?"

Carrie dipped a lump of cold blue crab in some cocktail sauce. She shrugged. "He was intubated at the scene. There wasn't much for us to do beyond the initial workup. We sent him to ICU. I took a look at the chart this afternoon. He's still there."

Jeffrey McDonald…had to be. "Thanks," Kurtz said. "I'll wander by there in the morning."

"It's too soon to tell." Joe Ressler was a medical intensivist. He was short, squat and hairy, with broad shoulders and a barrel chest.

"Go on," Kurtz said.

"He's got bisynchronous spikes and a lot of high amplitude delta waves, and the alpha waves are almost gone."

Kurtz, who had never had occasion to read an EEG, nevertheless could read the bottom line. "At least he's not brain dead."

Ressler shrugged. "You get patterns like this with high dose opioids, but it's been two days, already. It shouldn't be lasting this long."

No, Kurtz thought, morphine, heroin, even methadone should not have lasted this long, particularly since they had already administered IV naloxone, which was supposed to counteract narcotics. It could be that a higher dosage of naloxone might do the trick but naloxone had been associated with problems of its own, particularly sudden onset pulmonary edema. All things considered, it seemed wiser to wait the situation out. "We'll know in a few more days," he said. "Maybe he'll wake up before then."

Ressler shrugged. "Maybe."

Audrey Schaeffer sat at Jeffrey McDonald's bedside, staring at the monitor, her face pale. According to the nurses, she had said very little. Kurtz had met her on the prior admission and she obviously remembered him. "How are you doing, Miss Schaeffer?" he asked.

"Not so good. I'm wondering if I'm to blame for this."

That was unexpected. Kurtz looked at her. "In what way?"

"I had just told him that we were through. The very next night, this happens." She shook her head.

"It was his decision, not yours. You're not responsible for his actions."

"That's easy to say but it's hard to believe." She shook her head. "He's not a bad guy. He's just not the guy for me."

"I imagine that you've already been asked this, but have you any idea if he was taking anything? And what it was he might have been taking?"

"No. Not at all."

"Who might know?"

She frowned. "Steve Hayward, Howard Mather or Douglas Jefferson: his so-called friends. I don't like any of them."

"Steve Hayward, Howard Mather, Douglas Jefferson..." Kurtz said.

"Yeah," she said. "You could try them."

"Thank you, Miss Schaeffer, I will."

Well, actually, he wouldn't. Kurtz had stuck his nose into police investigations before, with variable results. This time, he decided to let the cops do their job.

"So, let me get this straight," Barent said. "You have information that might pertain to a crime and you've brought this information to us."

"Yeah," Kurtz said.

Barent scratched his head. "That's very mature of you."

Kurtz frowned at him. "I'm a married man. I have responsibilities."

"This is true. So, what do you want us to do with this information?"

"Investigate?"

Barent leaned back and thought about it. The initial screen had shown traces of heroin. Possession of heroin was of course, a crime, but the court system was jammed with people who abused narcotics and unless the guy was dealing the stuff, a case like this was hardly worth their time. "Let's wait until the mass spec comes back. If it's positive for anything else, we'll look up the guy's friends. Until then, we've got better things to do."

"Okay," Kurtz said. "Fine."

"Give my love to Lenore," Barent said. "Let me know how it turns out."

Chapter 8

"Huh?" Moran said. "What is this?"

Kurtz smiled. "Don't recognize it?"

"It's been awhile since High School chemistry, and even then I wouldn't have recognized it."

"Methyl 1- (2-phenylethyl)- 4- [phenyl (propanoyl) amino] piperidine-4-carboxylate is the chemical formulation of carfentanil."

Barent looked up. "What?"

"This is the tox screen on Jeffrey McDonald. Heroin mixed with carfentanil. A lot more carfentanil than heroin."

Barent sat back in his chair and frowned. "Well, that's not good."

"Gray Death," Moran said.

Kurtz winced. "Is that what it's called on the street?"

"It's got a few different names on the street," Barent said. "Gray Death, C-50, Serial Killer…"

"Carfentanil…" Moran said. "Gray Death, not China White."

"Either one is bad news," Barent said.

Carfentanil was an ultra-potent, long lasting analogue of fentanyl. While fentanyl was commonly used as an adjunct to anesthesia in humans, and alpha-methylfentanil had no legitimate uses at all, carfentanil was used to anesthetize large animals, like elephants and giraffes. It was ten thousand times more potent than morphine, colorless, odorless, water soluble and easily absorbed through the skin.

"In 2002, some Chechen terrorists took a theater full of people hostage in Moscow," Barent said. "The Russian Special Forces pumped an unknown agent through the theater's ventilation system and then moved in. They had medics on standby. The medics had been told to bring narcotic antagonists but they weren't told why and they weren't told how much. They didn't realize what was about to happen and they didn't bring nearly enough. Over two hundred fifty people died, including all the terrorists and about a quarter of the hostages, over two hundred of them. The Russians never disclosed what agent they used but a later analysis by a British firm on the clothes of some of the survivors revealed a mixture of different narcotics, primarily carfentanil.

"The stuff is more potent than nerve gas. A kilo of pure carfentanil can kill up to fifty *million* people."

"Oh," Kurtz said.

"Most of it comes from China," Moran said. "Amazingly, it's legal there. Anybody can make it and there are no restrictions on selling it. It's not hard to synthesize and it's a lot cheaper than heroin. If you go on the internet, there are Chinese websites that offer it for sale. They even give advice on how to import it into other countries illegally."

Kurtz shuddered. "In that case, I'm surprised there isn't more of it around."

Barent shrugged. "The problem tends to be self-correcting. It's easily absorbed through the skin and if you breathe in even a tiny amount, you'll never breathe again. People who mess with it have a habit of dropping dead. Also, the DEA works hard to keep it out of the country."

"Obviously," Moran added, "with less than complete success."

"So, now what?" Kurtz said.

"Now?" Barent picked up the phone. "We call the Narcotics Squad. Maybe they can give us some insight." He grinned. "And then we interview…what were their names?"

"Steve Hayward, Howard Mather and Douglas Jefferson," Kurtz said.

"Yeah. Them. And whatever happened to Jeffrey McDonald, by the way?"

Kurtz shrugged. "He woke up. They sent him home."

"Good," Moran said. "We'll talk to him first."

"Am I under arrest?" Jeffrey McDonald said. Barent and Moran stood on the front porch of Jeffrey McDonald's small house in Brooklyn. McDonald was standing inside with the door barely cracked, the security chain still attached.

Barent glanced at Moran and raised an eyebrow. "No," he said.

"Then I'm not saying a word."

Barent frowned. "We *could* arrest you. Would that make you feel better?"

"Huh?" Jeffrey McDonald said.

"Never mind. What exactly will it take to get you to cooperate?"

Jeffrey McDonald looked at him and frowned, then he seemed to come to a decision. "Come inside," he said.

McDonald led them down a narrow hallway into the den and sat on the couch. Barent and Moran took easy chairs. The room was neat. Somebody had made an effort to keep the place clean and organized.

Jeffrey McDonald sighed. "I realize that I have a problem."

Barent glanced at Moran. Moran's face remained impassive.

"It's nobody's fault," McDonald said. "I'm not blaming anybody, except maybe myself." He shrugged. "I don't even know why I do it."

Barent didn't know, either. He had some sympathy for the guy, but in the end, it was hard for him to relate. Why *did* people do things that were stupid and self-destructive? "This is twice that you've almost killed yourself. Have you considered rehab?"

"Yes. I'm going to Ambrosia tomorrow. In New Jersey?"

Ambrosia Treatment Center was a well-known and highly respected rehabilitation center. "I've heard good things," Barent said. "That's smart of you."

Moran leaned forward. "How long have you been abusing drugs?"

Jeffrey McDonald frowned. "Things are already tough enough. I don't need to go to jail."

Barent shrugged. "We have no intention of arresting you. You're entering treatment. A judge would take that into account and for a first offense, you would get probation. We're interested in arresting the people who are selling the stuff, not the victims."

Barent, like a lot of cops, believed in legalization. In Barent's opinion, most of the harm that drugs brought came from the criminality. The last people on Earth who wanted drugs to be legal were the criminals. If it wasn't a crime, the stuff would be cheap. If it was cheap, there wouldn't be any profit. Those countries where addiction was treated as a disease instead of a crime not only had less drug violence, they also had less addiction, the addiction that they had was less harmful to the patients and they had much better success at treatment.

Jeffrey McDonald nodded. "It's a compulsion, you know? I realize that it's stupid, that it's doing me more harm than good, but somehow, that realization just doesn't seem to matter. It doesn't even seem real. When you're high, it just feels so *good*…and without it, it's like I'm just going through the motions. Life has no meaning. Nothing is worth doing. Everything is just…gray. You know?"

Jeffrey McDonald was describing the classic symptoms of both clinical depression and drug addiction. A lot of depressed people turned to drugs. Barent knew this. The trouble was that, aside from the very temporary high, the drugs didn't help the depression. The drugs, by reducing the normal levels of dopamine and endorphins in the brain, made depression worse.

Barent nodded. "Do you know a guy named Mitchell Price?"

"Never heard of him."

"Where do you get the stuff from?" Moran asked.

"Friends." McDonald looked away.

"Steve Hayward?" Barent asked. "Howard Mather? Douglas Jefferson."

Jeffrey McDonald's eyes narrowed. "Audrey's been talking."

Barent just looked at him and after a moment, McDonald dropped his eyes. "Yeah," he said. "Steve Hayward. Not Howard. Howard has nothing to do with it."

"How about Jefferson?"

"No. Not that I'm aware of."

"We asked you before how long you were using," Moran said.

McDonald nodded. "It started in High School, marijuana mostly. This stuff? Only a couple of years."

"But you never OD'd until very recently."

"True."

"So, what's changed?"

McDonald frowned. "I'm divorced. That's different. I have a girlfriend." He grinned ruefully. "Well, I had a girlfriend." He sat back in the couch, apparently thinking. "Am I more depressed? I'm not sure. Maybe, but I'm not using more, not deliberately. I understand the difference between getting high and killing myself. Or I thought I did…"

Barent looked at Moran and shrugged.

Moran shook his head, looking skeptical. "And yet you've OD'd twice."

"Are the drugs any different?" Barent asked.

"Maybe." McDonald frowned. "I'm getting high quicker. It's like lights exploding in my brain. It feels…wonderful."

"And then you stop breathing," Barent said.

McDonald gave him a wounded look.

"Where does Steve Hayward get it?"

"No idea," McDonald said.

Steve Hayward worked for a company that manufactured household supplies. It wasn't glamorous and the pay was barely above minimum wage. It was a job, not a career.

Steve Hayward and Jeffrey McDonald had been friends for years. They had lived on the same block, gone to the same schools and had naturally gravitated toward each other, sharing an interest in sports, video games and, ultimately, drugs. Steve Hayward was a short, tubby little guy with a quick wit but little academic talent or interest. He got decent grades but was nowhere near the top of his class.

"It started in High School," McDonald had said. "Everybody knew that Steve was the guy you went to if you wanted to score."

Like a lot of guys who wanted to get rich but had neither the talent nor the motivation to put in long hours in a demanding field, Steve Hayward found himself a shortcut.

"High School kids rarely peddle heroin. Usually, it's marijuana, maybe a little cocaine," Barent said.

McDonald nodded. "That's how it started."

The two had gone to separate colleges and hadn't seen each other very often for the next few years, but they kept in touch. McDonald moved to New York after finishing school, and a few years later, Hayward did so as well. Hayward, like McDonald, was divorced. He had quickly re-married a much younger woman. He and the new wife liked to party. They also liked expensive wine, expensive cars and expensive vacations, none of which could legitimately be purchased by Hayward's legitimate employment.

"It's more of a front, really," McDonald said. "I don't think he spends much time, there."

No, he didn't.

The next day, Steve Hayward arrived at his office at about 10:00 AM. He left for lunch at noon, came back two hours later and went home at 4:00 PM. That seemed to be his routine. He repeated it the next day and the next.

One night later, Steve Hayward and his new wife went to a party. They both wore casual but expensive looking clothes. Hayward drove a Lexus SUV. The party was held at a brownstone in Riverdale. People came and went all through the evening, most of whom were white. Their ages appeared to range from late twenties to early middle-aged. Few stayed for longer than an hour. Steve Hayward was not the first to arrive but he was almost the last to leave. He and the new wife swayed a bit as they walked down the front steps. They giggled and had wide, happy smiles on their faces.

The surveillance van, parked across the street and recording the faces and license plates of all the guests, followed them at a distance as they drove home. The garage door opened. The garage door closed. The lights in the kitchen and then the bedroom went on and soon turned off. The van remained in front of the McDonald household for another hour and then, it being close to 3:00 AM, the van drove slowly off.

It was time for the forces of justice to get some sleep.

Steve Hayward did not show up for work the next morning. Neither did his wife, a secretary for an insurance brokerage. Calls to the home were not answered. Messages left on voicemail were not returned. The next day, the cleaning lady, a Mrs. Velasquez, who had been working for the Haywards for three years and was considered entirely trustworthy, arrived and let herself in with the key that she had been given. A few seconds later, Mrs. Velasquez came stumbling out of the house, gasping, her face white. She ran to her car, sat in the front seat and locked all the doors. Then she hesitated for a long moment, pulled her cell phone from her purse and dialed 911.

Lew Barent had seen a lot of dead bodies in the course of his career and at this point, very little could shock him. These dead bodies looked like most others, except for the fact that the heads had been removed and were sitting on the kitchen counter, surprised expressions on both. A search of the household revealed both headless bodies, still in bed. Both had been shot three times in the chest.

Harry Moran, Barent noted, looked no happier than himself. "Are we responsible for this?" Harry said.

Barrent had been asking himself the same thing. "We're not the ones who pulled the trigger. The guy who pulled the trigger is responsible." Even to himself, this sounded like a rationalization. In a strictly Platonic sense, what he had said was true, but still…it was hard to escape the feeling that Steve Hayward and his wife would both be alive if they had managed to stay off the police radar. Moran gave him a disapproving look and shook his head, disgusted.

The search of the house revealed nothing. No drugs, no weapons, nothing suspicious or out of place, just two dead bodies with their heads detached.

Chapter 9

Jason Klein was the co-owner and Manager at Kingsford Household Supply, the corporation where Steve Hayward had been employed. He was tall, thin and almost bald. He had a dark wooden desk in a small office. A picture of a plump, smiling woman and two smiling kids sat on the corner of the desk. He blinked at Barent and Moran, both sitting in wooden chairs opposite his desk. "He didn't do much around here, frankly."

"So, why did you keep him on?"

Jason Klein shrugged. "It was my partner's decision."

"Your partner?"

"Sal Marino. He's Hayward's cousin. It seems that their grandmother told him to." A slight, cynical smile played across Klein's face. "The old lady is eighty-seven and still rules the family with an iron fist. Better him than me."

"Okay," Moran said. "What was he like?"

"Hayward?" Klein tilted his head to the side seemed to think about it. "Not a bad guy. He kept to himself mostly. He didn't do a lot of work but then we didn't pay him a lot of money. He seemed happy with the arrangement. I always wondered why. Obviously, he wasn't making enough here to live on, but it wasn't hurting anybody, it kept my partner happy, or at least it kept his grandma off his back and I didn't see any reason to complain."

"What, exactly, did Hayward do?"

"He was a salesman. He was pretty good at it, actually. Got along with the customers, knew the merchandise. When he showed up, he made his salary."

"What about when he didn't show up?"

Klein shrugged. "Then somebody else did it."

"No," Moran said. "I mean where was he and what was he doing when he wasn't at work?"

"No idea."

"Great," Moran muttered. "That's just great."

Cindy Daniels was middle-aged and stocky. She had brown hair pulled back into a bun and a round, pleasant face. She was Klein's assistant manager. "He showed up when he felt like it, basically." She looked at Barent with a bewildered expression on her face. "Who would want to kill a guy like Steve Hayward?"

"That's what we're trying to find out," Barent said.

"Oh. Right." She frowned. "I don't know what else I can tell you."

Unfortunately, neither did Barent.

Sal Marino was also little help. "My Aunt Toni, Steve's mother, she's almost out of her mind." He shook his head. "Steve was her youngest, her baby. And Nonna is pissed." He frowned. "My grandmother is not a woman you want to make pissed."

Barent looked at Moran. "Why is that?"

"Nonna has connections." Marino gave an emphatic nod. "Connections," he said again.

Barent raised an eyebrow. "Connections with who?"

Marino squinted at Barent and blinked his eyes, apparently realizing that he might have said more than he intended. "Nonna's brother, my great-uncle Sal? The one I'm named for? According to family legend, he was a made man."

"Really?" Moran said.

Marino solemnly nodded.

"You're Sicilian," Barent said.

"Hey, I'm as American as apple pie. *I* am not Sicilian. *Nonna* is Sicilian. I want nothing to do with that shit. It's bad for your health."

"I think that's very smart of you," Barent said. "So why did you give your cousin a job, if he wasn't willing to do the job?"

"Cause Nonna asked me to."

"And why did she do that?"

Marino shrugged. "He's her grandson. He needed a job."

"But the job paid minimum wage. Meanwhile, he drove a Lexus."

Marino frowned. "None of my business," he said.

"You never wondered?"

"Sure, I wondered, but it was none of my business."

"You never asked him?"

Marino puffed his cheeks out and gave a little snort. "Frankly? I didn't want to know."

"Right," Barent said. "And now, it's too late."

Chapter 10

Dinner with the in-laws. Always fun. Kurtz had learned to relish the competition. Esther greeted him with a superficial kiss on the cheek and a reluctant smile. Stanley shook his hand. Esther's cousin, Sylvia Hersch and her husband Milton were there, along with a neighbor named Natalie Hale and her husband, Moishe. Moishe Hale wore a yarmulke and had a short black beard, and since Hale was about as WASP'ish a name as could be imagined, the name had most likely been changed at Ellis Island, when the first "Hale" had come to this country. Regardless, Moishe Hale had a ready smile and seemed like a pleasant guy. The Hale's youngest son, a quiet fourteen-year-old, clutched a paperback whose cover sported a rocket ship, a tentacled alien and a frightened looking blonde. The kid looked bored. Kurtz didn't blame him.

"You want a drink?" Stanley said.

"Absolutely." Stanley Brinkman was very proud of his collection of fine Bourbon.

"You know what I got?" Stanley didn't wait for him to answer. He positively beamed. He looked in both directions to make certain that nobody could hear him, leaned closer and whispered. "I got Pappy Van Winkle, 20 years."

Kurtz blinked at him. "You're kidding."

Stanley smiled a shark-like smile. "Nope."

The women were bustling around the kitchen: Lenore, Esther, Cousin Sylvia and Natalie Hale. Stanley frowned and grudgingly turned to Moishe Hale, who was standing nearby, oblivious. "You want to try some Bourbon?" Stanley asked.

Moishe shrugged. "Sure."

"Follow me."

Stanley led them into the den, closed and locked the door. "Sit down," he said. "Get comfortable." The den was Stanley Brinkman's domain. Esther never came there, not even to clean. The room was filled with trinkets and mementoes from vacations to exotic places like Miami Beach, Cancun, Branson, Missouri and Disney World.

The furniture was leather, soft and comfortable. The scent of cherry pipe tobacco clung to the furniture. A man cave.

A large wooden cabinet covered one whole wall, with a collection of bottles standing on top. Moishe Hale, who had evidently never been here before, looked around with avid interest. Kurtz, who had, watched Stanley as he delicately lifted one bottle, displayed the label and then poured a generous shot into each of three glasses. He took an eye-dropper, and carefully added five drops of mineral water to each glass. He handed one to Kurtz and another to Moishe and then sat down in a recliner with the third clutched in his chubby fist. "Cheers," he said.

Kurtz sipped. Flavors of maple, honey, a little vanilla. He swirled it around his tongue. Maybe some orange and clove. He closed his eyes and sipped again.

"Well?" Stanley said.

Moishe stared down at his glass with a quizzical expression. "I don't know," he said. "It's good, but it tastes like any other Bourbon to me."

Stanley stared at him. Kurtz suppressed a grin. Truthfully, while it probably was the best Bourbon he had ever tasted, Moishe Hale had a point. There wasn't any bad Bourbon and all of it tasted pretty much alike. The difference between the good stuff and the great stuff was subtle, and in Kurtz' firm opinion, definitely not worth the money. He was more than happy to drink it, however. "What did you pay for this?" he asked.

Stanley gave him a haughty look. "Three hundred and fifty."

Kurtz nodded, amazed. "Great stuff," he said. But not worth three hundred and fifty bucks.

"Yes," Stanley said. "It is." He looked at Moishe with disapproval.

"So," Kurtz said to Moishe. "What do you think of the Knicks this year?"

Moishe rolled his eyes. "What a bunch of clowns."

Can't disagree with that, Kurtz thought. Even Stanley had to purse his lips and acknowledge a truth so completely beyond dispute.

Five minutes later, somebody knocked on the door. "Yes?" Stanley said.

Lenore's voice answered. "Dinner."

They finished their Bourbon and trooped out.

Kurtz found himself sitting next to Cousin Sylvia. "So, how are you, *boychik*?" she said. Cousin Sylvia had a twinkle in her eye. She ran a real estate firm. Esther Brinkman, thank God, had recently joined the firm. Having an actual job had done wonders for Esther's disposition.

"Pretty good," Kurtz said. "I've been busy."

Natalie Hale looked up. "What do you do?" she asked.

Esther, carrying in a covered tray, said, "He's a surgeon." She frowned and wrinkled her nose. "A *general* surgeon."

Kurtz sighed.

Sylvia grinned and patted him on the hand. Lenore narrowed her eyes at her mother. Esther ignored Lenore and removed the cover from the tray. "Pot roast," she announced.

By now, Kurtz had eaten Esther Brinkman's pot roast many times. It was good pot roast, as pot roast went, but there was only so much you could do with pot roast. Thank god, she hadn't brought out the *gefilte* fish.

"Where do you work?" Natalie Hale asked.

"I have privileges at Staunton but I do most of my cases at Easton," Kurtz said.

Natalie frowned. "Did you know Steve Ryan?"

"Yes, I did."

Stanley was carving the pot roast into half inch slices. Lenore picked up a bowl of candied carrots, spooned some on her plate and then passed the bowl around the table, then did the same with a bowl of mashed potatoes. Stanley finished carving the roast, put two slices on his own plate and passed around the platter. "Wine?" Stanley asked.

"Please," Kurtz said.

Stanley, in addition to his fondness for Bourbon, also knew his wine. The bottle was Zaca Mesa Syrah. Kurtz sipped, let it roll around his tongue. Peppery, he thought.

"It was sad, what happened to him," Natalie Hale said.

"Steve Ryan?" Kurtz nodded. "Yeah. It's a shame."

Natalie shook her head. "His wife and kids are taking it hard."

The wife and kids usually do take it hard when Daddy decides to kill himself, but let's not be insensitive and say that out loud. "I'm sure. He was a nice guy. It's a shame," he said again.

"I went to school with his wife, Donna." Natalie smiled at Lenore. "Lenore and I both. We're old friends."

Kurtz had last seen Donna Ryan at the funeral but aside from briefly shaking her hand and offering his condolences, there had been nothing much to say. Donna Ryan was blonde, very thin, very pretty with sunken cheeks and sad eyes. The three kids had clung to her legs, overwhelmed.

For a few minutes, the conversation lagged while they ate. Finally, Sylvia sighed and said, "I know her mother. I sold them their house. She's a tough woman. She managed to get out of the Soviet Union with only her husband and the clothes on their backs. They hiked for miles through the woods before crossing the border into Finland. Tough."

Natalie Hale nodded. "Her parents had five kids. Donna has a lot of family. They're close."

"That whole Russian community is close," Sylvia said. "Her mother never did learn much English, but she made sure her kids got a good education and had a better life than she did."

Natalie sighed. "Yeah," she said. "Until now."

Shot. Strangled. Shot. Stabbed three times in the abdomen and once in the chest. Pushed onto the subway tracks and electrocuted, though that one might have been an accident, not deliberate. Killed in a bar fight, the alleged perpetrator having expressed remorse and regret; not that remorse and regret would keep him out of jail, but if he could successfully fake sincerity, Barent thought, it might at least reduce the guy's sentence. Barent flipped through the pages. Let's see…what else? Shot. Stabbed. Poisoned by a jealous girlfriend. Shot first in the testicles, then in the abdomen, then in the face. Barent winced.

None of these were Barent's cases but he liked to review the police reports from other districts and precincts, just to keep up with what was going on. What was the word? Oh, yes: *Schadenfreude*, the doleful pleasure to be obtained by observing other people's problems. Better them than me, he thought.

Now here was a tasty one, a half-eaten body pulled out of a landfill, the hands tied together. Male, slim, wearing a hooded sweatshirt and jeans. The body was decomposed to the point that the exact cause of death might have been speculative, except that the wire garotte left around the neck provided at least a tentative clue.

"Having fun?" Moran asked.

Barent shrugged. "Just thinking," he said.

A lot of police work was just thinking. You took a bunch of disparate clues and tried to fit them together. Sometimes you succeeded. This business with Jeffrey McDonald and Steve Hayward, for instance. Not much to go on, not yet. An overdose from a highly dangerous substance. The drug dealer turns up dead, killed in a spectacular, very morbid fashion. Who does that? Not your average two-bit hood. Not trying to keep it quiet, that's for sure. The papers, naturally, had run with the story, not that they knew the actual story. No, so far as the so-called journalists in this fair city were concerned, Steve Hayward and his wife were fine, upstanding citizens suspected of no crimes of any sort and murdered for no reason whatsoever.

The surveillance van had recorded the license plates of every car parked outside the brownstone where Steve Hayward and his unfortunate wife had partied. So far, they had all come up clean. None of the owners of any of the vehicles had any criminal record beyond a few traffic violations. There was a pattern, however. They were yuppies, every one. Except for Steve Hayward. Steve Hayward did not fit the pattern. Oh, he looked like them and no-doubt talked like them and probably seemed to fit in with them, but Steve Hayward, alone among the crowd, was not employed in any fashion that might support his lifestyle.

Steve Hayward, if Barent allowed himself to speculate, was the supplier, not the consumer.

So, who kills the supplier? A couple of obvious possibilities: first, an unsatisfied customer, second, a jealous competitor…but of course, it might not be the most obvious. Sometimes, it wasn't.

"So, what are you thinking?" Moran asked.

"I'm thinking we need more information."

Moran nodded. "Sounds right to me. Where do you intend to get it?"

Javier Garcia was angry. "Those who purchase illicit products are often reluctant to do so. They are fearful, and they are right to be fearful. There are risks involved in the purchase of such substances. They fear association with an obvious criminal element. They fear betrayal. They fear the police." Javier Garcia smiled. It was not a pleasant smile. "They even fear their neighbors."

Esteban Martinez, Javier Garcia's oldest friend, nodded.

"This is why we use men like Steven Hayward. We do not look like them. We do not sound like them. We are clearly foreign to them. They see us as dangerous and unpredictable. They would not purchase from us, not unless they were truly desperate. Steven Hayward looked like one of them. Steven Hayward gave them the illusion of familiarity. He was comfortable. He seemed…safe."

Esteban Martinez puffed out his cheeks. Javier Garcia was saying nothing that they both did not already know. He was merely venting.

"And now he is dead. Tell me, Esteban; who killed Steven Hayward?"

"I do not know," Esteban Martinez said.

Javier Garcia glared at him. "Whoever killed Steven Hayward will undoubtedly strike again."

Esteban Martinez sighed. "It is of course possible that it was a random occurrence. People are often murdered for the drugs that they carry, and those who sell drugs often have cash lying about the house."

Javier Garcia gave a tiny snort. "It is possible. It is not likely." He looked at Esteban Martinez. "Find out, Esteban. Find out who did this."

"Of course," Esteban Martinez said.

"Croft," Barent said.

Croft was a tall, black man wearing an expensive leather jacket, gold chains around his neck, and designer jeans. A small, curvy blonde with a pert nose, green eyes and full lips clung to his side. Croft looked up at Barent and winced. "Barent," he said tonelessly.

Barent smiled and slid into the booth. Croft and the blonde both stared at him.

"So," Barrent said. "What's new?"

Croft puffed up his cheeks. He said nothing and continued to stare. Barent signaled to a waiter, pulled out a small notebook and a pen. Croft winced. The waiter, a slender young man with a haircut that leaned heavily to one side of his head and probably cost several hundred bucks, wandered over. "Can I get you beautiful people something?"

"Cheeseburger and fries, medium well," Barent said. "Blue Moon."

The waiter gave him a big smile. "Coming right up."

Croft drew a deep breath. "What is it this time?" he said.

Barent's eyes flicked to the blonde.

"This is Regina," Croft said. "My fiancée."

Barent's eyebrows rose. Croft was an information broker. He had a head for figures, a high IQ and made it his business to collect random bits of information. He was also a pimp. A highly successful pimp. His girls were smart, good-looking and skilled. Croft treated them well, like the valuable commodity that they were. He never beat them or abused them in any way. They rarely stayed for long, though. Whoring, for most of them, was a way station on the way to something else. This was just fine with Croft. Always more where they came from, which was usually from the campus of one of New York's many institutions of higher learning.

Barent had been assuming that Regina was one of Croft's stable. Then again, maybe she was.

"Congratulations," Barent said.

Croft grunted. Regina bared her teeth.

"So," Barent said, "where was I? Oh, yes. I figured you could help me." He grinned. "I need some information." Barent had spoken with three contacts already this evening, and gotten nothing useful. After Croft, he planned on going home and calling it a night.

Croft sighed. He shook his head. "I know you put a word in to the parole board, Barent, but you and I were even a long time ago. Helping you would probably not be good for my bottom line. Or my health."

The waiter plunked down a frosted stein and a bottle of Blue Moon with an orange slice on top and wandered away. Barent watched him until he was out of earshot. "You employ a lot of girls,"

Barent said, "and your girls hear things. I'm not asking you to give me anything confidential or incriminating. What I need to know has nothing to do with you or your business."

Croft sighed. "What?"

Regina gave a small shake of her head but said nothing.

Barent looked at Regina. "Perhaps you might like to take a short trip to the Ladies' Room."

"I think I'll stay right here," Regina said. She had a smooth, deep voice. Strange to hear a big voice like that from such a tiny body.

"She can stay," Croft said. He grinned. "Regina, she know all my secrets."

Somehow, Barent doubted this but if that's the way Croft wanted to play it, then fine with him. He shrugged. "Any rumors on the street about new drugs?"

"Huh…" Croft said. He sat back. "Wasn't expecting that."

Barent waited.

"Some of my girls, they go with some rich dudes. You know?"

Barent nodded.

"Rich dudes got big egos. Sometimes, they got big mouths. It all a game to them; beat the competition, own something the other rich guy don't own, a car, a plane, a girl, something to put up their nose." Croft shrugged. "A lot of guys like a little blow before getting down to business. A lot of them like to share with their current lady. They think it impresses them, make them a little more pliable, more up for the evening's entertainment." Croft grinned and squeezed Regina a little closer to his side. Regina glanced at Barent and grinned. "But," Croft said, "and this is a very big *but*, this is a lot more common with the pros. A pro, she got herself a client list. She and the client, they know each other. They talk, they feel comfortable. Rich dudes don't generally get rich by being stupid. My girls, they more semi-pros, if you know what I mean."

Barent looked at him. "No," he said. "I have no idea at all what you mean."

Croft raised an eyebrow. "My girls, they young. A lot of them be college kids. Some of them doing it for a lark. They like the money but none of them plan on making it a career. They motivated. They have goals." He frowned down at the top of Regina's head then gave Barent a half-hearted grin. "I got no interest in going back to prison.

I pick my business associates very carefully. The guys I deal with, they want someone young and pretty and compliant. They like to spend a little time with girls young enough to be their daughters but they don't tell them any secrets, nothing that could come back to haunt them. It too big a risk. They don't know them. They don't trust them enough to keep their mouths shut."

"I don't understand that," Barent said. "They're employing young prostitutes but you claim that they don't want to take any risks and they don't want to do anything that could come back to haunt them. This seems a little inconsistent." Barent gave Croft a hard look. "I really should arrest you."

Croft gave him a look that clearly conveyed the opinion that Barent was an idiot. "I get paid for scheduling a meeting. I'm only the referral service. Payment to her is for time, conversation and companionship only. No sexual shenanigans are implied, committed or contracted for. She choose to boff his brains out, that strictly up to her. It got nothing at all to do with me. They be nothing illegal in that."

Strictly speaking, this was true. *Escorting*, as it was called, was not, in fact, against the law. The only thing that was against the law was the direct exchange of money for sex.

"It works both ways. My girls be smart. They smart enough to size the client up and give him what he wants. They call the client *Daddy* and tell him he so big and strong and handsome, even if he small and fat and ugly. None of my girls be interested in drugs. If they were, I would get rid of them."

"That's...disappointing," Barent said. But not exactly surprising. He shook his head. "So, you don't have any names..."

Croft grinned. "I didn't say that. I do have one name. I going to send you to an old friend."

Chapter 11

Arnaldo Figueroa was doing well. His left leg was still weak, his left hand clumsy, the feeling in both limbs diminished, but Arnaldo Figueroa knew the score. He went about his therapy with grim diligence, limping along the parallel bars, squeezing a rubber ball as if he wanted to crush it, which he did.

He had been moved from Bellevue to the Abrams Rehabilitation Institute of Easton Medical Center, Staunton College of Medicine, which was, frankly, something of a misnomer. The word 'Institute' carried gravitas. It impressed people. It sounded important. The actual Institute, however, occupied a mere eleven beds on a single floor of the hospital and the Department of Rehabilitative Medicine consisted of three physicians who spent the majority of their time at the school, not Easton. One of these, a portly little guy with thick glasses, bushy eyebrows and a bald head had outlined a treatment plan that the physical therapists were diligently following, but he otherwise saw Arnaldo Figueroa no more than once every few days. Kurtz was not a rehab specialist but he was a police surgeon and still nominally in charge of the case.

"How are you, Arnie?" Kurtz asked.

Arnie grinned at Kurtz, Drew Johnson, Linda Rodriguez and Richie Allen, the medical student. This was Richie's first clinical rotation. He stared at everything with wide eyes.

"Not bad, Doc."

"Could you hold out your hands?"

He sat up and held both arms out in front of him. It took a fraction of a second longer for the left arm to move into position. The arm was noticeably thinner than the right, the fingers flexed into a claw.

"Can you spread your fingers?"

A look of grim concentration crossed Figueroa's face. His lips thinned. Slowly, the fingers of his left hand opened and spread.

Kurtz nodded. "That's good. You're getting there."

Figueroa sighed. "Better than it was." He looked up at Kurtz. "Am I ever going to get back to work?"

Kurtz had never lied to a patient. He wasn't going to start now. "I don't know, Arnie. It's possible but the odds are slim."

Figueroa sank back into the bed. He swallowed.

"It's too soon to be discouraged," Kurtz said. "You're making good progress."

"Okay," Figueroa said. "Might as well go for it. Not much else to do here."

"Keep it up," Kurtz said. "I'll see you, tomorrow."

Barent met Christine Morales at the Modern. When they had first sat down, she had asked to see Barent's ID, which he turned over without comment. She examined it carefully, then handed it back.

She wasn't what Barent had been expecting. She wasn't young, for one thing. She had thick, black hair, a smooth, unlined face and even, golden skin. Her eyes sparkled, as if she found life endlessly fascinating. Her shoulders were broad, her breasts impressive, her posture straight. She wore a tailored business suit with just a hint of cleavage showing and looked like an adolescent's dream of his sexy, favorite aunt. She wore a large diamond and a wedding ring on her left hand. She reminded Barent not at all of his usual informant.

Christine Morales said very little at first. She sipped a glass of white wine and listened carefully while Barent spoke, focusing her wide, dark eyes on Barent's face, clearly paying attention. Barent found it...soothing, almost, even flattering. If she was putting on an act, she was very, very good at it.

"Tell me about your business," Barent said, while they waited for the food to arrive.

She smiled. "I'm not sure that would be wise."

"Money exchanged is for time, conversation and companionship only. Isn't that so? I'm not asking you to incriminate yourself."

She laughed softly. "What exactly do you need to know?"

It was a long shot. Barent knew that. The number of people in New York City who used and abused narcotics in any single day numbered in the thousands. The chances that this particular woman might have some special insight to offer was slim. Still, Barent had no place better to be and he was enjoying his lunch.

"First of all, I am a member of the Homicide Division of the NYPD."

Christine Morales nodded. Barent had already said this.

"My interest in any other crimes is peripheral. Specifically, three people were recently murdered, in two separate instances. The only similarity was the excessive level of violence. The crimes may be completely unrelated. However, one of them had been abusing heroin laced with a very unusual and very dangerous narcotic. The other two were a drug dealer and his wife."

Christine Morales raised an eyebrow. "And what makes you think that I can help you with this?"

Christine Morales ran a very exclusive, very upscale escort agency. The women she employed were, unlike Croft and his stable of college kids, professionals. Or so Croft had told him.

"Christine, she started out as one of my girls," Croft had said, "a long time ago. She was studying psychology at NYU, wanted a little extra money and got my name from a friend of a friend. Turned out, she a natural, had a real talent for the business." Croft smiled and shook his head. "After a year or so working for me, she decided that she already doing more good for both mankind and her bank account than she could with a Ph.D. Similar work, different methods." A thoughtful look crossed Croft's face. "Maybe not so different."

Barent frowned. Croft smiled. "You gonna pay my referral fee?"

Barent merely stared at him. Croft's smile grew wider. He snickered. "No? Why don't we consider it an act of charity for one of New York's finest?"

Regina had laughed.

"According to my source," Barent said to Christine Morales, "the women that you employ often hear things."

"Croft," she said. "He told me you would be calling."

Barent nodded.

"Croft is an anomaly in the business," Christine Morales said. "He actually cares about the girls that he employs. He never abuses them, not in the slightest."

"So I hear."

Every good cop had a stable of snitches, guys who could be depended upon to give a little information for a little consideration, which could range from a few bucks to a get-out-of-jail-free card, depending on the crime and the circumstances. Barent's crime, however, was murder. Barent's snitches, like Croft, were not at the level of the street. Barent had, of course, notified the Narcotics Squad of his needs and even now, he was certain, many cops other than himself were having discreet conversations with junkies and low-level suppliers all over the five boroughs. One of these, Barent was fully aware, was far more likely than himself to come up with a useful lead. Lunch with Christine Morales was more in the nature of a fishing expedition than a criminal investigation. He smiled to himself. Still, if his current efforts led nowhere, he was enjoying the conversation and he intended to enjoy his lunch.

"It is true," Christine Morales said, "that the ladies in my employ will often hear things that their clients would prefer to keep confidential." She grinned at him and sipped her wine. "It's a business built on mutual trust."

Barent had his doubts about this but he gave an encouraging nod.

"It's a strange business, in a way, very private, obviously. It takes place in some of the richest, most luxurious surroundings, and involves some of the richest, most influential men and women on Earth. Very few of these men and women are stupid. Very few are eager to endanger themselves."

"Please go on," Barent said.

She smiled. "One of my clients—let's call him Joachim, though that is not his real name—is a business man from South America. He stays at high-end hotels. Most often, he rents a suite and he requests my company for the night."

Barent blinked at her.

"What?" she said.

"I was under the impression," Barent said carefully, "that your position was more management than labor."

Christine Morales laughed. "This man is an old friend. I make exceptions for old friends, and I always loved my work."

"And what does he do, this old friend?"

"He's an executive with a trading company. They export products from Argentina: native art, carved figurines, wine…" She shrugged.

"What is he like?"

"A very pleasant man. Very polite." She smiled. "Very strong."

"What do you talk about?"

She frowned. "Our lives, mostly. His family and work. We have a very cordial, professional relationship. I would never betray his confidence, but truly, I know nothing at all about him that would reflect poorly on either his character or his activities. He is a gentleman."

Take that, Barent thought. He took a bite out of his sandwich. Christine Morales sipped her wine.

"And yet," Barent said, "he is spending time with you, rather than his wife. I assume that he has a wife?"

She stared at him, then smiled widely. "I do believe you're a prude."

Probably, Barent thought. He shrugged.

"Joachim is a wealthy man," she said, "and he comes from a wealthy family. He married when he was very young, to a woman of a similar social class. He barely knew her when they married—it was arranged by their parents—but neither objected and the marriage is a happy one. They have four children, all now adult. His wife spends much of her time on charity work. They are both sophisticated, cosmopolitan people. He would never say one word against his wife. He respects her. He is very fond of her, and she of him."

Barent must have looked doubtful. "Neither of them," she said, "are American. They do not necessarily share your values, your customs or your beliefs."

Perhaps not. In any case, this was getting him nowhere. "Did he ever offer you drugs?"

Christine Morales sat back, shocked. "Certainly not."

"Did you ever see him do drugs."

She shook her head. "No."

He looked at her. "Then why are we talking about him?"

"You asked me about my business."

"Oh. So I did." Barent scratched the back of his neck, slightly embarrassed. "Did he ever speak of drugs? In any way?"

Christine Morales frowned. "Joachim was a wild one, long ago, when he was young. He did many things that he now regards as foolish. He gambled. He raced cars. He took insane chances with his life and yes, he did a lot of drugs. And then one day, when he was very high, he crashed a car. The young woman with him was killed.

His family had influence. He was never charged, but the experience changed his life. He hasn't touched drugs since that day.

"Sometimes he would speak of the drug epidemic, particularly among the young, always with regret, and disapproval."

"How long have you been…associated with him?"

"Fifteen years," she said.

"And in that time, how often have you seen him?"

She appeared to think about it. "I'm not certain of the exact number. Perhaps twice a year. Some years, three."

"Do you ever leave the hotel room?"

"Of course. What did you think?"

Barent thought that she showed up, they had sex and she left. He was too polite to say it but his face must have expressed his thoughts. Christine Morales gave a low, throaty chuckle. "Joachim has a fondness for the ballet. I prefer the opera. My husband hates the opera." She shrugged. "When Joachim is in town, we typically attend at least one performance of each."

"Oh," Barent said.

"Silly man." She smiled at him, her face serene. "I, and the women in my employ, perform a very important social function, a function that modern American society does not approve of, but I neither need nor care for that approval, nor do my employees, nor do my clients."

Barent wondered what her husband thought of the whole thing but inwardly shrugged. He didn't need to know that and pissing off Christine Morales would not be doing him or his so-called investigation any good. Joachim Whoever would appear to be a dead end but Christine Morales was obviously an intelligent and perceptive woman. Barent didn't have to approve of her lifestyle nor her choice of a career but he recognized a potential asset when he saw one. Perhaps not now. Perhaps never, but it was entirely possible that in the future, on some other case, he might find it useful to speak with her again.

"I do have a name for you, however," Christine Morales said, and she smiled.

Reginald Rinear was a dumbass, Barent thought. His family had been New York aristocracy for over three hundred years. One ancestor had fought in the American Revolution. One had given his life at Shiloh and another had been wounded at Gettysburg. Reginald Rinear looked the part. He was tall, pale and thin, with blonde hair, a straight nose and cold, blue eyes.

"We will no longer accept Reginald Rinear's business," Christine Morales had said.

"And why not?"

She hesitated. "He is rude and offensive. He thinks that the payment for our time entitles him to things that it does not, such as a license to be physically abusive." Christine Morales had stared at Barent from under lowered brows. "He was a new client for us. We didn't know him. He is a phenomenon that all of us in the business prefer to steer clear of. He justifies his predilections as 'role play' and 'make-believe,' but actual bruises and what amounts to attempted forcible rape are considerably beyond the scope of role play. He is a braggart, a buffoon and a criminal."

Barent blinked. "Don't hold back. Tell me how you really feel."

Christine Morales gave him a half-hearted grin. "He used drugs in the presence of my employee. He stated that these drugs were 'new' and 'unique.' He claimed that they were unlike any other and only a select few had the privilege to indulge in them. He tried to talk my employee into sharing these drugs with him. She refused to do so. He didn't like that. Reginald Rinear does not enjoy being told 'no.'" Christine Morales ate a few bites of her salad, looking grim. "After he ingested this substance, whatever it was, he grew agitated. My employee stated that he then attempted forcible penetration, which she resisted, but he was, in her words, 'as limp as a wet noodle.' He began to curse. He hit her."

"Forgive my indelicacy," Barent stated, "but beyond the euphemisms regarding 'companionship' and 'conversation,' I find myself surprised that your employee would resist."

"He tried to stick it up her ass," Christine Morales said. "Some of us go along with that. Some of us don't. She doesn't. Shortly after, he grew somnolent. She stuck around long enough to make sure that he was still breathing, then she counted her blessings and left."

Presumably, she had also counted the money. "Still," Barent said, "considering the disappointment that the poor guy must have felt, the way in which his expectations for the evening were thwarted, don't you think his reactions were understandable? Perhaps you should try to see it from his point of view? He is a man, after all, and men have their needs."

"Well, fuck him," Christine Morales said, "and fuck you, too."

Barent chuckled. "I'll take it under advisement." He sat back in his seat and thought about what he had been told. "Tell me, would your employee be willing to proffer charges?"

"That would be up to her. An off-hand guess would be 'no.' Actually, 'hell, no' would be more likely."

"Right," Barent said. "Thanks for the information. I'll see what I can do."

Reginald Rinear worked as a commodities broker at Edward James, Financial, a medium sized firm with an exclusive list of very rich clients. He was, as Christine Morales had indicated, smug, arrogant, supercilious and uncooperative. He stared at Barent from the other side of his very large desk. Next to Reginald Rinear sat his lawyer, a man named Everett Johns.

"No," said Everett Johns.

Reginald Rinear sniffed. A small, cold smile crossed his face.

Unfortunately, Barent thought, Everett Johns was more than competent. Barent had encountered him before, on other cases. Everett Johns had come up the hard way, first a scholarship student at Columbia, then Harvard Law, then an associate at Pembroke and Elkington, one of New York's largest and most prestigious firms, where he had stayed and ultimately made partner.

"No. My client is not going to answer your questions. He has no reason to. You have no evidence of any wrongdoing on his part and he is not going to subject himself to a witch hunt."

Moran sighed. Everett Johns eyes flicked to Moran's face. Moran stared back.

Reginald Rinear may have been an idiot but he had been smart enough to refuse to talk without his lawyer being present. So far, the lawyer had done all of the talking.

"You may be correct," Barent said. "At the moment, we have a witness statement to the effect that your client is a chronic user of dangerous and illicit substances. Such statements do constitute evidence but admittedly, not enough evidence for us to obtain a warrant. Not at this time.

"You should be aware, however, that one Mitchell Price, a stockbroker, has been killed in a particularly gruesome way. His throat had been slit." Barent smiled at Reginald Rinear, who blinked. "Did you know Mitchell Price?"

"And what do you imagine my client has to do with this Mitchell Price?" Everett Johns said.

Reginald Rinear frowned. His eyes skittered away.

"I'll take that reaction as a maybe." Barent smiled. "Mitchell Price had ingested a very dangerous narcotic variant. It probably would have killed him even if his throat had not been slit. Certainly, it rendered him compliant. There were no signs of resistance at all. He bled out on his couch and died in his sleep.

"Recently, a similar, and even more dangerous narcotic has come to our attention. Both of these narcotics are imported from China and are used to cut heroin. You should be aware that both of them are a lot cheaper than heroin and about five thousand times more potent. People who use them tend to stop breathing and drop dead."

Reginald Rinear continued to frown. Everett Johns glanced at his client, his face expressionless.

"Still nothing to say? No?" Barent shrugged. "Then I want you to understand that the murder of Mitchell Price is not something that the NYPD is going to forget. We are going to pursue all available leads. We do not, at this time, suspect you of being complicit in Mitchell Price's murder. We do suspect that the information you could possibly provide us might assist in leading us to that murderer. One way or another, sooner or later, we will solve this case. You are not the only lead we are pursuing. If it comes out that you possess information that might have helped this investigation and that you refused to cooperate, we will make certain that your role does not remain a secret. How many of your clients, not to mention your employers, will wish to continue their association with a drug addict who is also an accessory after the fact to murder." Barent raised his eyebrows. "Any guesses?"

Reginald Rinear continued to frown into the corner of the room. Everett Johns glanced at him, gave a minute shake of his head and an equally tiny roll of his eyes. He looked at Barent. "Let me confer with my client. We will be in touch if he changes his mind."

As good as they were going to get, Barent thought. He rose to his feet, Moran following, and walked out of the room.

"Think he'll bite?" Moran asked.

"I guess we'll see."

Even at 4:00 AM, a hospital is never entirely dormant. Beepers are beeping; phones are ringing. Patients turn restlessly in their uncomfortable beds. Others, unable to sleep, wander the halls, pushing their IV poles along beside them. Nurses chatter, in between waking patients up to take their vital signs. Orderlies and pharmacy techs push carts down the hallways and resident physicians, always swamped with work, sit at the nursing station and write notes that they had no time to write earlier in the day.

Still, at 4:00 AM, even the busiest hospital grows somnolent.

Arnaldo Figueroa had served four years as an Army Ranger prior to joining the NYPD. He had been wounded twice and shot at more times than he cared to remember. Like most soldiers, he had learned to sleep at any time and in any situation. Like most soldiers who have had to survive in enemy territory, he had learned to sleep lightly.

A nurse opening the door carried a distinctive set of impressions and cues. The door opened wide and light would shine into the room from the hallway outside. The nurse would walk up to his bedside, not trying to be silent. Quite the contrary, as more often than not, a series of questions would be forthcoming, and even if the interaction was confined to the taking of heart rate and blood pressure, there was no way that a patient could sleep through it.

The orderlies also had no reason to be quiet. A food tray being delivered and then picked up, a change of linens, mopping down the floors, none of this was stealthy. Nothing was quiet.

The doctors, of course, and the students, they all wanted to talk. *How are you today, Mr. Figueroa? Are you in any pain? Hold out your hands and spread your fingers. Squeeze your fist as tightly as you can. Walk from one side of the room to the other. Do you have any questions?*

There was no reason that any legitimate personnel would very quietly, very stealthily pull open the door, quietly close the door behind them and then pad inside.

Noise in the middle of the night was annoying. Quiet—too much quiet—was infinitely worse.

Arnaldo Figueroa came awake. His slow, deep breathing did not change. He moved not a muscle. His eyes opened, just the merest slits. The room was dark, of course, but the window allowed light to shine in from outside. Not enough to make out the features but certainly enough to see the tall figure looming over his bed. The figure reached out, grasping Arnaldo Figueroa's IV line with his left hand, and pulled something from a pocket with his right hand. He fumbled with the injection port of the IV line.

The urinal, half filled, was hanging from the railing of the bed. Arnaldo Figueroa reached out with his right hand, grasped the urinal and threw its contents into the figure's face. The figure reeled back, cursing. Arnaldo Figueroa grasped the IV line and pulled it out of his arm. Then he screamed. The figure hesitated for a second and ran for the door. The door opened. The door closed. Arnaldo Figueroa collapsed back onto the bed, his heart thudding. "Close one," he muttered to himself.

"So," Barent said, "let's go over it again."

It is a common failing of humankind to discount events and testimony that are outside of one's own experience, and Arnaldo Figueroa was a recent victim of a traumatic brain injury. The nurses had at first refused to believe that he had suffered anything other than a bad dream, but after noticing the trail of liquid in the hallway outside that led to the staircase, and after discovering a syringe full of an unknown substance with a needle attached lying under the bed, they reluctantly agreed to notify hospital security. Security listened to Arnaldo Figueroa's story and then called Lew Barent and Richard Kurtz.

Arnaldo Figueroa sighed. "What more can I tell you? The room was dark. I couldn't see his face. He was tall, about six-one, maybe six-two. I'm not even certain it was a *he*."

Not a lot of women over six feet, Barent thought, and the footprints the guy had left out in the hall, nicely outlined in Arnaldo

Figueroa's pee, were Reeboks, size twelve. The syringe had been confiscated by the crime scene guys. By tomorrow, they should know what was in it.

"God damn hospitals," Barent muttered. "This place is about as secure as a sieve."

Kurtz nodded.

It was almost a month since Arnaldo Figueroa had been shot. The police guard had been removed two weeks ago, the brass having concluded that his shooting was most likely a random incident…evidently a mistake.

"You've never been up to the Eighteenth Floor, have you?" Kurtz said.

"No," Barent said. "Why do you ask?"

"The Eighteenth Floor is the VIP Floor. All private rooms. The stairways and the doors to each hallway are locked. There's security by the elevator. Nobody gets in without showing ID and being cleared."

"Huh…" Barent said.

"Arnie," Kurtz said, "you're about to get an upgrade."

"That's good," Barent said. He grinned wanly. "We'll bring the guards back too. Let's not make the same mistake twice."

This was becoming a habit. Barent and Moran sat next to each other, across from Kurtz. Kurtz was eating chicken salad on rye. Barent and Moran both had burgers on their plates.

"It was potassium chloride," Moran said.

Kurtz paused for a second, scowled down at his sandwich, then shrugged and took a bite. "A syringe full of potassium chloride would definitely be enough to stop the heart. It's instantly fatal, and it's undetectable. Every cell in the body is full of potassium. After death, all of that potassium gets released into the blood." He shrugged again. "We would never have known why he died."

"I always wondered about that," Moran said. "If every cell contains so much potassium, why would a little more be a problem?"

"A good question," Kurtz said. "The cells contain a lot of potassium but the blood contains mostly sodium. The balance of sodium and potassium is responsible for the conduction of electrochemical impulses. If the balance gets upset, then the impulses that make the heart contract will stop. If the electrochemical impulses stop, then the heart stops."

Moran nodded and took a bite out of his burger. "Okay," he said.

Arnaldo Figueroa was enjoying his new room, which was considerably larger than his old room. Security had been briefed. New guards had been posted. Nobody was going to sneak onto the Eighteenth Floor.

"No clue who the guy was?" Kurtz asked.

"If he worked in the hospital," Barent said, "it wasn't on that floor. He took off down the staircase. We don't know where he came out."

Staunton University Medical Center, Easton's sister hospital, had been plagued by a stalker, just a few months before. Security cameras had been placed on all non-patient care areas. Easton had cameras only in the parking lot.

"So, why Arnie, and why now?" Kurtz asked.

"He knows something," Barent said, "or somebody thinks he knows something."

"Maybe not," Moran said. "It could be personal. Cops sometimes make enemies."

"Killing cops is unusual," Kurtz said. "Criminals tend not to try."

Moran mirthlessly grinned.

"We're usually a pretty mild-mannered bunch," Barent said. "Protect and serve and all that; but when you kill a cop, the gloves come off."

Moran shrugged. He dipped a French fry into some ketchup and chewed it slowly. "We exist in an uneasy balance with the so-called criminal underworld. We know they're out there and we pick a few off now and then. We keep up the pressure. Most of the time, they keep their heads down. Both sides know that unless they go too far, they can get away with it: drugs, prostitution, illegal betting parlors, protection money. We can't eradicate it, not without devoting an enormous amount of resources, so most of the time, we don't even try, not unless they go too far."

"Like murder," Kurtz said.

"Yeah," Barent said, "like murder. Murdering a cop is definitely going too far."

"So, what would he know?"

"You mean before he got shot in the head?"

"Before, after…" Kurtz shrugged.

"After he got shot in the head, he was in the hospital," Barent pointed out, "mostly unconscious and barely able to move. I think we can assume that whatever the motivating factor might be is related to his prior activities."

"He was in Brooklyn the night he got shot," Kurtz said.

"Yeah, in Williamsburg. He was following three guys. He thinks they were Russian. That's all he remembers."

"Why was he following them?"

"Officer Figueroa, as you may have noticed, is Hispanic."

Kurtz blinked. "Yeah?"

"He was undercover. These guys came into the neighborhood. They stood out."

"I see. So, what happened, then?"

"That's what he doesn't remember."

"Does he remember what they looked like?"

"They were big. They wore suits and ties."

"Why does he think they were Russian?"

"He said that they looked Russian."

Kurtz sat back. "Do Russians look any different from any other white people?"

"Some do," Moran said. "Some don't. Russia covers a lot of territory and there are numerous ethnic sub-groups. Also, within any group, there's a lot of individual variation."

Kurtz had known plenty of Russians and people of Russian descent. Offhand, he couldn't think of any physical characteristics that might be distinctly 'Russian.' "So, what makes somebody look Russian?"

Moran rolled his eyes. "The Slavs supposedly have mostly round faces, pale skin and light brown to blonde hair, but plenty of other people in Europe have those same characteristics. Then there's the Mongolian influence. Russia was conquered by Genghis Khan and the Mongols. There was a lot of raping and pillaging. Some Russians, particularly those from the Eastern part of the country, do look at least vaguely Asian."

"Oh," Kurtz said. "So, did these guys look vaguely Asian?"

"Actually, he didn't get close enough to get a good look. Mostly, it was the way they walked."

Kurtz frowned. "And what does that mean?"

"Nothing that would stand up in court, that's for sure. Russian mobsters tend to be a tight knit group. A lot of them served in the military. They're disciplined and they're tough. When they walk down the street, they expect other people to get out of their way."

"That's not much to go on," Kurtz said.

"No. Arnie freely admits that he was making an inference when he said they looked Russian. Also, there are a lot of Russians in Williamsburg."

"So, what would Russian mobsters be doing in that particular neighborhood?"

"Nothing good, that's for sure," Barent said, "but the bottom line is that we have no idea."

Chapter 12

A phone call to someone who has nothing to do with the case could not possibly be construed as interfering with a police investigation. Kurtz told himself this, trying to believe it. He drew a deep breath, stared down at the phone and frowned. The phone seemed to stare back at him. The palm of his hand itched. Finally, he drew a deep breath, picked it up and dialed.

"Hello?"

Kurtz cleared his throat. "Sylvia? It's Richard Kurtz."

"*Boychik*," she said. "What can I do for you? You want to buy a nice apartment? Maybe a little house in Brighton Beach?"

"No, thanks. I'm calling about something else."

"Oh?"

"A few nights ago, at dinner, you mentioned something about Donna Ryan. You said that she was Russian."

"Donna? No. Her parents are Russian. Donna was born here. All of their kids were."

"Okay. You also said that the Russian community was close-knit."

"Did I say that? It's true, but I don't remember saying it."

"Anyway," Kurtz said, "who can I talk to about the Russian community?"

There was silence on the line for a long moment. "Why? What's going on?"

"Probably nothing, but I need some information on Russians in Williamsburg."

"Somehow, I'm not liking this."

Somehow, neither was Kurtz. "I'm sorry. I can't tell you anything else." He could, of course, but somehow, he felt that he shouldn't. Probably because the whole thing was far-fetched and stupid.

"Any particular part of the community?" Sylvia asked. "Doctors? Lawyers?"

Mobsters, Kurtz thought. He didn't say it. "Just the community," he said. "The community in general."

"Let me make a few phone calls," Sylvia said. "I'll get back to you."

"So, my son, what can I do for you?" the priest, wearing priestly robes and sharp gray eyes, gave Kurtz a wide smile.

Kurtz usually tried to limit Thursdays to a half-day in the office. He preferred to keep Thursday afternoon free for other pursuits. It occurred to him that he had never before stepped foot in an Orthodox Church. The thought made him a bit uncomfortable, as if he had somehow been letting somebody down. Maybe God.

"I got your name from Sylvia Hersch," Kurtz said.

"The realtor? She sold me my house."

"She told me. She also told me that you could give me some information about the Russian community."

The priest's name was Robert Kamenov. He looked younger than Kurtz had expected. According to Sylvia, he was well known and highly respected, a possible future candidate for Orthodox Catholic Bishop of New York and New Jersey.

"He knows everybody," Sylvia had said. "Whatever you need, he can help you."

When Kurtz had first arrived, the priest had introduced himself as 'Father Bob.' He had a small, comfortable office with a window looking out on a garden. A picture of a smiling, dark haired woman surrounded by three children sat on the corner of his desk. The Church, Saint Basil's, was a small but well-kept building in a middle-class section of Williamsburg, which was a well-to-do neighborhood in Brooklyn, close to the border with Queens.

The priest raised his eyebrows. "What sort of information?"

The bad kind, Kurtz thought. "General information."

The priest sat back and thought about that for a moment. "General doesn't tell me much of anything. I could talk forever. Are you interested in the condition of Verushka Popovich's arthritis? How about Vladimir Medbedev's recent purchase of a used Volvo?"

"No," Kurtz said. "Not exactly."

"Well, then, you're going to have to be a bit more specific."

The trouble was that Kurtz didn't know Father Bob. He didn't know if he would keep his mouth shut and he didn't know whose side he was on; but he was a priest, and one who did supposedly care about the well-being of his flock.

"How big is the community?" Kurtz asked. A nice nondescript way to start.

"How, exactly, are you defining the community?" Father Bob sat back in his seat and frowned at the little garden. "There are approximately 700,000 people who are at least marginally Russian in New York City. Many of these were born here and consider themselves fully American. Many speak Russian but are actually Ukrainian or Georgian or from one of the other former republics of the Soviet Union."

"How about in Brooklyn?"

"There are a lot in Brooklyn. A hundred-thousand or so." The priest blinked at him. "Have you heard of Little Odessa?"

Kurtz had heard the term but he knew nothing about it. He nodded.

"It's a neighborhood in Brighton Beach. It used to be mostly Jewish. Today, it's mostly Russian, primarily recent immigrants, though many of these are also Jewish. About a third of the population doesn't speak English. Once they get acclimated, learn the language, get jobs and have some money, they tend to move out."

"Williamsburg?"

"Williamsburg. Staten Island. Queens." The priest shrugged. "Podunk. Wherever."

"How much crime is there?"

Father Bob gave him a long look. "People sometimes think of America as a violent society, the Wild West and all that. In reality, the crime rate in the United States as a whole is somewhat below average for the industrialized world. However, there is tremendous variation in these statistics. The crime rate among the various communities in the United States tends to be similar to that of the country of origin. The crime rate among Russians living in America is similar to the crime rate in Russia, which is, on average, considerably higher than that of the United States as a whole."

Father Bob sighed. "My parents came here when I was six. I barely remember the old country, but I do remember my parents' frustration, their sense of anger and despair. There was no hope in the Soviet Union, no way to provide a better life, for yourself or your kids, not unless you could get out. One of the things about Communism is that it breeds the most selfish people on Earth. In Russia, it was every man for himself. Nobody had much of anything beyond the minimum needed to stay alive, and sometimes, not even that. Everybody was jealous of their neighbor. They hoarded whatever they could.

"Communism is dead, but the ravages of Communism remain. Now, the oligarchs are in charge, Putin and his cronies. For a little while, under Yeltsin, it seemed like Russia might make the transition to a pluralistic, democratic society, but not anymore. The rule of law means nothing in Russia, nothing at all, and it's still every man for himself.

"Yes," Father Bob said, "the crime rate is pretty high."

"Who?" Kurtz said. "Who runs it?"

Father Bob frowned. "I thought you were a surgeon."

"I am," Kurtz said. "I'm also a police surgeon."

"So? Police surgeons aren't police. They're surgeons. Why are you asking this?"

In for a penny, Kurtz thought. "One of my patients, a police officer, was recently shot. It's suspected that the assailants are Russian. I would like to understand what's going on."

The priest's face grew pensive. "What was that old saying? Curiosity killed the Kurtz?"

"Oh, that's funny."

Father Bob chuckled, then he shook his head. "Your colleagues in the police department are going to know a lot more than I do about who's who in the Russian mafia."

This was most likely true, Kurtz thought, but Barent and Moran would probably be reluctant to tell him. "I thought that a local, someone who was actually living and working in the community, might have some special insight into the problem."

Father Bob looked at him like he thought Kurtz was delusional. "Are you serious? Nobody in their right mind wants anything to do with those guys. It's a good way to not-so-quietly disappear."

Kurtz gave a half-hearted grin. "Who are *those guys*?"

"You are serious, aren't you?" Father Bob shook his head, then rose to his feet, walked over to a cabinet and pulled out a bottle. "If I'm going to talk about this stuff, I need a drink? You want one?"

"Sure," Kurtz said.

"Scotch? Bourbon?"

"Either one."

"Scotch, then." Father Bob poured a generous amount into two highball glasses, hesitated, then poured a little more. He handed one glass to Kurtz then sat back down behind his desk. "So," he said, "where to begin? First of all, there have always been outlaws in Russia. In the days of the Czars, when almost everybody was a peasant and dirt poor, those who robbed from the rich were regarded as popular heroes. The public admired them. Eventually, these outlaws organized into groups with their own codes of conduct, mostly don't betray the organization or you'll get your throat slit.

"Lenin, after the revolution, tried to wipe out the gangs but he wasn't very successful. Stalin exiled thousands to the gulags, where the criminal element organized themselves and in many cases, virtually ran the camps. During World War 2, amnesty was offered to those who would fight, and so many of the criminals not only gained their freedom, but also military training and an entrée into the military hierarchy. After the war, the gangs continued to grow. Eventually, they ran the black market, which greased the wheels of the so-called 'secret economy.' The government stores were often nearly empty of goods but if you wanted some coffee or a nice steak, maybe a bicycle or even a TV set, the black market could provide it. The government tolerated them. Associations between the gangs and government officials were common, even expected.

"After the collapse of the Soviet Union, thousands of ex-military and KGB offered their services to the gangs. Within a few years, organized crime, the oligarchs, virtually ran the Russian economy, and so it remains today. Russia is a criminal state. In a very real sense, Vladimir Putin is the richest and most successful crime boss in history. His tentacles reach everywhere.

"The so-called Russian mafia is an extension of the Russian government. Nobody knows where one ends and the other begins.

"The Italian mafia wasn't too different, back in the day. It also had ties to corrupt officials in Italy, gaining recruits and financial backing from the home country, but their reach and extent never compared to that of the Russians. The Russian mob is far larger and more organized. The local crime bosses are by no means independent. They are the neighborhood branches of a world-wide organization." Father Bob looked down at his glass, took a large sip and sat back in his chair. His face was grim. "This is not to say that rivalries do not exist. They do. The politics are Byzantine. Who is on top, who is rising, who will be stabbed in the back, who will be in charge next year or even next week are impossible to predict."

Father Bob gave Kurtz an amused grin. "Does this answer your questions?"

Kurtz, who had known almost nothing of this, took a sip of his own Scotch. It was excellent Scotch but he barely tasted it. The story that the priest told was…appalling. "So who is in charge?" he finally said.

The priest made a clicking sound between his teeth. "On your own head be it," he said. "A few years ago, if you had gone to the Bronx and you asked some random guy on the street who is in charge of the Italian-American mob, they would have told you, it's *John Gotti*. Everybody knew this, including the cops and the Feds. Proving it to the satisfaction of a jury was a very different matter, so Gotti went on for years, in and out of prison, mostly on minor charges. The Dapper Don, they used to call him. The guy was a New York celebrity.

"Russians, we like to keep things closer to the vest. A guy like Gotti would be regarded as not quite serious, almost a clown, a dangerous clown, but still…" The priest grinned. He looked down at his glass, which was almost empty. "You want some more?"

Kurtz put his hand over the top of his glass. "No, thanks."

Father Bob shrugged and poured another finger of Scotch into his own glass. "Still, you can't keep these things a secret, not entirely. We know who has the biggest house. We know who has armed guards patrolling the grounds. We know whose kids go to private schools and always travel with a bodyguard. Also, of course, we know that these things can be deliberate red herrings. The real bosses may be living quietly in some apartment somewhere, anonymous, the spider at the center of the web. This we do not know. Or at least, *I* don't know, and I most certainly do not want to know."

"Okay," Kurtz said. "I get the disclaimer. So, who is the one who has armed guards and whose kids always travel with a bodyguard?"

Father Bob grimaced. "There are a few. What relationship there might be between them, I have no idea. The names that you hear are Alexei Rugov, Sergei Ostrovsky and Iosif Kozlov. They all live in Brooklyn, not too far from here, in Brighton Beach. They all have large, tough looking men in their employ and they're all apparently very wealthy."

"Thanks," Kurtz said.

Father Bob grunted. He sipped his Scotch and stared out the window at the garden. He seemed disinclined to say anything more. Kurtz, for his part, had run out of questions. After a few moments, the priest muttered to himself, "Ah, well…" and turned to Kurtz. "Will there be anything else."

"No," Kurtz said. He put his empty glass down on the desk and rose to his feet. "No thank you."

Father Bob peered up at him. "A word of advice," he said. "Don't ask too many questions. Too many questions asked of the wrong people can get you killed."

"I understand," Kurtz said. "Thanks again."

"This hernia is killing me."

The cop's name was Gregory Samms. He was middle aged and not in the best shape. There was still muscle underneath the fat but Gregory Samms had not been spending as much time in the gym as he used to. A hernia was indeed bulging out of the cop's groin, swollen and faintly red. Gingerly, Kurtz palpated it. Samms sucked in his breath.

"How long has it been like this?"

"You mean, how long have I had the hernia?"

"How long have you had the hernia and how long has it been painful and red?"

"I've had it for about six months. It's been like this for a couple of days."

"Okay," Kurtz said. "Here's the story. This hernia is incarcerated, meaning that you have a piece of bowel that's stuck inside the abdominal wall. I can try to push it back in but that might not work and even if it does work, it's not going to stay in for very long, not unless the weak spot in the abdominal wall is repaired. What's worse, an incarcerated hernia often strangulates, meaning that the blood supply gets cut off. The bowel dies. Then you die." Kurtz raised his eyebrows. "When you said it was 'killing you,' you weren't kidding. This is not a pleasant way to go."

Gregory Samms blinked at him.

"You need surgery," Kurtz said. "You need surgery now. Not next week. Not tomorrow. Now."

Gregory Samms gulped. "Okay."

Fifteen minutes later, Samms was on his way to the ER. Kurtz had already made the arrangements and spoken to the surgeon on call. Samms would be in surgery within the hour.

He took a quick twenty minutes for lunch before the nurse showed his next patient into the office. Albert Morelli was a malingerer. According to what Kurtz had been told, Morelli had always been a lazy cop, the sort who went through the motions but never put himself out there. He was thirty-seven years old, had been a cop for fifteen years and had never risen beyond the rank of patrolman. His lack of ambition was almost legendary. That didn't mean that he never got sick, however.

Morelli had adhesive capsulitis, otherwise known as 'frozen shoulder.' It was a poorly understood condition where the joint capsule became inflamed, causing pain, stiffness and ultimately, immobility. Morelli had first noticed pain a couple of months ago and now he could barely raise his left arm above his waist.

"Any recent trauma?" Kurtz asked.

Morelli shook his head.

Frozen shoulder was more common in trauma and was more often found in association with diabetes, also in women and those over forty. Morelli had no predisposing factors whatsoever, but none of that mattered. He still had a frozen shoulder.

"Nobody knows the cause of this," Kurtz said. "It usually gets worse until the shoulder and arm are completely immobile, and then it begins to go away. The whole process can take up to three years."

"Three years...I can't work this way." Morelli's eyes grew round. A tremulous smile crossed his face.

Kurtz could almost see the implications sparking through Morelli's devious little brain. "No, but you won't be able to do anything whatsoever with the arm. That includes fishing and golf. The arm will be stuck to your side and it will hurt if you even try to move it." Morelli, Kurtz already knew, liked to play golf and he loved to fish. "Basically, you'll be stuck in front of the TV." Kurtz smiled. "Nothing to do but talk to the wife."

Morelli frowned, thinking this over, then he sighed. "Anything we can do about it?"

"Yeah," Kurtz said. "A steroid injection into the shoulder joint usually takes care of it. It's done by an orthopedist. You'll be back to work in a couple of months."

Morelli's eyes lit up. "Months?"

Kurtz solemnly nodded. "Sorry to deliver the bad news, but yeah, you're looking at two months off the job."

"Damn," Morelli said. "That's…"

Awesome? "A real shame, huh?"

Morelli gave him a wounded look. "Hey," he said. "It's not as if I did it deliberately."

"Nope," Kurtz said. "The Lord giveth and the Lord taketh away. If you have to be out of work, you might as well enjoy it. Right?"

A slow smile spread across Morelli's face. "Right," he said. Ten minutes later, Morelli left the office with an appointment to see an orthopedist.

The next patient wouldn't talk. His name was Gene Bauer. He had been a cop for almost twenty years. His record was routine. He had reached the rank of Sergeant, working mostly vice. He had hobbled in on crutches and sat stolidly while Kurtz examined him.

"I fell," Bauer said. "It was an accident."

By itself, a simple stress fracture of the tibia might not have stimulated much suspicion, except that Gene Bauer also had swollen knuckles on his right hand and obvious bruising next to his left eye.

Kurtz grunted. Bauer looked at him from under lowered eyebrows, his mouth set in a stubborn line. Supposedly, he had tripped on a kid's toy and fallen down the stairs, which could in theory have caused his constellations of injuries. He had gone to a local ER, where x-rays were taken and the leg put in a cast. This was a follow-up visit with a police surgeon, as required by regulations.

Bauer was a grown-up. Kurtz was not his nanny. If the guy wanted to keep his mouth shut, that was his business.

The orthopedist who had seen him in the ER had prescribed six weeks out of work. Kurtz shrugged and signed off on the paperwork.

"These things happen," Kurtz said.

Bauer grunted.

"Come back when the cast is removed. I have to certify that you're okay before you can return to the job."

Bauer nodded. "Right," he said. Then he frowned. "Thanks."

"Don't mention it."

Chapter 13

"I ran into Donna Ryan the other day," Lenore said.

Kurtz paused, the fork halfway to his lips. "Oh?"

"I don't think she saw me."

"Where was this?"

"Gramercy Tavern. I was eating lunch with some of my co-workers. I guess she was doing the same. She was with a group, guys mostly."

Donna Ryan worked for a small investment banking firm, called Hotchkiss and Phelps.

Kurtz spooned some tea smoked beef onto his plate and added a scoop of pork fried rice. They were eating at a hole in the wall in Chinatown that served world class food. Luckily, they had arrived early. The line was already snaking out the door. "I've always wondered exactly what it is that an investment banker does."

"A lot of it is schmoozing. Successful investment bankers have people skills. They're good at buttering up the clients."

"Yeah?" Kurtz gave her a doubtful look. "There's got to be more to it than that."

"One of my uncles is a stockbroker. He once said that a lot of the job is psychotherapy. When the market is going up, everybody is happy but when the market is going down, they have to do a lot of hand holding."

"Are investment bankers stockbrokers?"

Lenore shrugged. "It's the same general business. It's putting money to work and hopefully, watching it grow. In this case, most of it is the bank's money, but almost all the business owners have invested in the firm, as well. Most of the banks require it, actually. They want the business owners to be just as committed to the success of the new corporation or business venture as they are. So, the really successful ones are good with people. They also have to be good at math. A background in finance is a requirement. Some of them start out as accountants, math or economics majors, even physics. A lot of them wind up with MBA's. Donna got her MBA from Columbia, and then she became a CFA."

Kurtz blinked at her. "What's that?"

"*Chartered Financial Analyst.* They analyze business plans and balance sheets, look at social and economic trends, review the track record of the firm's officers and principals and try to decide if a proposed new idea or technology is going to make money or fall on its face." Lenore shrugged. "Basically, they read tea leaves. Is this corporation that's begging for money worth the investment?"

"You seem to know quite a bit about it."

Lenore smiled. "Remember Harrison Thomas?"

Kurtz frowned. Ah, yes, the former fiancé… "He's a banker, isn't he?"

"Yup. He knew all about this stuff."

Kurtz preferred not to think about Lenore's former fiancé. He shrugged. "So, you ran into Donna Ryan. How did she look?"

Lenore frowned. "Manic. She was talking a mile a minute, laughing, chugging down the wine. I thought she was trying much too hard."

"The job doesn't stop just because your husband commits suicide."

"No. No, of course not. There are still deals to be made. You show up and do the job or somebody else will."

"How did she meet Steve Ryan, anyway?"

"They met in middle school. They were childhood sweethearts."

Kurtz winced. "Tough," he said.

"Yeah." Lenore shook her head and they finished the rest of the meal in silence.

Mitchell Price was dead, murdered in a particularly gruesome way, as were Steve Hayward and his unfortunate wife. Jeffrey McDonald had OD'd twice. The common thread, obviously, was the narcotics. No evidence that Mitchell Price's supplier had been Steve Hayward but it remained a possibility.

It was important to gather the data. It was okay to toy with theories but you had to be careful not to start believing them, not too soon at any rate. The theory has to fit the data, and if you don't have enough data, it's all too easy to start winnowing the facts until they fit the theory.

Get the data. Getting the data was key.

Two different narcotics: alpha-methyl fentanyl and carfentanil, both commonly imported from China, plus heroin. Three deaths. One was drugged prior to having his throat slit. The two others dealt drugs, at least the husband did, and were torn to pieces.

"You want something to drink?" Betty asked.

"Sure," Barent said. "Thanks."

He sat back in his chair and stared at the TV set without really seeing it. Betty had on one of those programs where people found a house on the beach, renovated it and sold it for a higher price. Barent was dimly aware of this. It was a nice looking beach, with golden sand, blue water, blue skies and a lot of palm trees. The house was a dump.

Okay, what theory will fit these facts?

Betty placed a snifter of Irish Mist next to Barent's chair, then sat back down on the couch. Betty smiled at him but said nothing. She knew his habits well.

Nobody slits throats for no reason. The most obvious reason (since we're making up a theory) was competition: rivals in the drug trade. It fit the facts at least.

"You want to buy a house on the beach?" Barent said.

Betty blinked. "You serious?"

Rivals in the drug trade. Barent shook his head. Rivals in the drug trade wasn't getting him very far. He needed more data, but where to get it? "Probably not," Barent said.

"Too bad," Betty said. "Let's think about it."

"All clear," Vasily Lukin said.

Alexei Rugov rarely exposed himself in this way. And why should he? His compound in Brighton Beach sat at the water's edge, next to his yacht. It was a palace, the sort of palace that every Russian boy dreamed of having, and he, Alexei Rugov, was one of the very, very few who had achieved that dream. Alexei Rugov was a wealthy man. He had earned that wealth by the strength of his arms and the sweat of his brow, rising through the ranks of the Federal Security Services and then rising again through the ranks of the Brotherhood. And now here he was, still young, despite the gray in his hair, still fit, still strong enough to take what he deserved and to enjoy it. To grasp life by the throat.

Life is good, Alexei Rugov thought. He wanted to keep it that way.

He sighed, and then cracked open the door of the limousine and stepped out onto the pavement. Alexei Rugov had done many unpleasant things in his life and he had never shirked from his duty. There is always a price to be paid and to achieve success, and to keep it, one must pay that price.

The day was hot and humid. He could feel the sweat prickling on his forehead. His men had already secured the parking lot and fanned out through the neighborhood. This venture was as safe as it could be, but how safe, really was that? Explosives could have been placed hours or even days before. Agents could be hiding among the pedestrians strolling down the streets, posing as shopkeepers, housewives or even children. Snipers could be hidden in balconies high above, focusing their sights even now on Alexei Rugov's head. He smiled and scanned the apartment buildings surrounding the meeting place.

None of these things were likely, of course. It was only that a ruthless opponent, depending on how ruthless he wanted to be, had options that the more civilized would never consider.

Alexei Rugov had extensive experience with such things.

His men fell into step around him. They walked across the parking lot to the entrance of the restaurant. A jaguar made out of plaster and stucco, with the head of an Aztec god and surrounded by feathered serpents, crouched above the door. A sign said, *Casa Lindo*.

Inside, the restaurant was cool and dimly lit. It was a large room with tables and booths. Lunch was over; dinner had not yet begun. The restaurant was closed, the perfect time for a private meeting. A man, tall, bronzed and very good looking, dressed in a tuxedo, smiled at him. "Mr. Rugov," he said in unaccented English. "Welcome. Please come this way." He ignored the members of Alexei Rugov's security team. A few hard-looking Hispanic men sat in the booths. They carefully looked at Rugov and his team as they walked past, but none spoke to them and none left their booths.

They walked down a corridor hung with brightly colored banners, their feet sliding against a polished, hardwood floor. The corridor opened out into another room, almost as large as the first. A man sat at a round table in the center of the room. Javier Garcia. He was alone. He smiled at Alexei Rugov. "Please," Javier Garcia said, "sit down."

Alexei Rugov's men fanned out and took up stations across the room. Javier Garcia smiled at them benignly. "Can I offer you something? Something to drink?"

"Thank you, but no," Alexei Rugov said.

"Very well, then." Javier Garcia inclined his head toward Alexei Rugov. "You wished to see me."

"I did." Alexei Rugov drew a deep breath. "Our two organizations have had a long and profitable association, one that has enriched us both. Yet you have chosen to end this association. I would like to know why?"

Javier Garcia pursed his lips and frowned. "You could have asked me this question over the phone. There was no need to come to me in person."

"It is a mark of how seriously I take this issue that I chose to do so."

Javier Garcia gave a slow, regretful nod. "As you said, our relationship has been long and mutually beneficial. You offered me an excellent product at an excellent price. As it happens, however, one of your competitors has offered me a similar product at an even more excellent price." Javier Garcia smiled sadly. "These things happen."

Alexei Rugov stared at him. Out of the corner of his eye, he saw one of his men blink. Another puffed up his cheeks and frowned. A third cast a worried, sidelong glance at a fourth. "Do they?" Alexei Rugov said. "Just like that? No notification? No attempt to negotiate?"

Javier Garcia looked briefly annoyed. He shrugged. "There is nothing personal in this," he said. "It's business."

A slow smile spread across Alexei Rugov's face. He had heard this statement before. Supposedly, it meant something. "Some of us take our business personally."

Javier Garcia shrugged.

"And what if we offer you an even better price?"

"The contract that we have entered into precludes us from re-considering our decision at the present time. At the end of one year, you may enter a new bid."

"One year…"

Javier Garcia nodded.

"And who is it who has underbid us so decisively?"

A quick grin flit across Javier Garcia's face and quickly vanished. "Sergei Ostrovsky," he said.

Chapter 14

Reginald Rinear was used to getting what he wanted. It was a common characteristic of the very wealthy. He was not used to being followed and he didn't like it. When he left for work in the morning, a cop car was parked in the street. The car followed him at a sedate distance into Manhattan. When he left the office for lunch, a cop in a bright blue uniform picked him up on the street and walked casually along. Once, Reginald Rinear walked up to the cop and asked him what he thought he was doing.

"Just following orders, sir," the cop said, and gave him a big, toothy smile.

"You've been ordered to harass me?"

"No, sir. I've been ordered to follow you."

Reginald Rinear stared at him. "We'll see about that," he finally said.

The cop shrugged.

Reginald Rinear's father had served a term on the City Council, many years ago. His family donated generously to the Metropolitan Opera, the Museum of Modern Art and numerous political campaigns. Reginald Rinear knew a lot of very important people.

"So, Barent," Ted Weiss said. "What's with this Rinear guy?"

Ted Weiss was an assistant district attorney for the City of New York.

"A dirt bag," Barent said.

Ted Weiss stared at him. "What do you mean, a dirt bag? He's rich."

Barent shrugged. "A rich dirt bag."

Weiss sighed and pulled up a chair. "Tell me about it."

"Not much to tell. Three people are dead. Narcotics are involved. Reginald Rinear, we've been told by a confidential informant, uses narcotics."

"So do fifty-thousand other people in this town. Minimum. Why are you following him?"

Frankly, because they had no leads, and because Reginald Rinear was annoying. "The drugs involved are alpha-methyl fentanyl and carfentanil: China White and Serial Killer, as they are known on the street. They're both unusual, though not nearly as unusual as they should be. Our informant has stated that the drugs Reginald Rinear has been indulging in are supposedly 'new' and 'unique.' This is what we commonly refer to as a 'clue.' Admittedly, not much of a clue, but we don't have anything else to go on. The guy is an uncooperative witness," Barent said. "He could talk to us but he won't."

Ted Weiss continued to stare. "That's it?" he said.

Barent shifted uncomfortably. "Also, he's an annoying little shit. I admit that he probably can't help us on this particular case, but maybe he can. He knows a lot more than he's saying, that's for sure."

"Which, according to you, is probably nothing. And all of us know a lot more than nothing."

Barent shrugged.

"Alright," Ted Weiss finally said. "Let me know how it goes."

"Believe me, you'll be the first to know."

After three more days, Reginald Rinear cracked.

Barent received a call from Everett Johns. "My client wishes to speak with you."

"Excellent," Barent said. "Where and when?"

"His apartment. Tonight, at 7:00 PM."

Barent considered this. Obviously, the guy would prefer that the cops not be seen at his office. This would not inspire confidence in either clients or co-workers. Similarly, being seen entering the Precinct House might also raise questions that Reginald Rinear would prefer not to answer.

"We'll be there," Barent said.

The apartment took up an entire floor in a very old building on Central Park South, with its own elevator. Barent could only speculate how many rooms the guy had. Reginald Rinear was divorced, with two children who were boarding at Milton Academy. He didn't live alone, however, as the apartment had a staff of hot and cold running butlers and maids, one of whom, a thin, balding old goat with a beady eye and disapproving expression, met them at the door and ushered them inside. "Master Rinear is in the den," he said, "with Mr. Johns."

"Master?" Barent said. "You really call him 'Master?'"

The butler shrugged. "He insists on it."

"Then lead the way, Jeeves," Moran said. "We mustn't keep the Master waiting."

The butler's lips twitched. "That will be James, sir."

Moran gave a regal nod. Barent said nothing. They followed James into a large, brightly lit room. The floor was polished marble. Glass cases filled with fragile looking knick-knacks from all over the world covered the walls. A large, floor-to-ceiling window looked down on Central Park.

Reginald Rinear and Everett Johns sat together at a large, cherry wood table. "Gentlemen," Everett Johns said. "Please sit."

Barent and Moran sat. Everett Johns smiled and rubbed his hands together. "So," he said, "first, thank you both for coming. My client, as always, wishes to cooperate with the police. He is prepared, within limits, to answer your questions."

"What limits?" Barent asked.

"Nothing that is said here can be used against him. He will not be required to testify in any legal proceedings that ensue as a result of the information that he is about to give you."

They had already discussed this with Ted Weiss, who had discussed it with the DA. "No," Barent said. "We are prepared to offer you transactional immunity. You won't be charged, but it is entirely possible—not likely, but possible—that your testimony may be required."

"No," Reginald Rinear said.

Everett Johns appeared worried.

"No?" Moran said.

"No," Reginald Rinear said.

"Sooner or later," Barent said, "we will find the people responsible for the deaths of Mitchell Price, Steven Hayward and his wife, Marilyn Hayward. If it should come out that you refused to divulge information that could have led to the apprehension of said criminals, and possibly have prevented further crimes on their part, we will not hesitate in letting the public know of your involvement."

Reginald Rinear's lips thinned.

"This is a good deal," said Barent. "You should take it."

Everett Johns sighed. "Give me a moment to confer with my client."

"Certainly." Barent and Moran both rose to their feet. James was waiting for them outside the door.

"Please come with me." He led them to a small sitting room. "Can I get you some tea? Coffee, perhaps?"

"Coffee would be good," Moran said. "Cream. Two sugars."

"You, sir?" James asked.

Barent glanced at Moran. "Black," he said.

James nodded and left. A few moments later, he re-appeared, accompanied by a young white woman wearing a maid's uniform and pushing a cart. Under James' watchful eye, the maid placed a pot of coffee, two cups, spoons, cream and sugar on the table. James and the maid both left.

Moran poured a cup for Barent, then prepared his own and carefully sipped. "Yep," he said. "It's coffee, alright."

Barent looked down at his cup and shrugged. "The very rich are different from you and me, Harry," Barent said. "But sadly, their coffee tastes much the same."

The door to the sitting room opened. "Master Rinear would like you to come back, sirs," he said. They trooped back into the office, taking the coffee with them. Everett Johns greeted them with a huge smile. Reginald Rinear looked grim. "My client," Everett Johns said, "agrees to your terms."

A weird dude, Barent thought. Reginald Rinear appeared just a tad embarrassed by his escapades into the seamier side of life. He seemed to be trying to cling to his view of himself as above the mundane cares and concerns of the quotidien world but seemed vaguely aware, somewhere deep inside, that shoving narcotics up his nose was not an activity that a respected member of the upper classes would ordinarily be doing. He was defensive.

"I began using drugs in college," Reginald Rinear said. "It was the thing to do at the time, and I have no doubt that it still is. Marijuana, a bit of cocaine." He shrugged. "It was common at parties. Almost as much so as the wine, the beer and the hors d'oeuvres. A small pile of rolled joints, a silver tray, a small spoon, a container of white powder…" He shrugged again. "You simply weren't one of the group if you didn't participate. It was a rite of passage, as it were." He blinked. "You know how it is."

Not entirely, no, but Barent could imagine. He gave an encouraging nod.

"It seems so innocent, now," Reginald Rinear said.

"College was a long time ago," Barent said.

"Indeed. We have better drugs, today. Much better." Reginald Rinear's lips twitched upward. "The new ones...they're like a symphony in your head, the sensation is almost indescribable."

"Where does it come from?" Moran asked. "How do you get it?"

"You have to know somebody." Reginald Rinear frowned. "And the somebody you know knows somebody else, who also knows somebody else, a chain of suppliers reaching across the ocean to God knows where."

Reginald Rinear made it all sound quite amazing and exotic but Reginald Rinear was telling him nothing that Barent didn't already know. Marijuana and meth were the only drugs home grown in the US in large enough amounts to be significant. All the rest were imported, starting in Afghanistan or China or Mexico or a dozen other places. Unscrupulous men refined them or paid to have them refined. Not all of these were violent men. Many were businessmen simply looking for an opportunity, but somewhere along the chain, somebody had to smuggle it in, and the smugglers were almost always prepared to fight and kill, if necessary. And then these killers, or the people that the killers sold it to, had to find salesmen, people ingrained in the community, people who looked normal, people with weaknesses or simply down on their luck. Some of these were desperate. Some did it for the thrill. None of them had a highly developed sense of empathy or concern for their fellow human beings. And so you wound up with the kid in school who could get you a few joints or the salaryman at the next desk who happened to have a little bag of something extra stuffed in a back drawer, or the friendly neighbor down the block who you could go to in a pinch for your daily (or three or four times daily...) fix.

Sometimes, of course, the farmer, the supplier, the manufacturer, the smuggler, the hard-eyed killer and the local entrepreneur were all part of the same huge organization. If enough money were involved, even the government, or multiple governments along the transport chain, would take its cut and give its unofficial blessing before sending the product on its way. So it was with Afghanistan and China today, with Colombia and Mexico in the not-so-distant past.

Barent gave Reginald Rinear an encouraging nod. "I understand," Barent said. "But where did you get it, you personally?"

Rinear hesitated. "You mentioned Steven Hayward. He was one of them. He has an associate, a man named Andrew Fox."

"Did either of these men ever come to you, or did you go to them?"

"Most often, a group of friends would get together. Either Hayward or Fox would bring it."

"It's good to have friends," Barent said. Not exactly anonymous, but this was a common model. There was safety in numbers. It all felt more normal, less exposed, though of course, this safety was an illusion. A crowd of people in the living room while a few friendly transactions took place in the den would not protect you if the police decided to raid the place. And more people meant more people who might be able to identify you.

"This is good," Barent said. He glanced at Moran, who smiled back. "Give me all the details you can remember. I want to know everything."

Chapter 15

"I am concerned," Sergei Ostrovsky said.

Ilya Sokolov, Sergei Ostrovsky's principal lieutenant, frowned at him. "I think that you should be. I am concerned as well."

Sergei Ostrovsky suppressed a smile, though in truth, there was little about this situation to smile about.

Sergei Ostrovsky was sixty-seven years old, a feared and venerated figure in the Russian community, and even more so in the sub-community that existed on both sides of the law. He had been a Major in the Intelligence Directorate (GRU) prior to the dissolution of the USSR before offering his services, as so many of his colleagues had done, to the rising tide of organized crime. Despite his history, however, Sergei Ostrovsky regarded himself as a voice of moderation and good will. Sergei Ostrovsky had a sense of proportion. He only killed when he had to…or when he was ordered to do so.

"This latest venture," Sergei Ostrovsky said, "may not be worth the cost."

Ilya Sokolov said nothing.

"You do not agree?"

"You rule men because they understand, deep inside themselves, that your wisdom, judgment and strength are greater than their own," Ilya Sokolov said. "They will stay loyal only so long as they believe that your will is iron and your word unbreakable. They will not follow a leader they consider to be weak."

And that, simply stated, was the problem. Action had been taken, not against himself, but against their ally, Javier Garcia, and by association, against their joint venture.

"And what do you advise?" Sergei Ostrovsky asked.

Ilya Sokolov hesitated.

Sergei Ostrovsky gave a small, disgusted laugh. "Steven Hayward was in the employ of Javier Garcia. Despite our probably temporary alliance, the affront is to him, not us. Would you recommend that we offer our assistance?"

Ilya Sokolov frowned. He said nothing.

"Exactly," Sergei Ostrovsky said. "Asking for our help, even accepting our help if we were to offer, would make him look weak. Javier Garcia cannot afford to look weak."

Sergei Ostrovsky leaned back in his chair. He raised a cup of tea to his lips and took a sip, then set the cup carefully back on his desk. "This adversary has chosen to remain hidden. He is fearful. This is wise of him. He should be fearful."

Ilya Sokolov gave a small smile. "Javier Garcia is a dangerous man to play games with."

Sergei Ostrovsky shrugged. "What do our contacts in the police have to say?"

"The perpetrators are unknown to them. They are not natives of New York."

"Set up a meeting with Garcia," Sergei Ostrovsky said. "Let us hear his thoughts on this matter. We will offer our condolences and our aid. He will, no doubt, refuse, but we should offer. We should take care to present a united front in this matter." Sergei Ostrovsky smiled. "One never knows who might be watching."

Ilya Sokolov bowed his head and walked from the room. After he left, Sergei Ostrovsky sipped his drink and gave a long, tired sigh. He was getting a little old for this. Maybe it was time to go down to Florida and sit on the beach. The whores in Miami were said to be beautiful and skilled.

He sighed again and shrugged. A wistful fantasy. Young lions wished to rule the pride. Old lions knew that the burden of kingship can never be put down.

No, Sergei Ostrovsky thought. Here I am, and here I remain.

At least the Security up here was serious. Arnaldo Figueroa recognized one or two of the men at the station outside the Unit, cops moonlighting for a few extra bucks. Also, of course, the newly reconstituted official police guard. You had to have a pass to be admitted, in case Paris Hilton or Kim Kardashian chose to spend a few days getting an anonymous nose-job or tummy-tuck. At the moment, however, the Unit was almost empty, a couple of D list celebrities that Arnaldo Figueroa vaguely recognized from some reality TV shows.

Rehab was going well. His hand was getting stronger. He still limped, but he could toddle across the room without assistance. He was still clumsy but he could hold a knife and a fork and cut his own food. Not much of a triumph, in the normal course of things, but Arnaldo Figueroa cherished it.

"How are you, Arnie?"

Kurtz was a guy Arnaldo Figueroa felt comfortable with. Not quite a cop, but almost. Kurtz had the look, the look of a guy who watched his surroundings, not suspicious exactly, but aware of everyone and everything that went on around him. Arnaldo Figueroa had heard stories about Kurtz. He wasn't sure he believed them.

Wordlessly, Arnaldo Figueroa held out his left hand, clenched it into a fist, then spread the fingers.

"Nice," Kurtz said.

"When am I getting out of here?"

Kurtz looked down at the chart in his hands, considering. "You still need rehab," he said, "but that can be done as an outpatient. Let me talk to the neurosurgeons."

"Great."

Kurtz smiled. "A few more days, probably. I'll let you know tomorrow."

"Great," Arnaldo Figueroa said again.

"How do I look?"

Lenore always asked that and the answer was always the same. "You look terrific," Kurtz said.

"Good enough to impress the other wives?" Lenore grinned.

"Yeah, and the husbands, too."

Lenore gave a tiny snort. "They're a lot easier."

Sean Brody was the Chairman of the Department of Surgery at the School. He was hosting a "small" get-together. As a chairman, Brody always seemed to feel an obligation to impress the troops with the quality of the food, if not the entertainment. Tonight, Brody had stressed, would be 'casual.' Kurtz wore a button down shirt, no tie, with a blue blazer. Lenore wore a green skirt with a matching blouse, which did nothing to hide her impressive figure.

Unexpectedly, Donna Ryan was one of the guests. Steve Ryan's unfortunate demise was still only a few weeks in the past and Donna still seemed subdued, hardly a surprise. She was accompanied by a large guy, probably about her own age, who wasn't saying much and frankly, seemed a little out of place. The two of them were sitting on a couch, each with a drink in hand. The guy watched the crowd, hovering at Donna's side. She stared at the carpet.

"Huh…" Kurtz said.

Lenore pursed her lips.

"That's Arkady Lukin," Lenore said. "Her cousin."

Kurtz frowned. "Cousin?"

"Second cousin. Or is that second cousin once removed? I can never get that straight. Anyway, his mother is Donna's mother's first cousin."

Arkady Lukin had dark, hard eyes. He looked around with a flat, level gaze. He wore tailored gray pants and a black sweater. There was a sizeable amount of space around the two of them. The guy just looked intimidating.

"You want to say 'hello?'" Kurtz asked.

Lenore frowned, then glanced at Kurtz' face and slowly smiled.

"Sure," she said.

The two of them wandered over to the bar, where Lenore grabbed a glass of white wine and Kurtz made himself a Bloody Mary. They greeted a few people, said hello to Sean Brody and his wife, Mary, and slowly made their way across the room. "Donna," Lenore said. "How are you?"

Donna Ryan gave a brittle smile. "A little better," she said. "It helps to get out." Arkady Lukin stared at Kurtz, who blandly smiled back.

Kurtz held out his hand. "Richard Kurtz."

"This is my cousin," Donna said, "Arkady."

Arkady Lukin looked at Kurtz' outstretched hand, seemed to think it over, then reached out and enfolded it in his own. Quite a grip, Kurtz thought. You could tell a lot from the way a guy shook hands. This guy, for instance, thought he was tough. Looking at the width of his shoulders and the depth of his chest, he probably was tough. And he liked to let people know it. His grip was strong, strong enough to hurt. Kurtz grinned at him and squeezed back. Arkady Lukin blinked. After a few moments, they both let go.

"And what do you do?" Arkady Lukin asked. He had a deep voice with no accent.

"I'm a surgeon," Kurtz said. "You?"

Arkady Lukin grinned. "Business."

"Arkady works for the Rugov Corporation," Donna said.

Kurtz blinked. "Alexei Rugov?" he said.

The two women stared at him. Arkady Lukin gave a long, slow smile. "You've heard of him? Few people have."

"Yes," Kurtz said. "I've heard that he's wealthy."

"This is so," Arkady Lukin said.

"Tell me, what exactly does your business do?"

"Rugov is a holding corporation, much like Berkshire-Hathaway, or Bain Capital. We own bits and pieces of other businesses."

"That sounds like it might be lucrative."

Arkady Lukin nodded. "We have found it to be so."

Kurtz grinned. "Also, risky."

Arkady Lukin shrugged. "There is no gain without risk. The larger the risk, the larger the potential gain."

"If you know what you're doing."

"As you say, Alexei Rugov is a very wealthy man. He knows what he's doing." Arkady Lukin gave a cold grin. "The people who work for him do so as well."

Kurtz found that he had nothing to say after that. He nodded and after a few pleasantries, he and Lenore wandered away. "What was that all about?" Lenore asked.

Kurtz imagined that Arkady Lukin's eyes were boring into his back. The space between his shoulder blades itched. He twitched uncomfortably. "Nothing, probably."

Lenore rolled her eyes. "Let me get another glass of wine."

The party passed uneventfully. The food was good, the company congenial, the conversation, if not exactly entrancing, was at least not boring. Kurtz opined on the Knick's awful past season and dreadful prospects for the future and agreed that the Yankees hopes for another title were at least reasonable.

David Chao was there, hovering near Carrie Owens side. Donna Ryan and Arkady Lukin left early, which somehow lightened Kurtz' mood.

On the drive home, Lenore said, "I once read a comment that sounded very cynical to me, and very sad. Possibly truthful, though."

"Oh?"

"Something to the effect of, 'You show me the most beautiful woman on Earth and I'll show you a man who's tired of sleeping with her.'"

Kurtz blinked. "Oh?' he said cautiously.

"What do you think of that comment?"

So many choices, Kurtz thought. So many ways to go wrong. "Isn't beauty supposed to be in the eye of the beholder?"

She frowned at him. "Excellent attempt at deflection, *boychick*, as Cousin Sylvia would say. That may or may not be so, but it isn't exactly answering the question."

Kurtz sighed. "What exactly is the question?"

"Is the charge going out of our relationship?"

"Are you serious?"

"I want to know what you think."

"Alright," Kurtz said, "I think that we've been fucking like bunnies for nearly two years now and I'm not tired of it, yet."

"It just seemed to me that we've been doing it a little less than we used to."

They used to do it three times a day. After living together for over a year and being married for two months, it was down to ten times a week, not that Kurtz was counting. "Maybe a little," Kurtz conceded.

Lenore frowned and said nothing.

They drove in silence for a little while, then Kurtz said, "What brought this on?"

"I bought some new lingerie." Lenore smiled. "I was thinking of trying it out."

"Oh," Kurtz said. Crisis averted. He breathed an inward sigh of relief. "That's a good idea."

She smiled wider. "I thought you would say that. I just wanted to be sure."

Barent glowered at him. "You want to know what?"

Kurtz sighed. He had been afraid that Lew would react this way. "What do you know about Alexei Rugov?"

"No," Barent said.

Kurtz blinked. "No, what?"

"Just *no*. You are going to stay far, far away from Alexei Rugov and everything to do with him. Is that understood?"

"Hey," Kurtz protested. "It was just a question."

Barent sat back and stared at Kurtz' face. "With you, there's always a sub-text."

"Yeah, well…so what's the story?"

"Oh, boy." Barent let his breath out, gave his tuna salad on whole wheat toast a jaundiced eye and sipped his coke. Kurtz picked up his own pastrami on a Kaiser roll, took a bite and stolidly chewed, giving Barent a little time to deal with it. Finally, Barent shook his head. "Alexei Rugov is a member in good standing of the Russian mafia."

Kurtz nodded.

"Nothing to say?"

"I already knew that," Kurtz said.

"I'll just bet you did." Barent shook his head. "There are three of them: Alexei Rugov, Iosif Kozlof and Sergei Ostrovsky. They're like the five families. They each control a branch of the Russian mob in New York."

"Okay. Do they ever cooperate?"

"Sometimes, sure," Barent said. "And sometimes they're at each other's throats."

"I met a guy at a party a couple of days ago: Arkady Lukin. He said he worked for the Rugov Corporation."

"Each of the three has a corporation. They're actual corporations that do a fair amount of legitimate business."

"And what else do they do?"

"What else is there? Prostitution, gambling, loan-sharking, guns, drugs. You name it, they're into it…though gambling isn't what it used to be. What with Foxwoods, Mohegan Sun and Atlantic City, there are plenty of legal places to throw away your money. Not much profit anymore in illicit gambling."

"Arkady Lukin said that the Rugov Corporation is a holding company. He said that they own bits and pieces of other businesses. I don't understand this. Why do the criminal stuff if you can make money legally?"

"Legal. Illegal." Barent shrugged. "It's all the same to these guys. It's just another way to make money. And don't kid yourself; the 'legitimate business' baloney is largely a front. If they're putting money into other businesses, it's mostly a way for them to stash it. Private corporations don't have to file quarterly reports to the SEC. They aren't required to disclose their shareholders, their officers or their directors. That's why they're private."

"Money laundering," Kurtz said.

Barent nodded. "Yeah. The money goes in and whatever comes out is entirely up to the two parties involved."

"But they have to pay taxes."

"Sure. They pay taxes on declared income, but is the income that they're declaring the actual income? Hard to tell.

"There are five different entry programs into the FBI," Barent said. "One of the five is accounting. About fifteen percent of FBI agents are accountants."

Kurtz ate his sandwich while he considered this. "I didn't know that. Doesn't exactly jibe with the image."

Barent shrugged. "That's how they got Al Capone: income tax evasion."

"So how do these guys get away with it, if everybody knows what they're doing?"

"Everybody doesn't *know* what they're doing. Everybody *thinks* they know what they're doing. I'm sure that the Feds have sniffed around the Russian mob. They probably have a whole division devoted just to them, but they can investigate all they want. They can't look at the books without a warrant and they can't get a warrant without at least some confirmatory evidence. Also, these guys have very good lawyers."

"Hmm…" Kurtz sat back and thought about it.

"What brought this on?" Barent asked.

"Steve Ryan," Kurtz said.

"The plastic surgeon. He committed suicide."

"Yeah. It turns out that his wife, Donna, is Russian. Her cousin is Arkady Lukin, the one who works for Rugov."

Barent frowned. "So?"

"Lenore knows them. She went to High School with Donna. They're friends. We used to socialize."

"Okay. So?"

"So, nothing. I was just curious."

"God, help us," Barent said.

Kurtz gave a tepid grin. "Arnie Figueroa was following some Russians when he got shot."

"There are a lot of Russians in New York and we already know that some of them are criminals. We have no reason to link Arnie Figueroa's shooting with the Rugov organization and certainly not with Steve Ryan's suicide."

"If it was suicide…"

Barent paused with his sandwich half-way to his mouth. "Let's not invent problems that don't exist. The guy left a note declaring his intentions to end it all, and aside from a little alcohol, there weren't any drugs in his system other than the ones he had prescriptions for."

Kurtz grudgingly nodded. "And then, of course, there's the guy who tried to inject potassium chloride into Arnie's IV line."

Barent sighed. "Shall I give you the usual advice?"

"Yeah, yeah. Mind my own business. Don't get involved. Stay away from these guys and don't get in over my head. I've heard it all before."

"It's good advice," Barent said. "You should take it."

"Right," Kurtz said. "Understood."

Barent gave Kurtz' mulishly smiling face a searching look and shook his head. They finished their lunch in silence.

Chapter 16

Arnaldo Figueroa knew that his brain was not working as well as it used to, but still, an undercover cop is trained to observe things. When you're in the lion's den, you'd better pay attention and be ready to move fast if you don't want to get eaten.

He had been home for a day. It was nice. Cynthia made his favorite dishes. The kids fussed over him. It was a little boring, he had to admit, with nothing to do but sit around and watch TV but the happy feeling of simply being alive and home had not yet faded. He squeezed a rubber ball with his left hand, willing the strength and dexterity to come back. He walked up and down the stairs, trying to regain his former balance.

He sat in his favorite chair in front of the TV, stared out the front window and suppressed a wolfish grin. The guy wandering down the street had passed this way twice already in the past hour. He looked familiar. He was paying just a bit more than casual attention to the house. Not that there was anything blatant about it, but still, he had walked by three times now.

Where had he seen this guy before? Big, beefy, broad shoulders, barrel chest. The guy looked strong. He was dressed in casual clothes, nothing that would stand out. He was white. It was possible that the Department was providing him with a little surreptitious protection, but if so, he should have been informed. Arnaldo Figueroa was still a cop, after all, and cops had guns. An unfortunate misunderstanding could very easily result in somebody getting killed. He clutched his service pistol in his right hand and considered his options.

The kids were in school. Cynthia, after spending the past day hovering over him, had finally begun to relax and had resumed her regular schedule. Right now, she was over at her sister's for cookies and tea. Arnaldo Figueroa was all alone. All alone, a poor, unfortunate cripple, all alone and vulnerable…so sad.

Arnie grinned.

The guy did look familiar, though. Something about the gait, the way he looked over his shoulder. Hard to say, really, but Arnie was pretty certain that he had seen this guy before, and he thought he knew where. A vision of waking up in the night flashed through his memory, seeing a vague figure hovering over his bed, reaching for his IV line.

Come on, you bastard, Arnie thought. *Stop beating around the bush. Grow a pair.*

Sitting calmly in the darkened room, he clutched his pistol in his right hand and waited.

The two men stood in front of Iosif Kozlov, their posture erect, their eyes fixed straight ahead. "Whose idea was this?" Iosif Kozlov said.

One of them, the taller one, cleared his throat. "Yevgeny's," he said.

"Yevgeny's," Iosif Kozlov repeated. "Yevgeny was an idiot." He considered the two men. "And what did you know of this?"

"Nothing," the smaller one said.

"He was acting on his own." The taller one frowned.

Their words had the ring of truth, unless they were much better actors than they seemed to be, which was unlikely. These two were young and perhaps not too bright but they knew how to follow orders. "Yevgeny has paid the price for his stupidity," Iosif Kozlov said. "This is the way of the world and I am not unhappy with such an outcome. The authorities in this country would love an excuse to move against us. We cannot afford to give them such an excuse and we cannot afford stupidity." He shrugged. The three men, now two, were foot soldiers. There were thousands just like them, all eager to come to America, eager for a chance to prove their worth. Pawns, Iosif Kozlov thought. Easily replaced.

"You are dismissed," Iosif Kozlov said.

Without a word, the two men turned on their heels and marched from the room.

"Who is he?" Barent said.

"No idea," Arnie said.

The dead man had brought with him an excellent set of lock picks, which he apparently knew how to use. It had taken him less than five minutes to jimmy the lock and enter through the front door.

"Stop," Arnie said. "Put your hands up and make no sudden moves."

The guy wasn't too good at following orders. He hesitated for a brief instant, then went for his gun. Arnie shot him, three times in the chest.

"Oh, boy," Arnie muttered. Cynthia was not going to be pleased. He sadly contemplated the dead body lying on the floor and the rivulet of blood slowly trickling into the carpet, then picked up the phone and dialed 911.

Not much for the crime scene boys to do. Cause of death was obvious. The guy had no ID and no obvious identifying features except for the absence of the little finger on his left hand.

"He didn't say anything?" Harry Moran asked.

"Not a word. I told him to raise his hands, he went for his gun and I shot him."

"Hopefully, his prints are on record," Barent said. "We'll see."

They weren't, as it turned out, but the dead body did reveal some additional clues. A tattoo of a snarling tiger peered out at the world from the left side of his chest. Another, smaller tattoo, of the Madonna and child sat on his right pectoral. Both tattoos were a uniform, grayish color.

Barent peered down at the photographs and sighed. "These mean anything to you?" he asked Moran.

Moran frowned. "Sure," he said. "You don't see these very often, not in this country."

"Not too surprising, though," Barent said.

A number of books had been published on Russian criminal tattoos, a weird and previously clandestine art form. Each tattoo had a unique meaning. They were almost a language of their own. Almost all the prisoners in Russia's maximum security facilities had them, but there weren't a lot of supplies in prison. The ink was most commonly made from scorched rubber mixed with the subject's own urine. Infections, ranging from tetanus to gangrene, were common. Risking such infections was only one small way for a Russian mobster to demonstrate his courage.

The snarling tiger meant defiance for the Soviet authorities. The Madonna and child meant loyalty to the criminal organization.

The gun was a cheap piece of crap and the little finger…that was a typical Russian punishment for some sort of fuck-up. The Chinese triads did something similar. Barent shuddered. Most likely, the guy had been required to cut off the finger himself.

"These people are not known for their restraint, and certainly not for their subtlety," Moran said. "One guy with a syringe of potassium chloride. Another guy, or maybe the same guy, barging in with a gun." Moran shook his head. "If the Russian mafia had wanted to kill Arnie, they would have sent more than one, and they wouldn't have bungled the job."

"Seems right. Presumably, the guy was acting on his own. Not too bright of him."

The obvious next step was to run off a few thousand photos of the dead man's face. Somebody out there must know who he was and who he worked for. The odds of finding that somebody, however, were slim. Russian mobsters were not a forgiving bunch, and anybody with loose lips would be likely to die a slow, painful death and never be seen again.

Still, no reason not to try. Sometimes you got lucky.

A holding company, even a holding company that was less than legitimate, owned bits and pieces of other companies. Sometimes they owned those companies outright. Arkady Lukin worked for the Rugov Corporation, a holding company, and Donna Ryan worked for Hotchkiss and Phelps, an investment bank.

A lot of similarities, Kurtz thought, between a holding company and an investment bank. A search through the internet revealed very little of interest, however. Alexei Rugov was mentioned in a few articles, mostly supposition and speculative bullshit. Basically, nobody knew anything about him except that he had a military background and had emigrated to the United States shortly after the fall of the Soviet Union.

Arkady Lukin had been born in this country. He had an older brother and two sisters. There was nothing about him on the web except for a few college photos. He had gone to Fordham and graduated with a degree in finance. He had a profile on neither MySpace nor the newer one, Facebook.

Donna Ryan, née Petrovich, had just a bit more of a presence on-line. As Lenore had said, Donna Ryan was smart. She had majored in economics at Wellesley, graduating Summa cum Laude, and then gone on for an MBA. She had been hired by Hotchkiss and Phelps immediately after graduation and had become a Certified Financial Analyst a few years later. She and Steve Ryan had married less than a year after she finished college, while Steve was in Medical School at Columbia. They had three kids, the oldest only ten.

Hotchkiss and Phelps was a medium sized, privately held investment firm. In the past five years, they had brokered some prominent deals regarding software startups, biotech firms, small defense contractors and real estate development. Donna had made partner only the year before.

Kurtz sat back and considered. Nothing leaped out at him. Nothing rang a bell. What he had was an inchoate mass of random information. There were nearly three quarters of a million Russians in New York and neither Kurtz, Barent nor Moran knew of anything whatsoever to tie Arnaldo Figueroa and his assailant to Alexei Rugov or Arkady Lukin.

Kurtz didn't like Arkady Lukin, though. There was just something about him, and he felt sorry for Donna Ryan. He hadn't known Steve Ryan all that well, despite the fact that they had socialized a few times, but he had been a nice guy who tried his best, despite being a piss poor surgeon.

What next? By now, Kurtz was well acquainted with the basics of police work. When you hit an impasse in a case, seek more information…

"I'm not too thrilled about this," Lenore said.

Neither was Kurtz, truth to tell. Donna Petrovich and Lenore Brinkman had gone to High School together. They had taken many of the same classes. They had been friends. This visit seemed a little underhanded. "Yeah. I understand," Kurtz said.

Lenore sniffed.

The door opened. Donna's pale, wanly smiling face greeted them. "Come in," she said. They followed her down a hallway into a den that overlooked a small backyard with a neatly laid out garden that featured a trickling waterfall, a small pond and a couple of lily pads. "Please sit down."

Kurtz and Lenore sat together on a couch. Donna sat on a hassock on the other side of a glass coffee table. A plate of assorted cookies and a pot of tea sat on the table. "Help yourselves," she said.

Kurtz selected a couple of cookies and poured himself a cup of tea. Earl Gray, not his favorite. "Thanks for seeing us," he said.

"No problem," Donna said. "What's it all about?"

Nothing much, Kurtz thought. Only murder and attempted murder. Maybe.

Lenore raised a brow and gave him an arch look.

"What can you tell me about the Rugov Corporation?" Kurtz said.

Donna seemed momentarily taken aback. "Very little. Why do you want to know that?"

Yeah, genius. Why *do* you want to know that?

"Curiosity," he said. It was the truth, though truthfully, none of this was his business.

"Curiosity..."

Kurtz nodded.

"Strange thing to be curious about," Donna said.

"I won't argue," Kurtz said. "Nevertheless, I'm curious."

Donna sighed. "As I said, I know very little about the Rugov Corporation. It's a privately held firm. Their business doesn't intersect with ours."

"No? Rugov is a holding company. Hotchkiss and Phelps is an investment bank. I was under the impression that what you do is similar."

She shrugged. "They buy established corporations, usually corporations that have previously been successful but have fallen on hard times. We supply venture capital. We finance the growth of new corporations and then help them grow. Our focus is different. The firms that interest us are different."

"I see," Kurtz said, though truthfully, the two business models sounded pretty much the same.

"Rugov is primarily owned by a man named Alexei Rugov. He's a somewhat shadowy figure in the Russian community. He's said to be a gangster."

"I knew that," Kurtz said.

Donna Ryan grinned. "Somehow, I suspected that you did."

"And yet your cousin, Arkady Lukin, works for the Rugov Corporation."

"As I've said, I don't really know anything about Alexei Rugov or his corporation except for the rumors. I do worry about Arkady, though." Donna stared out at the garden and took a small bite out of a cookie. "Arkady and I have always been close. We played together as children. It's a large family. A lot of get-togethers, a lot of holiday dinners."

"Tell me about your family," Kurtz said.

"Why? Because you're curious?"

"Yes, actually," Kurtz said.

"Why?"

Yes, genius. Why? Kurtz cleared his throat. "I had a very small family. My mother died when I was very young. It was just my father and me. I've always wondered what growing up with a large family was like."

She gave him a doubtful look, then shrugged. "When you're young, you tend to take it all for granted. It's just the way life is. They're always there, the aunts, the uncles, the cousins, not necessarily appreciated and sometimes even disliked, but they're still your family and you can't choose your family. It's comforting, in a way, knowing that all these people exist who have at least some minimal interest in you and your life, being a part of something larger." Donna shook her head. "And then you grow up and you don't see them quite as often. And then Aunt Galina dies and a few years later, Uncle Boris passes away and then, suddenly, you hardly see them at all. You find that the current generation doesn't have the same interests, the same allegiance, as their parents did. It's sad. I hardly ever see most of my cousins, anymore. We've drifted apart, but I was always close to Arkady."

"He seemed very protective of you," Kurtz said.

Donna smiled wistfully. "Kids sometimes gang up on other kids. They're uncivilized little beasts, most of them, until they get older, and sometimes not even then. I was always the bookish sort. Most of my cousins were more rowdy. Some of them picked on me. Arkady always defended me."

"Picked on you how?"

"The usual baloney. Steal my books, hide my pens, unravel my braids when my back was turned. None of them meant much harm. I suppose they would tell you that they were just having fun."

"What does Arkady do for Rugov?"

"He's a financial analyst, like me."

"Does he ever talk about the deals he's involved in?"

Donna blinked at him. "Not at all. That would be highly unethical. Our clients have an expectation of confidentiality. We wouldn't stay in business very long if we violated that expectation."

"But Arkady, unlike you, did not seem to be the bookish type. He seemed very fit."

"He is fit. Arkady was all-state in track and field. He threw the shot-put and the javelin. He also wrestled." Donna shrugged. "Ability at athletics is not incompatible with having an excellent mind." She pursed her lips and examined the width of Kurtz' shoulders. "You should know that."

A point, Kurtz thought. A definite point. "And did Arkady have an excellent mind?"

"When he was young, he had little interest in school. He was smart but his grades didn't reflect it. Somewhere along the line, he grew up."

"Tell me about his family," Kurtz said.

Donna frowned. "Arkady's father runs a store that specializes in men's clothing. He's successful. His mother stayed home and raised the children. He has one older brother, Vasily. Vasily was born in the old country, a few years before his parents emigrated. His sisters are Olga and Natasha, both younger, both born here. Vasily was always getting into trouble when he was young. I believe that he spent some time in a juvenile correction facility. Olga and Natasha are both pretty girls. They're interested in fashion, makeup, partying and not much else."

"I remember Olga and Natasha," Lenore said. "They don't have three brain cells between them."

Donna shrugged.

"I don't recall much about Vasily," Lenore said. "He never seemed to be around."

"I don't know," Donna said.

And that was that. They chatted for a few more minutes and then took their leave. In the car, on the drive back to Manhattan, Kurtz was silent. Lenore let him think for awhile and then said, "Did you get anything useful out of that discussion?"

"Hard to say. I'm forming more of a picture of the guy. Will that lead to anything?" Kurtz sighed. "Probably not, but you never know."

Lenore smiled. "There are things that Donna didn't want to say. Arkady was protective of Donna when they were kids but Donna was just as protective of him. Arkady had a tough time of it in school."

Kurtz glanced at her. "How so?"

"Because Arkady is gay."

Kurtz blinked. "Really…"

"Really," Lenore said.

"Hey, come on in."

Holding a large gin and tonic in his left hand, Alan Saunders smiled blearily at his friend, Reggie Johnson, and held the door open. Reggie Johnson nodded to the woman at his side. "This is Alicia."

Alicia, a small brunette with red lips and a tiny, up-tilted nose, smiled. "Pleased to meet you," she said.

"Welcome," Alan Saunders said. "Come on in and help yourselves."

Inside, most of the furniture had been pushed to the sides of the large living room. The music blared. Three couples were already dancing. A long table covered with cold cuts, sliced bread and mixed hors d'oeuvres had been set up along one wall. Another table on the opposite wall held wine, beer, various bottles of liquor and ice.

"You want a drink? Something to eat?" Reggie Johnson said.

Alicia shrugged. "I'm not really into this scene. Let's get what we came for and hit the road."

Reggie grinned. "Sure," he said, and turned to Alan Saunders, who had walked in behind them. "The man of the hour here, yet?"

Alan Saunders wrinkled his nose. "He's got somebody with him. They're in the small office next to the den."

Reggie blinked. "Who's with him?"

Alan Saunders' eyes skittered to the side. "He says he's a bodyguard."

"A bodyguard?"

"He just sits there. He doesn't say much."

"He's never had a bodyguard before. I don't like that," Reggie said. "I don't like it at all."

"Me, neither, but if you want to buy what he's selling, then that's the way it is."

Reggie glanced at Alicia, who looked worried. "You want to do this?"

"They've been here for over an hour," Alan Saunders said. "There hasn't been any trouble."

"Let's do it," Alicia said. "Fast." She frowned at Alan Saunders. "And then let's leave."

Reggie shrugged. He walked down a corridor, then turned left. Alicia followed. The door to the office was open. "Hey, there," a man said. He was maybe thirty years old, wearing designer jeans and a long-sleeved pullover. He sat on a small sofa, a black carry bag at his feet. Another man, with light brown skin and black hair, sat next to him. This man looked at Reggie and Alicia, gave them a slight nod but said nothing.

Reggie gave a tentative smile and pulled out a roll of cash.

The first man smiled back. His eyes flicked to Alicia, who was staring at the cash. He smiled wider, opened the carry bag and pulled out a sandwich sized zip-loc bag half filled with white powder. He hefted the bag in his open palm and handed it over. Reggie gave him the money and carefully placed the zip-loc bag in his pocket.

Both men had done this before. "Pleasure doing business with you," the man said.

Reggie grinned. "You bet."

They walked back down the corridor and into the living room, which was starting to get crowded. The music was loud. Three guys huddled in a corner, chugging back wine and discussing something that couldn't be heard over the music. Four women were dancing together.

"Let's get out of here," Alicia said.

"Sure," Reggie said.

The door opened. A man walked in, followed by another, then three more. Two of them carried handguns in their fists. The others held rifles. Reggie blinked at them. The five men spread out, lifted their guns and opened fire at the crowd. Reggie felt both of his legs give way and he fell heavily. Alicia crumbled next to him. One of the gunmen put a couple of short bursts through the stereo system. The music stopped. Within seconds, everyone but the gunmen were lying on the floor.

Three gunmen calmly walked through the back of the room and down the corridor. A few seconds later, more shots rang out. The gunmen re-appeared in the living room.

"Attention," one of the gunmen said. Alicia was curled up near Reggie's side, moaning. Reggie, both legs shattered, could hear him clearly.

"Attention, please," the gunman said again. He smiled. "With appropriate care, most of you will live. You should be grateful. If we had wished to kill you, all of you would now be dead. Consider this a warning." He briefly surveyed the room and gave a small, satisfied nod. All five gunmen walked out.

"A warning of what?" Barent said.

Moran puffed up his cheeks and shrugged.

The wounded had been bundled up and taken by ambulance to area hospitals. None of them were dead, though at least three had suffered so much blood loss that they were unlikely to survive. The two men in the back office, however, were very dead indeed, having been hit by at least ten bullets each in the abdomen and chest. Not the head. Whoever had done this had wanted the dead men to be easily identifiable.

Curious that the carry bag full of white powder had also been left behind. A rival gang might kill a man to steal his very valuable stash of narcotic. The fact that they had left it in place was, presumably, a part of the message.

"A turf war?" Moran said.

"Seems likely."

Joe Danowski, a Lieutenant on the Narcotics Squad, walked back into the office, took a look at the dead men and grunted. "Alejandro Gonzales," he said.

"What's his story?"

"The usual. In and out of prison, petty crimes, mostly. Marijuana. A little cocaine. He's Mexican. We haven't seen him around lately. I guess he graduated into bigger, if not better things."

"Sad," Moran said. "All that education, wasted."

Danowski barely cracked a smile. "I don't recognize the white guy."

"His wallet says he's Andrew Fox. His partner was Steven Hayward, who recently had his head cut off. Also, Hayward's wife."

Danowski puffed up his cheeks. "I've heard that."

"So, what do you think is in the bag?" Barent said.

Danowski shrugged. "We'll find out."

Javier Garcia was not pleased. "First the Haywards. Now this. Who were they?"

Esteban Martinez frowned. He was worried. Esteban Martinez had started out as a typical young gang-member, but he turned out to have a head for figures. *La Familia* had found this talent to be useful. Esteban Martinez no longer carried a gun and no longer needed to involve himself in the more sordid aspects of their mutual business. Also, he had grown fat. Esteban Martinez was not looking forward to a war.

"We don't know." Esteban Martinez hesitated. "They were white. They had no discernible accent. They could have been anybody."

"And yet they knew where the event was due to take place. They knew where Fox and Alejandro would be. It was a message, they said. A *message*." He almost hissed it.

Esteban Martinez winced. He cleared his throat and swallowed. Javier Garcia was clearly furious. Esteban Martinez had seen this aspect of his old friend and colleague only a few times, and not at all in recent years, but he knew that somebody was going to die.

Javier Garcia glared at him. "You will find out who did this," he said. It was not a request.

Esteban Martinez sighed. "You know that the obvious candidate is Alexei Rugov. We have ended our distribution arrangement with his organization. He was not pleased."

"It may be Rugov and it may not. Perhaps we are meant to think that it is Rugov. In chaos, there is opportunity. Is this not so? Perhaps there are those who would benefit by a war between Alexei Rugov and ourselves. I will not attack the Rugov organization without proof that he is responsible." He glared again at Esteban Martinez. "Find out."

Esteban Martinez nodded. "Yes," he said. "Yes, I will."

Chapter 17

Mrs. Shapiro's voice sounded worried. "There is a man at the front desk, Doctor. He's asking to see you."

Kurtz sighed. It had been a long, frustrating morning. First a gallbladder that had been more difficult than expected, then an unscheduled appendix in the ER that couldn't wait. He had hurried back to the office and had been hoping for a little time to inhale a sandwich before his first patient. He stared down at the roast beef on rye that he had just opened, gritting his teeth. "Is it an emergency?"

"He says it's urgent."

"Urgent," Kurtz muttered.

"He says to tell you that his name is Vasily Lukin."

Slowly, Kurtz smiled. He folded his sandwich back up and placed it into the middle drawer of his desk, then opened the side drawer, pulled out a Sig Sauer P365, checked the slide, made certain there was a bullet in the chamber and gently placed the gun back in the center of the drawer, where he could reach it easily. Police surgeons were authorized to carry. Kurtz had only recently purchased the gun. Small, easily concealable, with a nitron slide and a ten-round magazine. A truly nifty little weapon. He left the drawer open.

"Send him in," Kurtz said.

Vasily Lukin looked a lot like his brother. He was just as tall, a little leaner, with a hard face and glittering black eyes. He wore black pants and a matching black blazer with a telltale bulge under the left shoulder. There were tattoos on his hands. He stalked into the office, sat down in one of the two chairs across from the desk and stared at Kurtz.

Kurtz smiled back. "Can I help you?" he said.

Vasily Lukin continued to stare. The smile still on his face, Kurtz stared back. After a moment, Vasily Lukin frowned and looked away. "You are a physician," he said.

"That is correct."

"A surgeon."

Kurtz nodded.

"Two nights ago, you paid a visit to Donna Petrovich."

"Her name is Donna Ryan, now. She hasn't been Donna Petrovich in a long time."

Vasily Lukin shrugged. "Her husband is dead."

"Yes," Kurtz said. "He committed suicide."

"He was weak," Vasily Lukin said.

"Perhaps so," Kurtz said, "but now he's dead, and the dead can no longer trouble the living, so why are you here?"

Vasily Lukin leaned forward in his chair. "You will stay away from Donna Petrovich."

"Will I?" Kurtz sat back in his chair and steepled his fingers together beneath his chin. Kurtz did not like Vasily Lukin any more than he liked his brother, which on first impression was not at all. Vasily Lukin seemed somehow to think that he was hot shit. Truthfully, Kurtz had not expected to have anything further to do with Donna Ryan after their conversation the other night, but he liked the idea of pulling Vasily Lukin's chain. "Tell me, does Alexei Rugov know that you're here?"

Vasily Lukin stared at him.

"Nothing to say? I expect not, then."

"You are foolish," Vasily Lukin said. "You are more than foolish. Alexei Rugov is not a name that you should be speaking carelessly."

"No? Let's see…how about Iosif Kozlov? Sergei Ostrovsky, perhaps? Are these names that I should be speaking carelessly? I was given to understand that Russian mobsters believe in discipline. The needs of the organization are paramount, and all that. What need is served by your visit here today?"

Vasily Lukin narrowed his eyes, then shrugged, rose to his feet and stalked out of the office. Kurtz moved to the window. A few seconds later, he saw Vasily Lukin exit the building and get into the back seat of a black Mercedes sedan that was double parked on the street. Too far away to see the license plate, not that the license plate would tell him anything useful. The sedan drove away.

Kurtz sighed and picked up the phone.

"You said *what?*" Barent stared at him, incredulous.

"The guy pissed me off," Kurtz said, defensively. So okay, maybe he had been a little indiscreet.

Barent stared at him, then let out a low whistle and shook his head. "I always knew you were a loaded gun but this is seriously nuts."

"I don't like it when mobsters try to tell me what to do."

"And this happens every day? That mobsters try to tell you what to do?"

"It's happened before," Kurtz said. "It annoys me, and even once is once too much."

"So, what do you plan on doing, now? You've stuck your head into a hornet's nest, not for the first time, I might add. And for what? What did you expect to get out of that idiotic conversation?"

Kurtz had been asking himself the same thing. He shrugged.

"Why couldn't you have just told the guy that you had no intention of approaching Donna Ryan ever again? Why couldn't you have just given him what he wants?"

"But I don't know what he wants."

"What do you *mean*, you don't know what he wants? He wants you to stay away from Donna Ryan. You do know that, right? Because he said so?"

Barent's voice, Kurtz noted, had gone just a tad high-pitched.

But *why* did Vasily Lukin, or the organization of which he was a member, want him to stay away from Donna Ryan? Offhand, Donna Ryan didn't seem like the sort of woman to interest Russian mobsters. "Alright," Kurtz said. His voice sounded petulant even to himself. "Fine."

Barent let out a long, slow breath. "Are you carrying?" he asked.

"Yeah," Kurtz said.

"Great," Barent said. "That's just great."

"I'm a police surgeon," Kurtz said. "It's a dangerous job. Sometimes people threaten us."

"Yeah," Barent said. "And sometimes they deserve it."

"This man was not what I expected," Vasily Lukin said.

Alexei Rugov sat back and pondered this. "How much does he know?"

Vasily Lukin shrugged. "Probably nothing, or at least nothing that we care about. Your name is hardly a secret. Neither is that of Iosif Kozlov, nor Sergei Ostrovsky."

It was easy to kill people, Alexei Rugov reflected, and sometimes it was necessary, but killing people tended to have consequences, some of them unexpected and some unpleasant. Killing a physician, particularly a physician associated with the police was not a step to be taken lightly, not when Alexei Rugov's name had already been mentioned. He and his organization existed in a delicate web of relationships and obligations and some things were simply not worth the cost.

"Keep an eye on him," Alexei Rugov said.

"Of course," Vasily Lukin said.

Barent was a cop. Cops had a certain degree of immunity to retribution. Even the most hardened mobster would hesitate to deliberately and in cold blood murder a cop. Kurtz was not a cop, exactly, but he was a police surgeon, which might or not be enough in the mind of a Russian mobster to provide him with the same nebulous protection.

There was nothing to tie Donna Ryan to Arnie Figueroa, except the fact that both had something to do with Russians, and there was certainly nothing to tie either of these individuals to the murders of Mitchell Price, Steven Hayward or his wife, and now, Alejandro Gonzales and Andrew Fox. Still, the fact that Vasily Lukin, and possibly Alexei Rugov had displayed an interest in Donna Ryan was at least, potentially, a clue.

The offices of Hotchkiss and Phelps occupied the twenty-fourth floor of a skyscraper in Midtown. The carpet was thick, the artwork on the walls looked expensive, full of flowing lines and bright colors. Barent was hardly an expert on abstract art but he liked the paintings. The splotches of color looked lively, like good things happening. Donna Ryan's office was large, with a glass and aluminum desk, comfortable chairs and a corner alcove with a couch, a coffee table and a bookshelf. Donna Ryan herself seemed dwarfed behind the desk, particularly with the large glass wall behind her looking down on the city.

Donna Ryan nodded as Barent walked into the room. "Detective," she said. "What can I do for you?"

Her face was thin and pale, her eyes shadowed. Nevertheless, Donna Ryan was a beautiful woman.

"A few days ago, Richard Kurtz and Lenore Brinkman paid you a visit," Barent said.

She nodded. "Yes?"

"Yesterday, a man named Vasily Lukin warned Richard Kurtz to stay away from you."

Donna Ryan winced. "That idiot," she muttered.

Barent said nothing. After a moment, Donna Ryan shifted uncomfortably in her chair. "Vasily Lukin is my cousin. Did you know that?"

"I did."

"I have never been close to Vasily. He's quite a bit older than me and we had little to do with each other, growing up. I am close to his brother, Arkady. Arkady has always been protective of me. I would think that Vasily is acting on his brother's behalf."

"What do you mean by that, exactly?"

"Probably not what you think. There was never anything at all romantic between Arkady and myself, though at one point, the family seemed to think that there might be. We had similar outlooks on life, similar taste in books and movies and art. We talked to each other. We were good friends."

"What did you and Richard Kurtz talk about?" Barent had already gotten Kurtz' side of the conversation. He was curious to hear what Donna Ryan might have to say.

"Nothing very significant. He was curious about the Rugov Corporation. He asked about my family."

"And after he and Lenore left, who did you talk to about his visit?"

"I mentioned it to Arkady. There seemed no reason not to."

"Anybody else?"

She shrugged. "Only my mother."

Barent sat back in his seat. "Richard Kurtz is a police surgeon. He's also a friend of mine. He has on occasion displayed an interest in things that are none of his business."

Donna Ryan cracked a smile. "I know Richard. His wife and I are old friends. I'll speak with Arkady. I'm not quite the fragile flower that he seems to think me."

Barent nodded. "Not to change the subject, but the Rugov organization has a rather sinister reputation."

"So, I've heard. Beyond the fact that they're a holding company, I know nothing at all about the Rugov organization."

"And yet Arkady Lukin, your cousin, to whom you are close, works for them, and presumably so does Vasily."

Donna Ryan shrugged. "I know nothing about the Rugov organization," she repeated. "My cousins have never discussed it with me. I imagine that this is deliberate."

"Does it bother you, that they work for a man who is said to be a mobster?"

"Frankly, yes, but they're grown men and there's nothing I can do about it."

"I understand that your parents escaped from the Soviet Union. I would imagine that the politics of the old country must have been a routine topic of conversation in your family."

"Absolutely. My parents did escape. My aunts and uncles as well. The borders were actually rather porous at that time. Many people took vacations and simply walked away. They had to be willing to leave everything that they had behind, but since nobody in the Soviet Union had much of anything, this wasn't that much of a sacrifice." Donna Ryan nodded. "They did discuss it. They talked about it constantly. Every family get together, every dinner." She grinned. "Sometimes the discussions grew heated. I remember my Uncle Ivan pounding on the table and shaking his fist in my father's face."

Barent blinked. "What was this heated discussion about?"

"I have no idea, other than the words 'Stalin,' 'Andropov,' 'Yeltsin' and then, a few years later, 'Putin.' Among themselves, they spoke only Russian."

"And you never learned the language?"

"No. It was deliberate. My parents didn't want the younger generation to learn Russian. The United States was a new country and we were living a new life. They loved Russia. They were passionate about it, but they had no expectation of ever going back.

141

They wanted us to grow up and become good little Americans." She smiled. "Vasily and Arkady's parents felt differently. They learned the language from an early age. Their parents wanted them to feel that they were Russian. I imagine that this was one of the things that my parents disagreed with."

"And now Arkady and Vasily Lukin have supposedly become members of a Russian criminal gang."

Donna Ryan sighed. "That is the rumor. I hope that the rumor isn't true but as I said, they're grown men and there's nothing that I can do about it." She hesitated. "I'll speak to Arkady. I wouldn't want Dr. Kurtz to come to any harm."

"Thanks," Barent said. "Neither would I."

Chapter 18

"Fucking clowns," Kurtz muttered.

What the hell did they think they were doing? Kurtz liked to run in Central Park. It wasn't hard to spot people who just happened to be running along behind him, day after day. It had taken him only a little longer to spot the blue Toyota that followed him to work and the red Volvo that followed him back home.

"We're being followed," Kurtz said. Lenore often ran with him in the Park, particularly if the day was sunny and the skies clear. They had just passed the one-mile mark.

Lenore blinked. "Are we?"

"Two guys. Big, white, casual dress. They're annoying me."

Lenore gave him a worried look.

Lenore's presence concerned him. He had no desire to drag Lenore into anything that might turn violent.

"Don't be annoyed," Lenore said.

Kurtz grunted.

"Maybe we should go home," Lenore said.

"Sure." They turned. The two men turned with them. They were making no effort to get closer. They followed at a leisurely pace behind. A few minutes later, they were out of the Park and soon after, they entered the lobby of their building.

"Call Lew," Lenore said.

Kurtz nodded. "Yeah."

"I was afraid of this," Barent said.

"What are you going to do about it?"

"We'll follow the followers. What else?"

Something inside Kurtz unclenched. He had toyed with the idea of doing something…drastic. Like turn around and beat the two guys to a pulp, but that might have been a bit immature of him. Also, of course, maybe they would have beaten him to a pulp, instead. No. Much better to let the forces of law and order protect and serve. "Good," Kurtz said. "Where and when?"

"Follow your routine. We'll take it from there."

The next day, Kurtz donned his sweats and his running shoes and set out for the Park. By mutual agreement, Lenore stayed behind. He jogged an easy mile. Sure enough, two large, white men picked him up at the half-mile mark. He turned down a trail and picked up the pace. They followed. Behind them, four other men, two white, one black, one Asian, turned onto the trail and began to run.

Kurtz slowed. Ahead of him, around a bend, stood a bench. He stopped and sat down on the bench, apparently winded. The two men also slowed. One looked at the other, who ignored him, his eyes fixed on Kurtz.

The four men behind them trotted up. "Excuse me," the black guy said.

The two looked at them, their faces hard.

The black guy smiled. Suddenly, the two white guys were surrounded. "We're police. We've been told that you're harassing this man." Kurtz smiled and gave the white guys a little wave.

One of the white guys cleared his throat. "This is untrue," he said. "We do not know this man. We are running in the park. Running in the park is allowed." He had an accent that might have been Russian.

"Harassing people isn't," the black cop said. "Can we see some identification?"

The white guy who might have been Russian gave Kurtz a level look. Something in his gaze spelled trouble. Kurtz smiled back.

"Certainly," the white guy said. He reached into a back pocket, pulled out a wallet and produced a card, apparently a driver's license. The black cop took it, turned it over and examined both sides. "Joseph Smith," he said. He turned to the second guy, who silently produced a similar card.

The cop frowned at it. "Jonathan Jones." The cop sighed. "Okay," he said, "let's go downtown."

"What is the reason?" the white guy said. "We have done nothing."

The cop shrugged. "Harassment is a crime. Also, we have to check out your ID's. It's possible that these are false names." He gave the white guy a toothy grin.

The white guy frowned but said nothing. The cop turned to Kurtz and winked one eye. Kurtz gave him a little nod. "Don't beat them too badly," Kurtz said. "No permanent damage. Who knows? They might be innocent."

The cop snorted. "Fat chance."

Once they arrived at the station house, the two white guys were allowed their one phone call. They were locked in a cell. Nobody approached them. Nobody spoke to them. An hour later, a lawyer showed up. His name was Abner Goodell. He was slim and balding. His dark blue suit appeared slightly rumpled. He asked for a room to discuss things with his clients and after a half hour, announced that they were ready to be interviewed. The interview was short.

Abby Blake was the Assistant District Attorney assigned to the case, such as it was. She was only one year out of law school but was not, Ted Weiss had grudgingly conceded at her first performance review, incompetent. "We're looking at charges of criminal harassment, stalking and attempted assault," she said.

Abner Goodell blinked. "Are you out of your mind?"

"Not the last time I checked."

"They were running in the park. People run in the park all the time. They never came near this guy…what's his name?" Abner Goodell looked down at his notepad. "Kurtz."

"Doctor Kurtz is a member of the New York City Police Department. He is a respected physician and surgeon."

"So?"

"They were harassing him."

"Says Kurtz. They say differently."

The two white guys, whose names may or may not have been Joseph Smith and Jonathan Jones, sat at the table, trying to look innocent. Abby Blake glanced at them. "Their ID's are phony. We have no idea who they are."

"There is no legal requirement in this supposedly free country to carry any identification whatsoever, despite the wishes of a government that is increasingly fascist in both its outlook and procedures."

"True," Abby Blake said. "There is no legal requirement to carry identification. There is, however, a very definite legal requirement that official documents, in this case two licenses supposedly issued by the State of New York allowing the holder to operate a moving vehicle, be legitimately issued. Their licenses are phony. According to New York Penal Law 170.30, criminal possession of a forged instrument in the First Degree is a 'C' class felony and may be punishable by up to fifteen years in jail."

The two white guys frowned. The frowns did not go unnoticed by either Abby Blake or Abner Goodell. "She's full of shit," Abner Goodell said. "First Degree Criminal Possession is possession of a false document in association with grand larceny, forgery, criminal possession of stolen property or outright theft. The charge is ridiculous."

"We could be looking at a RICO case here," Abby Blake said thoughtfully.

Abner Goodell gave her a long look. "Possession of a phony driver's license in association with no other crime is an 'A' class misdemeanor."

Abby Blake clicked her tongue between her teeth. "Even an 'A' class misdemeanor can still bring up to one year in jail. At Riker's Island. Not the most pleasant place to spend a year."

"A first offense," Abner Goodell said, "typically involves probation and a small fine."

"You're forgetting the harassment charge." Abby Blake gave a long-suffering sigh. "Okay, I'll concede that a 'C' class felony is probably reaching. Possession plus harassment is Second Degree. That's 'D' class." Abby Blake gave the two white guys a shark-like smile. "That's seven years in jail."

Abner Goodell gave her an incredulous look. "Okay," he said. "Enough with the BS. Let's deal."

In the end, the false driver's licenses were confiscated. Instead of being charged under Penal Law 170, the two men would instead plead guilty to a violation of Section 509(6) of New York's Vehicle and Traffic Law and pay a fine of three hundred dollars each. In return, the two gave their real names, which turned out to be Ilya and Dimitri Fedorov. They were brothers. They worked for a bakery that specialized in Russian pastries, owned by their aunt, Masha Fedorov.

A few phone calls verified that they were telling the truth, at least about the aunt and the bakery. As to the charges of harassment, they would admit nothing. They were running in the park. Running in the park was not a crime.

They each had a few teenage arrests on their record, ranging from petty vandalism to assault. Nothing in the past five years, which could mean that they had repented of their youthful misbehavior or perhaps had learned how to conceal their crimes. In any case, the police had no real evidence of intent to commit harm. Running in the park was not a crime. Neither was running behind Richard Kurtz.

"They sent a message," Barent said to Kurtz, later in the day. "We sent a message back."

"Do you think the message was received?"

"Let's hope."

"Yeah," Lenore said, and frowned, first at Kurtz, then at Barent. "Let's hope."

"This man Kurtz could be a problem," Alexei Rugov said.

Vasily Lukin said nothing.

"He is intelligent. He acted decisively."

Vasily Lukin cleared his throat. "It took little intelligence to contact his colleagues among the police."

"Really? We deliberately allowed our people and their actions to be seen. A warning. He deliberately responded in a manner that was appropriate but did nothing to escalate the situation. He understands that we know who he is and that he can be reached. We understand that he has the protection of the authorities." Alexei Rugov shrugged. "It is a stalemate."

"For now," Vasily Lukin said.

"For now. Dr. Kurtz could possibly be an annoyance but he is peripheral to our plans. Unless he interferes in a much more serious way, we will not bother him again."

"Very well," Vasily Lukin said.

Alexei Rugov smiled. "You sound not entirely happy. For every action, there is a reaction. If Dr. Kurtz does decide to be an annoyance, we can always re-visit this decision."

Arnie Figueroa had made steady progress. His left hand was still a bit clumsy and definitely weaker than the right, but it was getting there. Feeling had returned to his leg. The limp was almost gone. He was aware that his days as an undercover cop were most likely behind him, even if his physical condition might allow it (still doubtful). Getting shot in the head and all the ensuing publicity had quite dramatically blown his cover. The newspapers had printed his name and his face.

Arnie Figueroa was looking forward to a desk job and frankly, at this point the prospect did not dismay him.

He had taken a cab back to his old haunting grounds. Arnie had lost weight. He wore contact lenses that changed the color of his eyes and he wore a wig, a blazer and a button down shirt. Nobody would recognize him, or even look at him twice. He sauntered up and down the street, circling the block, trying to remember…

"So, tell me," Kurtz said, "what was Steve Ryan doing the night he decided to commit suicide?"

Barent stared at him. Moran gave a long, slow smile. "Thinking again?" Moran said.

"It occurred to me to wonder."

Moran shook his head, still smiling.

It was Thursday afternoon. Kurtz had called first, to make certain that Barent and Moran would both be available, then had dropped by Barent's office.

"A family dinner," Barent said.

"Both sides of the family?"

"The wife's. Steve Ryan has one grown sister. She and her husband live in Seattle. His parents retired and moved to Florida about five years ago. None of his family is left in New York."

"The wife's…" Kurtz repeated. "I've been told that she has a rather large family. How many of them were there?"

Barent sighed. "Give me a second." He hit a few buttons on his computer, stared at the screen. "A lot of them," he said.

Kurtz smiled. "Yeah?"

"Donna Ryan's parents, her brother, two of her sisters plus their husbands, her cousins, Vasily and Arkady, their parents, four more cousins, six assorted kids."

"A party," Kurtz said.

"Yeah."

"Any particular occasion?"

"No. Just a family get-together. They have them fairly often."

"Where was this party, exactly?"

"The Ryans' house."

"It's a big house," Kurtz said.

Barent nodded.

"Anybody else?" Kurtz asked.

"Their priest, Robert Kamenov. Also, his wife."

"Father Bob?"

Barent gave Kurtz a long-suffering look. "Yes. Father Bob."

"Quite a crowd."

"Donna Ryan has a close-knit family."

That must be nice, Kurtz thought. Comforting, even, having all those people around who cared about you. Donna had said as much. Lenore's family was similar. Despite his occasional exasperation with his mother-in-law's impulses toward insanity, he enjoyed their frequent get-togethers. They were entertaining, if nothing else.

"And what did any of them have to say about Steve Ryan?"

Barent scratched his head, stared at his computer screen. "He seemed subdued."

"Subdued…"

"Not in the best of moods. He had just lost a patient."

"This, I know. She was my patient, too."

"Apparently, he had also decided on a change in careers."

"Okay."

Barent looked at him. "You've heard this before."

"I have. Steve told me."

"Then why are you asking us?"

Kurtz' mouth twitched upward. "Go on," he said.

"Go on, what? What more do you want to hear?"

"He was subdued. The autopsy revealed high levels of alcohol plus diazepam, for which he had a prescription. Okay, I get it, but subdued doesn't necessarily mean that he was planning on killing himself. From what I know of him, Steve was always the quiet type. Maybe he felt a bit out of place with his wife's family, many of whom were presumably speaking a different language. Maybe he just had a lot on his mind. Did anybody, anybody at all, say they were worried about him?"

"No," Barent said. "No, they didn't, but he left a suicide note and there was no evidence of violence. If anybody slipped diazepam into his wine glass, we have no way to prove it, and no reason to think that it happened."

"But it's possible."

Barent shrugged. "We try not to jump to conclusions in this business. Judges and juries tend to disregard conclusions that are not warranted by the evidence."

"God damn juries," Kurtz muttered.

"You got that right," Moran said. "You can't trust a jury. Juries do whatever the fuck they feel like. Just look at the OJ case."

Moran, Kurtz knew, tended to dwell on the OJ case. To Moran, the OJ case was emblematic of everything that was wrong about the so-called justice system.

Kurtz gave Moran a sour look. Moran smiled back.

"Anything else on your mind?" Barent asked.

"No," Kurtz said. "Not at this time."

Chapter 19

"Hello, Detective?"

"Yes?" Barent said. The voice on the other end of the line was vaguely familiar.

"This is Gerald Cox. At Adler and Bowen?"

A slow smile spread across Barent's face. "Yes, Mr. Cox. What can I do for you?"

"I think I know who Mitchell Price was going out with."

"Really?"

"Really."

"And how did you come by this revelation?"

"My secretary told me."

"Your secretary…"

"Yes. Her name is Celia Bauman."

"And why didn't your secretary tell us?"

Barent could hear Gerald Cox sigh over the phone. "When Mitchell Price was murdered, my secretary was on her honeymoon. You didn't talk to her. She wasn't here."

Most murders were solved, when they were solved, by the application of slow, tedious footwork. You went door to door. You talked to the friends, the family, the co-workers and the neighbors. You talked to a hundred people and maybe one of them remembered something that might be a clue.

Over the last fifty years, the clearance rate for murder in the United States had gone from over ninety percent down to about sixty-five percent. "Clearance" did not mean that somebody was convicted or even brought to trial. It simply meant that somebody was arrested for the crime. Much of the difference between then and now was thought to be that the standards for arresting a putative suspect, whether rightly or wrongly, were a lot tighter than they were in the past. Some of it was the breakdown in relations between the community and the police. A lot of people in a lot of cities were simply not willing to talk to the police under any circumstances. The clearance rate for murder in New York City, thankfully, had gone in the other direction, thanks to Giuliani and then Bloomberg, and was now above the national average, at almost seventy percent. Still, this was the clearance rate for murders that were reported, where a body was present and accounted for, murders that were known to be murders. Nobody really knew how many murders were never discovered to be murders, were thought instead to be runaways or accidents or death by natural causes.

But sometimes, you got lucky. Sometimes a clue just dropped into their laps. It didn't happen often. Enjoy it when it did.

"Officer Moran and I will be there shortly," Barent said.

"Her name is Stephanie Rogers," Celia Bauman said. "I saw them together about a month ago. It was in Macy's. They were shopping."

"And how do you know this Stephanie Rogers?"

"We were in school together." Celia Bauman compressed her lips into a thin line. She clutched a handkerchief, which she unconsciously twisted back and forth between her fingers.

Barent glanced at Moran. "You don't seem happy," Barent said.

Celia Bauman gave an abrupt nod. "I am not happy. Someone that I knew and worked with has been murdered. Someone else that I know may be responsible. It's…unpleasant."

Murder often was, Barent thought. "I understand…So, you saw the two of them together in Macy's. How did they look?"

She frowned. "What do you mean?"

"Happy? Sad? Together?"

Celia Bauman gave a small, tight smile. "She was clinging to his arm. They were definitely together."

"She was clinging to his arm…and what was he doing?"

Celia Bauman frowned, evidently giving the question careful consideration. "He seemed a little stiff," she finally said. "He was looking away."

Barent pondered this. "What was she like, this Stephanie Rogers?"

"Back in High School? Pretty, blonde." Celia Bauman shrugged.

"Were the two of you friendly?"

"Sort of. We were both cheerleaders."

Celia Bauman looked the part. She had a heart-shaped face with auburn hair, large green eyes and an up-tilted nose.

"Would you say that you knew her pretty well?"

She sniffed. "Well enough."

"What was she like?"

"Self-centered," Celia Bauman said. She stopped and looked down at the floor.

"Go on."

"She didn't spend a lot of time studying, I can tell you that. Her grades were mediocre. I don't think she was stupid. It's just that she didn't care about learning anything. She cared about looking good, ruling the social roost and having the hottest boyfriend."

"Captain of the football team?"

Celia Bauman barely grinned. "As a matter of fact, yeah."

"Homecoming queen?"

Celia Bauman grinned a little wider. "Actually, that would be me. Stephanie never forgave me."

"I'm sure that her disapproval upset you no end."

Celia Bauman shrugged. "I managed to get over it."

"Okay," Barent said. "Have you any idea where Stephanie Rogers lives? Or where she works?"

"Not a clue."

Barent glanced at Moran. "Google will know."

Stephanie Rogers was not hard to find. She lived in a small apartment in Soho and worked at a lady's boutique. According to what was available online, she was thirty-one years old, twice married and twice divorced. No kids.

Barent and Moran knocked on Stephanie Roger's door at seven o'clock at night.

The door didn't open. "Who is it?" a voice said.

"Miss Rogers?" Barent said. "We're the police. We need to talk to you."

There was a momentary silence. "What do you want?"

"Please open the door," Barent said.

"You have some ID? You're not getting in here without some ID."

Barent held his badge up to the peep hole. After a moment, the door opened. Stephanie Rogers peered out at them, her face pale.

"May we come in?" Barent asked.

Wordlessly, she stepped to the side. The apartment was small, Barent noticed. One bedroom, almost shabby. The furniture was clean but not new and there wasn't a lot of it. They trooped inside. Barent sat on a chair. Moran took the couch. Stephanie Rogers hesitated for a moment, then sat on another chair and stared at Moran, who grinned mirthlessly back. "What's this all about?" she said.

"Mitchell Price," Barent said.

She blinked. "Who?"

"Mitchell Price," Barent repeated.

"I don't know anybody by that name."

"No?" Barent frowned and looked at Moran. "We've been told that you knew him very well." Barent barely grinned. "Mitchell Price is dead."

She blinked again and stared at Barent's face.

"His throat was slit," Barent said. "Also, he had been drugged. He didn't struggle at all, because of the drugs. Makes it easier to slit somebody's throat when they don't struggle." Barent smiled.

Her breath came faster.

"Nothing to say?" Barent sighed. "You won't mind if we search this place, will you?"

"No," she said. "Look all you like."

"I can't believe it," Moran said. "She's an idiot."

"Good for us," Barent said. "Bad for her. Not so good for Mitchell Price."

A small bag of white powder had been discovered in a supposedly hidden compartment in a jewelry box in Stephanie Rogers' bedroom. A large, very sharp chef's knife that matched the set in Mitchell Price's apartment sat in a drawer in her kitchen.

Stephanie Rogers was indeed a very good-looking woman, but there were faint lines at the corners of her eyes and she was about ten pounds above her optimal weight. Stephanie Rogers' cheerleading days were far behind her.

She was allowed her one phone call and a lawyer showed up within the hour. His name was James Reilly, a middle-aged, bald guy in a neat blue suit.

"We're not even going to question her until the forensics come back," Barent said. "Until then, there's nothing to say. We're holding her on suspicion of murder in the first degree."

James Reilly nodded, his face impassive. "Let me talk to my client," he said.

They talked in a private room. Reilly departed and Stephanie Rogers went back to her cell. The next afternoon, at 2:00 PM, Barent, Moran, Stephanie Rogers and Reilly sat down for the interview.

"So," Barent said, "what was the nature of your relationship with the deceased."

Stephanie Rogers stared at him. James Reilly frowned.

"Nothing to say?" Barent sadly shook his head. "We have one witness, a woman who's known you since High School, who says that she saw you together with Mitchell Price. You were clinging to his arm." Barent smiled a shark-like smile. "He, apparently, was ignoring you."

Stephanie Rogers continued to stare and continued to say nothing at all.

Barent peered down at a sheet of paper attached to a clipboard. "The white powder is heroin mixed with alpha-methylfentanyl, commonly referred to on the street as 'China White.' The knife that we found in your drawer matches the set of knives from Mitchell Price's kitchen. It's been cleaned but in the spaces between the blade and the handle, traces of Mitchell Price's blood were found." Barent shook his head. "You can hardly ever remove all the blood traces from a knife. This is why people who make a habit of murder and know what they're doing throw away the weapon. Trying to clean it is just asking for a conviction."

Stephanie Rogers was the stubborn sort. She sat there with a mulish expression on her face, arms folded across her chest and glowered at Barent.

Moran gave a small, satisfied smile. Stephanie Rogers' eyes shot to his face, then back to Barent's.

"Mitchell Price had ingested a mixture of heroin plus alpha-methylfentanyl shortly before his death and as I've already said, the knife has his blood on it." Barent leaned forward and pasted a sincere expression on his face. "We don't need your confession to convict you. The physical evidence will be more than enough." Barent glanced at James Reilly. "What do you have to say, councilor?"

James Reilly sighed. "Let me talk to my client." He frowned. "Again."

Wordlessly, Barent and Moran rose to their feet and trooped from the room. Ten minutes later, armed with fresh cups of coffee, they returned. Barent knocked on the door, waited five seconds, then opened it. James Reilly looked grim. Stephanie Rogers had clearly been crying. Barent and Moran sat. "So, let me ask you again: what was the nature of your relationship with Mitchell Price?"

Stephanie Rogers cleared her throat. "I met him at a bar. I was out with some friends." She shrugged. "He seemed nice. We started dating. After a couple of months, we discussed moving in together." Her voice ground to a halt.

Barent waited. After a moment, Stephanie Rogers went on. "I took a look at his cell phone." Her lips thinned, more of a snarl than a smile. "It turned out that I wasn't the only one he was spending time with. Not at all. Mitchell liked to play the field, you see. I might have been okay with that if he hadn't lied to me." She raised an eyebrow and for some reason, looked at Moran. "Hey, I've had a few casual relationships. Go out, have a little fun, enjoy the evening, fuck. No strings." She shrugged. "More than a few, actually. That's okay, so long as the ground rules are made clear. I won't tolerate being lied to. It's…disrespectful."

"I see," Barent said.

Moran leaned forward. "So, when did you decide to kill him?"

"You don't have to answer that," James Reilly said. "I advise that you don't."

Stephanie Rogers shrugged. "Help me out, here," she said to James Reilly.

"Certainly," the lawyer said. He smiled at Barent. "Let's deal."

Stephanie Rogers was returned to her cell. Abby Blake and James Reilly had a nice little chat over a cup of coffee. Barent, Moran, Stephanie Rogers, Abby Blake and James Reilly re-convened an hour later.

"First of all," James Reilly said. "I've asked Ms. Blake to be present so that there will be no misunderstandings, now or later. Ms. Blake, would you please tell my client what we've agreed to?"

Abby Blake smiled. "Certainly. In order to spare the City of New York the time and expense of a trial, and considering that the evidence in this case is iron-clad,"—Abby Blake paused for an instance and looked at James Reilly, who shrugged—"you will plead guilty to the charge of Manslaughter in the First Degree. We've cleared this with the DA. He agrees."

"What does that mean?" Stephanie Rogers asked.

"In New York, Manslaughter in the First Degree means that the guilty party has acted with deliberation but without prior intent. Basically, it was a crime of passion." Reilly puffed his cheeks up and glanced at Abby Blake. "You could almost claim temporary insanity."

Abby Blake grinned. "Temporary insanity is not part of the deal."

Stephanie Rogers looked at James Reilly. "Why not?"

"Because," Abby Blake said, "you waited until he was drugged out of his mind before slitting his throat, thus indicating the ability to both reason and control yourself. Pretty cold-blooded, if you ask me."

Stephanie Rogers sighed. "Go on," she said.

"You will be sentenced to seven years in prison," Abby Blake said.

"I don't want to go to prison." Stephanie Rogers glowered at James Reilly, who shrugged.

"Tough," Abby Blake said.

"You had been betrayed by a cold-hearted man with a history of lying to women," James Reilly said. "If you prefer to take your chances with a jury, I can work with that."

Abby Blake looked at him like she thought he was an idiot. "Good luck," she said.

James Reilly shrugged again. "I recommend that you take the deal. With time off for good behavior, you'll probably be out in less than five years."

Stephanie Rogers stared at him, then she seemed to slump. "Okay, I plead guilty and get seven years in jail. What do you get out of it?"

"That's simple," Barent said. "You tell us everything you know."

Chapter 20

"The problem is," Kurtz said, "that she doesn't know anything."

Lenore paused, a dumpling covered in sesame sauce held in her chopsticks. "Nothing?"

"Nothing useful. Nothing pertaining to any other crime."

"Except illicit possession of narcotics."

"Yeah. Except that."

Lenore nibbled on one end of the dumpling, smiled widely, took another bite and then swallowed. "Spicy," she said.

"The drugs," Kurtz said, "belonged to Mitchell Price. She has no idea where they came from, or so she claims."

"Arnie Figueroa? The Haywards?"

"She knows nothing about anything. Nothing at all."

"Or so she claims."

Kurtz smiled wanly. "Yeah."

Was it all becoming routine? It occurred to Kurtz that he and Lenore spent a lot of time in restaurants. They had their favorite places and they returned to them often. He thought about what Lenore had said to him, the other night, about the most beautiful woman on Earth and the not-so-lucky guy who was tired of sleeping with her. Was he getting tired of sleeping with Lenore? Could it possibly be true? Were they stuck in a rut?

He smiled. Maybe it was true, in a faint, distant sort of way, but it was a hell of a rut. God knows, just looking at Lenore nibbling on a dumpling with those full, plush lips almost made him groan out loud. He toyed with the idea of dumping her across the table, yanking her panties off and fucking her brains out, right here. She would pretend to fight him at first and then, overcome by the passion of the moment, fuck him right back. The other diners would applaud. He would then be invited on all the late-night talk shows and probably be elected mayor.

"Something on your mind?" she asked. Lenore picked up another dumpling.

"Have I ever told you that you're very sexy when you eat a dumpling?"

She grinned. "Not yet."

"Very sexy."

"Enjoy it while they last. The hot and sour soup is next."

Kurtz smiled. "You should slurp it a little. I find that really enticing."

She smiled back. "You do enjoy your food, don't you?"

He nodded. "Harry and Lew have been talking to the guys on the narcotics squad. It seems that there has been a small but significant increase in drug related deaths, all across the city. It's not a lot in absolute numbers, but it's more than it used to be."

Lenore nodded.

"Most of them are low-lives," Kurtz said. "Nobody that anybody is going to miss, except maybe their mothers, and probably their mothers are just as sick of them as anybody else."

"China White? Serial Killer?"

"A little of both, mixed with heroin."

"Where is it coming from?"

"That's the question." Kurtz shrugged. "Probably China."

"And of course," Lenore said, "none of this is any of our business."

"That's for sure."

She gave him a somber smile. "It's good that you know it."

"Oh, yeah. These guys would squish me like a bug."

Inwardly, Kurtz sighed. He wondered sometimes if he had made a mistake, back in the Army, when he had clerked for CID and his superiors had quietly let him know that he could have a career there if he wanted it, but it would have required a long-term commitment to the military. At the time, he had been tempted but he had reluctantly decided that he didn't want to be a cop. He knew where he was going: college, then medical school…and now here he was, a surgeon, respected practitioner of the art and somehow, involved once again in some criminal insanity.

Kurtz had a sense of proportion, a desire that the books balance, that the good be rewarded and the bad be punished. It was like an itch. Injustice had always grated on him.

The first time, with Sharon Lee, had been a fluke. The second time as well, when Rod Mahoney was murdered, but Kurtz had come to realize, almost with dismay, that he had more in common, deep down inside, with Harry Moran and Lew Barent, than he did with his medical colleagues. Cops, the good ones, were all predators, men and women hunting the hunters of other men. They had no illusions. They understood the quirks and foibles of human nature. They knew that nothing stands between civilization and chaos but the willingness of those like themselves to put it all on the line.

"Not the most pleasant dinner conversation we've ever had," Lenore said.

"Sorry."

They ate in silence for a little while. Then Kurtz said, "What can you tell me about Arkady Lukin?"

Lenore sighed. She patted her lips with a napkin. "You think that Steve Ryan was murdered, don't you?"

"*Think* might be too strong a word," Kurtz said. "More of a suspicion."

"And you *suspect* that Arkady Lukin had something to do with it?"

"Either him or his brother."

"Why?"

"Why do I suspect that Arkady Lukin killed him or why do I suspect he was murdered?"

"Either. Both."

"I suspect he was murdered because the alternative seems unlikely. He didn't have enough reason to kill himself. He was planning on changing his practice. It seemed to me that he was looking forward to it. He seemed relieved. I suspect that Arkady Lukin killed him because he wanted Donna Ryan for himself."

"Except that Arkady is gay."

"How well did you really know him, back when you were kids? Maybe he swings both ways. Maybe he's willing to make an exception for Donna, with whom he's been close since childhood."

Lenore frowned, evidently not persuaded. "You don't really know what was going through Steve Ryan's mind. You had one conversation with him on this subject. Didn't Bill Werth say that suicide in such situations is common?"

"He did."

"Well, then."

Kurtz shrugged.

"And as for Arkady, if he was going to kill Steve Ryan, why now? If he was so jealous, why didn't he tell her how he felt? Why didn't he act sooner? Why would he wait until Donna was married, with three kids?"

"No idea."

"This is basically bullshit. It's all theory and speculation. It could have happened, but you have no good reason to think so."

"And I have no good way of proving it." He toyed with his food, then sighed and shook his head. "It's just a feeling."

"Feelings are not admissible in court," Lenore said.

"No," Kurtz said. "I suppose not."

"So, Barent," Joe Danowski said. "Let me tell you what we've got."

Joe Danowski was middle aged and grizzled and wore his suit like he slept in it. He always looked just a bit befuddled, a deliberate act intended to disarm the opposition. He had been a cop for twenty-five years.

"Give me a second," Barent said. He went over to the pot of coffee on the cabinet against the wall, re-filled his cup and glanced back at Danowski. "You?" he asked.

"No, thanks. I'm good."

Barent sat back down. "Okay," he said.

"Most of this is inference, not evidence," Danowski said.

Barent nodded.

"The Russians, all of them, hire either from recent immigrants, from the first generation born here, who also grew up in the neighborhood, or from their own people back home. They all know each other. We have been unable to place anybody inside any of the local organizations. What we've found is that the older and more established an organization is, the more members it has from outside that circumscribed community, which obviously helps us. In the past, we had some luck getting informants on the Italian mafia, the Chinese tongs and the Irish mob, all of which first came to this country in the late 1800's. Plenty of their members were born in the US, went to school here and thought of themselves as primarily American. It took time, but we were able to get eyes inside. We could tell what they were doing, in a general sense, at least.

"The newer organizations are tougher. We've got nobody inside MS-13, for instance." Danowski shrugged. "Maybe the FBI does, but I doubt it. Same with the Colombians and now the Russians."

Barent nodded again. He knew Danowski. Danowski was the methodical sort. He would work up to whatever it was in his own way.

"However," Danowski said, "all of these organizations use local suppliers and they all have local contacts, and those contacts have contacts of their own. It's impossible to keep everything secret. So here is what we're sure of: the stuff is manufactured by any number of companies in China. Peony Flower Trading, in Shanghai seems to be the main source of the alpha-methylfentanil right at the moment. Most of the carfentanil comes from Zhang and Sons, in Chengdu, but it could just as easily have been the other way around."

Barent shrugged.

Danowski nodded. "Yeah. Not that it matters," he said. "The stuff is legal there. Until their own government decides to crack down, there's not a thing we can do to stop it, not at that end.

"From there, it gets a bit hazier. The bottom line is that the stuff arrives in this country as parts of routine shipments, disguised as routine merchandise. It might be inside the tires of a kid's bicycle, or inside a container of laundry detergent, or maybe half a kilo is stuffed inside the head of a Darth Vader doll. Again, no real way to find out and no real way to stop it."

Barent sipped his coffee. Danowski smiled.

"Javier Garcia, or so we are told, is pissed off."

"Not surprising. His guys got whacked."

"Yeah. We've been able to determine that the guys doing the whacking were brought in from out of town. They weren't trying to cover their tracks. Quite the opposite. We have local hotel, car rental and gas station receipts, all with the same phony names on the credit cards. They came in, did the job, and left."

"Surveillance cameras?"

"A couple of shots. They're white. None of the faces are on record." Danowski shrugged. "Probably disguises. Wigs, contact lenses, cheek inserts, nose putty…"

"Where are they supposedly from?"

"Credit card addresses are all from Boise, Idaho. The addresses don't exist. The credit card numbers were never actually issued."

"The whole thing could be a set-up," Barent said. "Maybe they're actually local, pretending to be from out of town."

"We have surveillance from LaGuardia, two of them boarding a plane to Boise, Idaho, waving at the camera. They're cheeky bastards."

"Any surveillance from Boise?"

"It shows them getting off the plane and vanishing into the crowd. By now, they could be anywhere."

Barent considered this. "We were assuming that it was a rival mob."

"A rival mob probably paid for it. That mob is presumably local, but maybe not. If they're local, they didn't do it, themselves."

"In that case, I don't understand the motive. They stirred up some trouble, caused a little mayhem but did nothing that would stop the traffic. So, Javier Garcia is pissed. Was that what they were trying to accomplish? Piss off Javier Garcia?"

Danowski made a faint noise. "Pissing off Javier Garcia is not a good idea. Javier Garcia is no dummy, but it's the law of the jungle out there. If any of his people get the idea that Garcia is weak or otherwise over the hill, then his people will turn on him. His position won't last a week."

"You mean he'll be killed."

Danowski shrugged. "He's going to have to strike back. He has no choice, and he can't wait too long to do it."

The next afternoon, as he was running in the park, a large man, his face covered by a ski mask, stepped out from behind a row of hedges and swung at Kurtz with a baseball bat. Luckily, Kurtz caught a glimpse of him from the corner of his eye and jerked to the side. The bat barely grazed his shoulder. It still hurt, though, and his arm went momentarily numb.

"You piece of shit!" the man screamed. He swung the bat again.

Kurtz leaned back and ducked. The bat passed over his head. Kurtz stepped in, hammered a punch into the man's abdomen. It was a hard abdomen, with a lot of muscle. The man groaned, turned with the punch and snapped a kick at Kurtz' kneecap, which he barely evaded. They circled for a few moments. From the corner of his eye, Kurtz saw a slew of pedestrians watching the fight. Two of these were snapping pictures. At least three others were talking into their phones, hopefully calling the cops.

Kurtz stepped in, feinted left and threw a punch with his right hand. The guy moved his head to the side, slipping the punch, then he turned and ran, waving the bat at the crowd. The crowd parted and then closed in behind him.

Kurtz slumped down, breathing deeply.

"You alright, buddy?" somebody asked.

"Sure," Kurtz said. "Never better."

"The ski mask is certainly suspicious," Barent said.

"No shit," Kurtz said.

Barent's mouth twitched upward. "Unfortunately, none of the pictures are going to do us much good. He was white. We can see that much from his hands. Burly, about six-one, maybe two-twenty. He seems to know how to handle himself in a fight. You were lucky."

Kurtz wasn't feeling lucky. He was feeling pissed off. "Think he'll try again?"

Barent shrugged. He scratched his head. "Since we don't know why he tried in the first place, there is no good way to answer that question." He hesitated. "You were carrying, right?"

"Yes," Kurtz said.

"Why didn't you shoot him?"

"Too many people around. Bullets keep going until they hit something. It wasn't safe."

Barent nodded. "Good. That's the right answer."

"So, now what?"

Barent hesitated. "All I can do is give you the usual advice: stick to crowded areas. Don't go out alone."

"Carry a gun?"

"Yeah. That, too. Don't use it unless you have to."

Arnie Figueroa never had liked doctors' offices. Even as a kid (especially as a kid), waiting for the shot that always seemed to be coming despite everybody's denials, there was something about the cold, white efficiency that just creeped him out. No help for it, though. If he wanted to get back to work, this was what he was required to do.

Even the waiting room gave him the shivers. The rows of cheap seats, the TV set in the corner near the ceiling, the scattered piles of old magazines. He could feel his skin crawl. He tried not to stare at the other patients, all of them cops, none of them looking happy. One had a cast on his leg. One had her arm in a sling. One had bruises on his face. Three others had no discernible injuries but all of them seemed glum.

One in particular caught his attention. Medium height, medium build, short brown hair, hazel eyes, white. There was just something about the guy. So far as he could tell, Arnie Figueroa had never seen him before but he seemed familiar, somehow. Maybe it was the glower. The guy didn't just look unhappy, he looked mad. Also, he had glanced over at Arnie more than once, apparently sizing him up.

"Officer Figueroa?"

He looked up. A pretty, middle-aged nurse clutched a chart and smiled down at him. "The doctor will see you, now."

Arnie Figueroa seemed a bit depressed, Kurtz thought, which was not a surprise, considering everything he had been through. The euphoria of finding himself alive was past. The simple satisfaction of being out of the hospital and home had receded. He had been home for long enough to get bored. Kurtz had seen it many times before.

The exam had gone well. Arnie had made progress, frankly, more progress than Kurtz had ever expected. Too soon to say if and when he might get back to work, but it was looking more likely by the day.

"What's bothering you, Arnie?"

Arnie sighed. "Hard to say, actually. Maybe I'm imagining things."

"Oh?" This too, was not surprising. People who suffered traumatic brain injury often did imagine things: people who were never there, events that had never happened...dreams that seemed real. The opposite happened too, of course. Chunks of memory that vanished into bloody mist as a portion of their brain turned into sludge.

Arnie shrugged. He looked at Kurtz. "So, when can I get back to work?"

Kurtz pondered his patient's eager, beseeching face. "I can't tell you that," he said, "but you're making progress."

Arnie sighed.

"Cheer up," Kurtz said. "You're getting better. The odds are good. Frankly, I didn't think I'd be able to say that."

"Right," Arnie said. He sighed again.

Kurtz grinned. "I'll see you in two weeks."

"Sure."

Chapter 21

"Why are we going to this, again?"

Lenore smiled. "Because Donna is an old friend and we were invited."

Kurtz sighed. He had been trying without success to forget about Russian mobsters and Donna Ryan's Russian family; and yet here they were, on their way to dinner at Donna Ryan's, where they would be mingling with Donna Ryan's family, none of whom he knew except for Arkady and Vasily Lukin…who he didn't like.

Kurtz frowned. Lenore, as she usually did, looked serene.

"I know we were invited, but why did we accept?"

"It seemed the considerate thing to do."

"Oh," Kurtz said. "Yeah."

"Why is this bothering you?" Lenore asked.

Truthfully, Kurtz was not entirely sure. The sky was gray. A thin mist drizzled off the windshield as he drove. The weather, he morosely reflected, reflected his mood. "I don't understand what's going on," Kurtz finally said. "It worries me."

Lenore's family was Jewish. Her mother came from Germany and had lived through the Holocaust. Esther Brinkman's family history was immediate and real to her, less so to Lenore.

Lenore's grandfather on her father's side, also Jewish, had emigrated to America in the late 1800's, from Latvia. Supposedly, according to family legend, the Latvian Jews had originally emigrated to Latvia from the Caucasus, in Russia, but that was long ago and the story may not have been true. With each generation, the history of that side of Lenore's family receded further into time.

They were Americans. They were from Brooklyn and Manhattan and New York. None of them knew about or cared one iota for whatever country their distant ancestors might have come from.

Donna Ryan's family was different. The generation that had escaped the Soviet Union was still alive, the events that had propelled them from the old country still clear in their memories, their psychic wounds still bleeding. Most of them lived in neighborhoods filled with recent immigrants, just like themselves.

They spoke Russian at home and read newspapers that were printed in Brooklyn but written in Cyrillic.

But despite their differences, Donna Ryan and Lenore Brinkman both came from close knit, extended families. Lenore was used to the ways that close knit families behaved. She felt comfortable in such an environment. Kurtz did not. Kurtz felt awkward. Also, if his suspicions were correct, one or more members of this particular close knit family belonged to the Russian mob and had murdered Steve Ryan.

In the end, however, it turned out to be a pleasant enough evening, more a neighborhood party than a family dinner. The front door of Donna Ryan's large house was left open. Nobody rang the bell. People came and went as they pleased. Most of them seemed to know one another. There were hand shakes and hugs and laughter and talk, all of it animated and most of it in Russian.

Father Bob was there, sitting in an arm chair, sipping what looked to be Scotch, pleased with himself. He saw Kurtz and raised an eyebrow, smiled in appreciation at Lenore. "Father Bob," Kurtz said, "my wife, Lenore."

"I've heard about you. I understand that you're an old friend of Donna," Father Bob said.

"We went to school together," Lenore said.

"Then you probably know most of the rest." Father Bob waved the hand holding his Scotch at the crowd. Father Bob, Kurtz noted, was a bit drunk. "A lovely family," Father Bob said.

Lenore frowned. "It's been a long time. I imagine that you know most of them better than I do."

"I suppose I do." Father Bob smiled.

At that moment, a huge man with a thick black beard walked into the room. He had bushy eyebrows, a hawk-like nose, enormous shoulders and a barrel chest. He saw Lenore and blinked. Then he saw Kurtz. His eyes narrowed.

"Uh-oh," Father Bob murmured. "Get ready for the third degree."

The huge man waddled across the room, stopped in front of them, smiled at Lenore and said something in Russian.

"Now, Mr. Petrovich," Lenore said, "you know I don't speak Russian."

The huge man chuckled. "You have grown up," he said. "This should not surprise me, but somehow, it does. I still think of you as the little girl with the..." He blinked. "How do you call them? The pigtails?"

Lenore winced. "I haven't had pigtails since I was fourteen."

The big man made a clucking sound between his teeth. "Too many years," he said. He fixed Kurtz with a beady eye. "And who is this?"

"Richard Kurtz," Lenore said. "My husband."

"Husband?" Mr. Petrovich's eyes opened wide. "A husband? You are much too young to have a husband."

"He likes them young." Lenore glanced at Kurtz, then leaned forward and whispered to Mr. Petrovich. "I think he may be a pedophile."

Mr. Petrovich smiled. Then he gave a booming laugh. He looked at Kurtz. "What do you say to this? Your wife claims that you like little girls."

Kurtz frowned. "I'm going to make her wear pigtails."

Mr. Petrovich snickered. "What happens between a husband and wife is nobody's business but their own. I am certain that this one will keep you on your toes."

Kurtz grunted.

Mr. Petrovich turned toward Father Bob and said something in Russian. Father Bob nodded and answered back in the same language. Mr. Petrovich turned back to Kurtz and Lenore. His eyes grew momentarily cloudy. "My daughter has recently had a very difficult time. She has told her mother and myself that you have stood by her. We are grateful for this. You honor us with your presence. Thank you for coming."

"Thank you for the invitation," Kurtz said.

Mr. Petrovich gave Kurtz a keen glance, reached into a pocket and handed Kurtz a small envelope. "Allow me to extend our hospitality even further," he said. "Please accept this, with my thanks. It's good for any time you wish to use it, but I suggest you come this Friday. We're having a special dinner." He nodded, smiled, patted Lenore on the hand and wandered off.

Kurtz opened the envelope. It contained a small black card with embossed writing in Cyrillic. "What does he do, again?" Kurtz asked.

"He owns a restaurant," Father Bob said. "Classic Russian cooking. The food is terrific. The place is always packed." He peered at the card in Kurtz' hand. "That will give you seats at the chef's table, and the food will be on the house." Father Bob's lips quirked. "You should go."

Kurtz slipped the card into his pocket. "Thanks," he said.

Parties are parties the world over, and this one was probably the same as most others. The fact that he couldn't understand more than one word in ten, however, proved daunting. "Stick with me," Kurtz said. "I'm feeling a little out of place."

Lenore grinned. "Sure."

In a corner of the room, seven chairs were arranged in a circle. A small woman with graying hair and dark blue eyes sat in the center of the circle, discussing something in Russian with three older ladies. She sat very straight. "Donna's mother," Lenore said.

"The one who didn't want the kids to speak Russian?"

"That's the one."

"Let's not disturb them, then," Kurtz said.

They wandered around the room. A side door led to a backyard with a sand box and swing set. A couple of kids threw a baseball back and forth. Three young women pushed younger kids on the swings, speaking to each other in Russian. Two other women watched over toddlers dumping sand on each other. The toddlers and the mothers were all laughing.

"How long are we going to stay here?" Kurtz said.

Lenore frowned. "Where's Donna? We should at least say hello."

They came upon Donna Ryan in a den across from the living room, Arkady Lukin hovering near her shoulder. As Kurtz and Lenore entered the room, Arkady bared his teeth. It might have been a smile. If so, he wasn't putting a lot of effort into it. Kurtz met Arkady's smile with one of his own. Lenore frowned.

Donna was sitting on an uncomfortable looking settee. A cocktail sat on a low, wooden table in front of her. She smiled when she saw

Kurtz and Lenore and rose to her feet. "I didn't think you would come."

"We wanted to say hello," Lenore said, "but we won't be staying for very much longer."

"No?" Donna grinned. "I understand. It's not exactly your crowd. Too much Russian, I suppose?"

"It's nobody's fault," Kurtz said, "but we're feeling a little out of place."

"Most of them do speak English," Donna said, "when they want to."

Kurtz shrugged.

"Well, anyway," Donna said. "You should congratulate us." Donna gave a tremulous smile. "Arkady and I are celebrating."

Arkady, standing next to her and a little behind, looked insufferably smug.

"Celebrating?" Lenore said. She blinked and glanced doubtfully at Arkady's face.

Donna Ryan was only recently a widow. A little soon for a new engagement, Kurtz thought. So much for Arkady Lukin being gay.

Donna looked at Lenore quizzically, then suddenly seemed to get it. She blushed. "Oh, my goodness, not that." She gave Arkady a wry smile. "No, we're celebrating our new business association. Very soon now, Arkady will be working with me, after the merger goes through."

"Merger?" Kurtz said.

"Haven't you heard?" Donna frowned. "But then, why would you? I only heard myself a couple of days ago. Hotchkiss and Phelps will be merging, with the Rugov Corporation."

"I've remembered something," Arnaldo Figueroa said.

Barent looked at him. "Go on."

"You know the three guys I was following? The night I got shot?"

Barent nodded.

"The neighborhood is mixed, mostly Hispanics. Most of those are Mexican."

Arnie's background was Mexican. His job as an undercover cop had centered around infiltrating various gangs but mostly, the smaller gangs primarily composed of recent immigrants from Mexico.

"I first picked up the three guys in a restaurant. They stood out. Big, white guys. They kept to themselves in a booth in the corner. They had a plate of nachos but they weren't really eating it and they didn't order anything else. They seemed to be waiting for somebody. After a half hour or so, another white guy showed up, this one smaller. He came into the place, looked around like he had never been there before, saw the three Russians (if they were Russian), walked over and sat down at their table.

"They talked for awhile. One of the three guys handed the new guy an envelope. He put it his pocket, got up and left. Five minutes later, the three big guys got up, too. I followed them." Arnie shrugged.

"Okay," Barent said.

"I didn't remember this until recently."

Barent glanced at Moran, who had listened without saying a word. "Okay," he said again.

Arnie's mouth twitched upward. "The fourth guy, the one who left?" He drew a deep breath. "I think he's a cop."

Moran winced. Barent stared at Arnie. "Why do you think that?" he finally said.

"I saw him again, in Dr. Kurtz' office. In the waiting room."

"Did you get his name?"

Arnie shook his head. Barent let out a breath. "Shouldn't be too hard to get it." He picked up the phone.

Normally, a physician's fidelity is totally and solely to his patient. All medically related information regarding a patient, up to and including the patient's identity, is to be kept strictly confidential. There are allowable exceptions, including a legitimate investigation by an officer of the law. In this case, however, even this exception was unnecessary. Richard Kurtz was a police surgeon and his treatment of police officers was done under the auspices of the NYPD, which, as an organization, was entitled to all relevant information regarding such officers.

"Albert Morelli," Kurtz said. "I saw him right after I saw Arnie."

"Don't know him," Barent said. Moran shook his head.

"He had a frozen shoulder. It's resolving."

"Is that so? Any reason to suspect that this frozen shoulder was faked?"

Kurtz thought about it. "I suppose it's possible. The diagnosis is made from the symptomatology. Later in the process, the joint capsule fibroses and thickens. Sometimes it can be picked up on x-ray. Early on? There's nothing to see." He grinned. "I sent him to an orthopedist. He got a steroid injection into the joint capsule. That hurts."

"If he was faking it, then he deserved it. If he wasn't faking it, then he needed it. Either way, you did your job."

Kurtz shrugged. "Albert Morelli, or so I've been told, has a reputation as a lazy cop."

"Maybe he's been faking that, too." Barent picked up the phone. "Let's see what Internal Affairs has to say about Albert Morelli."

Jason Blair was about forty, a good-looking guy with short, sandy blonde hair, weathered skin and faint lines around the eyes. He looked like he spent a lot of time in the sun. He wore jeans and a sweatshirt. "Morelli," he said, and shook his head.

"Tell me about Morelli," Barent said.

"About ten years ago, Morelli worked narcotics. The amounts he turned in often seemed just a little bit short."

"Nothing proven?"

Jason Blair shook his head. "No."

"Anything else?"

"A couple of complaints regarding alleged brutality. Nothing came of them." Blair frowned. "The witnesses were considered unreliable."

Barent nodded.

"He did beat up a pimp, once." Blair shrugged. "The pimp had been beating up one of his girls. She wound up with a broken nose and a fractured jaw. Morelli was walking the street and came upon the assault while it was in progress. The pimp tried to complain about it afterward but Morelli's actions were obviously in defense of the hooker, and the pimp did try to resist arrest. Nobody blamed Morelli for that one. Actually, it was the high point of his career."

"Supposedly," Kurtz said, "he's lazy."

"He is lazy, but lazy is not a crime. His evaluations aren't the best. They're not the worst, either."

"That's it?" Moran said.

"He worked vice for nearly three years. A couple of hookers claimed that he was sampling the merchandise." Blair shrugged. "His word against theirs."

In the United States of America, approximately one thousand officers of the law are charged with a crime each year, the most common of which is assault. This is not to say that the cops in these cases are guilty, merely that they have been charged. Driving under the influence was second. Official misconduct and abuse of authority (whatever that meant) was number three. Forcible rape, so far as Kurtz could recall, was number ten on the list. Domestic abuse was in there, somewhere, as well.

Cops are under a lot of pressure. They see a lot of sad, tragic and miserable things. Sometimes they take it out on the people around them.

And sometimes, of course, they're merely crooked, greedy and corrupt, but the thin, blue line did exist, and cops did tend to pull together. Nobody loved a snitch. In the abstract, the job that Internal Affairs did was one that all of them were supposed to applaud. In reality, it took a pretty blatant example of corruption before a crooked cop would be cast out of the club. Every cop was uncomfortably aware that he too, in a moment of weakness, was capable of doing something violent and stupid.

Still, stealing drugs from drug dealers indicated considerably more than a moment of weakness, but even that could be excused, depending on what he was doing with the stuff. Using it himself? To escape from the horrors of the job? Bad, but understandable. A stint in drug rehab, a slap on the wrist and the offending officer would soon be returned to the job, chastened and determined to sin no more. It would be different if the cop was selling the stuff to the local school kids. Maybe. And the rest of it? From a cop's point of view, minor offenses, hardly worth thinking about.

"Not much there," Kurtz said.

"No," Jason Blair said.

"If he's sold out," Moran said, "then he's presumably doing it for money. Where's the money?"

Jason Blair nodded. "I'll see what we can find out."

Chapter 22

"Well?" Javier Garcia said.

Esteban Martinez was unhappy. His efforts to determine the person or persons behind the assassinations of first, Steven Hayward and his wife, then Alejandro Gonzales and Andrew Fox had so far come to very little. "They were from out of town," he said.

"And?"

"They have covered their tracks well."

Javier Garcia looked at him, his face impassive. Esteban Martinez drew a deep breath. "After the latest assault, they split up and vanished."

"The weapons?"

If they were found, the weapons could be linked to the crime. Nobody would be so foolish as to take their weapons with them. "Vanished as well. Presumably shoved down a sewer grate, or a furnace vent, or merely thrown into the East River."

"Nothing?" Javier Garcia blinked at him. "Nothing at all?"

Esteban Martinez gave him a small, uncertain smile. "There is one lead. We are pursuing it. I should know more soon."

Javier Garcia sat back in his chair. "Let me know when you do."

"How is it," Kurtz asked, "that Donna Ryan knew nothing about this merger?"

Lenore frowned. "How should I know?"

Kurtz looked at her. "I was speaking rhetorically."

"Ah…"

It was a Friday night. On most Friday nights, they ate out, but it had been a long, frustrating week and when Lenore had suggested the idea of relaxing at home for a change, Kurtz had quickly agreed. Lenore did not exactly regard herself as a gourmet chef and Kurtz, while he could grill a burger or a steak, also had a limited repertoire in the kitchen. But that was alright, since the local Thai place delivered.

"Another curry puff?" Lenore said.

"Please."

Kurtz had read somewhere that every culture on earth had at least one version of a dumpling. Thai Curry puffs—spiced potatoes and peas covered by a delicate, soft pastry, were among his favorites. Lenore had ordered a lot of them.

He took a bite out of his curry puff, sipped a beer and felt himself slowly unwind. Lenore grinned at him. She had taken a bath before dinner and was wearing a black thong and a red silk robe, loosely tied at the waist. Nothing else. She leaned over to grab some cucumber salad and a beautiful, pink nipple poked enticingly out of her robe. Lenore, obviously, had plans for after dinner. Her breasts bounced, just a little as she moved.

Kurtz quickly swallowed and drank down his beer.

Lenore had ordered plenty of food, more than enough for dinner and then lunch the next day.

"I still don't get it, though," Kurtz said. "Donna is a partner. Don't the partners have to approve a merger?"

Lenore shook her head. "Not all partnerships are equal. Donna is one of the youngest partners in the firm's history, but she's still a junior partner. Typically, the junior partners own a very small share of the corporation. If the buyout was negotiated by senior management, then they presumably had a majority of the shares. They could approve it on their own and keep the whole thing under wraps."

"I took a little stroll through the internet the other day," Kurtz said. "Supposedly, investment banking firms are divided into various divisions."

"The larger ones are. The smaller ones tend to specialize. Hotchkiss and Phelps isn't Goldman-Sachs."

"So, what do they specialize in?"

"I don't know. Would you like me to give Harrison a call? He might know."

The former fiancé… "Uh, no," Kurtz said.

Lenore shrugged. "Probably just the basics. Research, mergers and acquisitions. The smaller ones don't issue bonds, they don't function as market makers and they don't have a brokerage division. Mostly, they arrange for loans between other corporations and make loans of their own."

"And Rugov buys them, other corporations, I mean."

"Supposedly."

"And now, they're *merging* with Hotchkiss and Phelps." Kurtz finished his curry puff, decided against having a fourth and moved on to the Panang shrimp, considered for a moment and spooned a small portion of tamarind duck and yellow rice onto his plate.

"So it seems."

"That term, *merger*, is sort of a euphemism, isn't it? It makes it sound like it's an actual merger, where two companies are joining together to create a new, larger company. What's really happening is that one company *buys* the other, gets rid of the assets that they don't want, fires the corporate officers, fires half the workers and then subsumes its business into itself. At best, the company that's being bought will become some sort of a new division, but maybe not. Maybe it will simply vanish."

"Pretty much."

"So, who is buying whom?"

Lenore shrugged. "I have no idea."

Keep your friends close and your enemies closer. Machiavelli. Sergei Ostrovsky patted his lips with a linen napkin and smiled across the table at Iosif Kozlov. The two ate lunch together every few months. Truthfully, Sergei Ostrovsky was not certain if Kozlov was more of a friend or more of an enemy. In his world, the two were often interchangeable. They were, however, business partners, in a limited sense, at least.

"Rugov has suffered reversals," Sergei Ostrovsky said.

"This I have heard." Iosif Kozlov shrugged.

Sergei Ostrovsky nodded as if the other man had said something very wise. Truthfully, Sergei Ostrovsky could not have cared less if Rugov and his organization were obliterated, except for the concern that whatever obliterated Rugov might next choose to obliterate himself. One had to be wary about such things.

"Javier Garcia is also displeased," Kozlov said.

Sergei Ostrovsky blinked. A small smile hovered over Iosif Kozlov's face as he said this. Kozlov, it seemed, was enjoying Javier Garcia's discomfort. Sergei Ostrovsky wondered why. "So I would imagine," he said, "since it is his employees who were killed and his business that has been disrupted."

"And by whom, I wonder?" The smile on Iosif Kozlov's face suddenly vanished. He looked intently at Sergei Ostrovsky.

Interesting. Sergei Ostrovsky had wondered the same thing. He had almost convinced himself that it must have been Iosif Kozlov. Kozlov apparently had concluded, or at least was wondering, the same regarding Sergei Ostrovsky.

"It wasn't me," Ostrovsky said.

Iosif Kozlov patted his lips with his napkin and shrugged.

Of the three men, Ostrovsky had the smallest organization. His people were well trained, his interests profitable. He had been content to grow steadily but slowly, with minimal risk. The venture that he had entered into with Iosif Kozlov had enriched them both. Kozlov had the connections in Macau and the Phillippines that allowed for the product to be transported easily, with minimal losses to the ever vigilant narcotics agents of numerous governments. Ostrovsky had done business before with both Juan Moreno and Javier Garcia and, if not trusted exactly, was a known quantity to both the Mexican and the Colombian gangs. Garcia had his people on the street, throughout the city and beyond. It seemed a natural association.

Rugov, of course, had his own organization and his own contacts, some of which were the same as those of Ostrovsky and Kozlov. Inwardly, Sergei Ostrovsky sighed. The world was big enough for them all. Truthfully, though they sold similar products, narcotics represented a small percentage of both Alexei Rugov's and his own profits. There was no need to fight over the scraps. So much better to live peacefully and enjoy one's life.

He realized that Javier Garcia might not see things in exactly the same way.

"Javier Garcia," Iosif Kozlov said, "is a dangerous man."

"We are all dangerous men. Javier Garcia did not get to where he is today by being either impetuous or stupid."

"No, but he is going to strike back. He has to. He cannot allow such an affront to pass unanswered."

"Since neither of us would seem to be responsible for his recent misfortune, then neither of us should have anything to fear." Sergei Ostrovsky smiled as he said it. Iosif Kozlov smiled back.

"Dessert?" Sergei Ostrovsky asked.

Iosif Kozlov seemed to consider this. "Please."

The shack was small and rarely used. It did have electricity, however, and running water, though there was no heating system and the water was room temperature only. The shack sat near the side of a dirt road that connected to a larger paved road that led into the very small town of San Sebastien, New Mexico.

The shack served as a way station for drug runners, a fact that was officially unknown to the local police, who had been well paid to stay away.

Rodrigo Diaz stepped warily around a small pool of blood on the floor. It would not do to get blood on his fine, leather shoes, but also, scorpions were common in the desert. No matter how tightly the windows and doorways seemed to be closed, the little monsters did somehow on occasion find their way inside.

"Why do you persist in this foolishness?" Rodrigo Diaz said.

A large, naked white man lay strapped to the one table in the small central room. He looked up at Rodrigo Diaz through dull, swollen eyes. He gave a little cough and spat a glob of blood in Rodrigo's direction. He grimaced through broken teeth.

Rodrigo shook his head. "All we are asking for is a name. One little name. A simple thing. Who hired you?"

The man shook his head.

Truly, Rodrigo Diaz was amazed. Low level cannon fodder was rarely known for its intelligence or its strength of will. A few threats, perhaps a symbolic kick or two in the most sensitive places, and most of them were quite happy to sing whatever tune their captors required. Not this one. They had already progressed far beyond threats. His nose was broken, his front teeth shattered. Still, he refused to speak.

"You know that we have merely begun," Rodrigo said. "What you have already suffered…" Rodrigo shrugged. "It is only the beginning. We all know how this will end. Let us end it now."

"Fuck you," the white man said.

Rodrigo sighed. "Your defiance will make no difference. No difference at all." Rodrigo nodded toward the much larger man standing at the side of the table. "Sebastian is very good at his work. He enjoys it."

The white man's eyes flicked toward Sebastian, who smiled. "Fuck him, too."

"So foolish," Rodrigo said. "So very foolish." He nodded toward Sebastian, who picked up a hammer and carefully shattered the white man's left thumb. The white man screamed. Sebastian brought the hammer down on the index finger, then crushed the rest. By the end, the man was hoarsely whimpering.

"All we want is a name," Rodrigo Diaz said. "Just a name." He smiled. "Then you can rest."

The man was crying but seemed no closer to telling them what they wanted to know.

"There are so many parts to the human body," Rodrigo mused. "So many parts that can be rendered useless, or even removed." Rodrigo paused, gave a slow, sad shake of his head. "We are not used to such defiance. Sebastian, I fear, is growing angry. Your refusal to cooperate is insulting to him. If he starts again, it will not end with your fingers or your toes."

The man drew a deep, sobbing breath and looked at Rodrigo's face. He blinked his eyes. "Ostrovsky," he whispered. "Sergei Ostrovsky."

"There now," Rodrigo said. "Was that so difficult?" He turned toward Sebastian. "You may continue," he said. "When you are satisfied, bury what remains in the desert." He left, carefully closing the door behind him, content with the outcome that had been achieved. His superiors in *La Familia* would be pleased.

"Sergei Ostrovsky," he said to himself, and shrugged.

Chapter 23

Jason Blair gave Kurtz a moody look. "Why is he here?"

Kurtz wondered the same thing. He stood in the corner and smiled at Jason Blair.

"I want him where I can keep an eye on him," Barent said.

Jason Blair shrugged. "We've looked at Albert Morelli as closely as we can without a warrant. He bought himself a boat recently. Boats are expensive. This was a Grady-White Express, thirty-three feet. He got it used for $126,000."

"That's a good price, actually," Moran said.

"Maybe it is, but he's a cop. Most cops don't have 126,000 bucks to throw around."

"Maybe he bought it on credit," Barent said.

"He didn't. He paid cash."

"Okay…" Moran said.

"There's more. A year ago, he bought a condo on Amelia Island. That's in Florida, in case you didn't know, a very upscale community. Nothing ostentatious. A mere three bedrooms on the beach for seven hundred and fifty thousand."

Barent scratched his head. *Nice*, Kurtz thought. Maybe he should buy a condo on the beach.

"Cash?" Moran said.

"He put down half. He's got a mortgage for the rest."

"No chance a favorite aunt died and left him the money?"

"Not so far as we have been able to determine."

"Okay," said Barent, "so now what?"

"What we have been able to find out, simply by accessing public records, combined with Arnie Figueroa's testimony, should enable us to get a warrant. We're going to cover Albert Morelli like a blanket."

"And then we'll see," Moran said.

"Yeah," Blair said. "Then we'll see."

"This makes no sense," Javier Garcia said.

Esteban Martinez puffed up his cheeks. He said nothing.

"Sergei Ostrovsky is our principal supplier. Why then, would he attack us?"

An obvious question, Esteban Martinez thought, without an obvious answer.

"I don't believe it," Javier Garcia said.

"Our source was not lying," Martinez said. "We have this on good authority."

Garcia shrugged. "The source may have been deceived or misinformed. He may not have known who really hired him. He was a foot soldier. Such men go where they are told and do what they are ordered to do."

"You are of course, correct. The question now is: what are *we* going to do?"

"Set up a meeting with Sergei Ostrovsky. We will confront him with the evidence and see what he has to say."

Esteban Martinez spread his hands. "He will deny it, and regardless of the truth, he will manage to sound convincing."

Javier Garcia glowered at Esteban Martinez, who frowned but did not look away. "True," Javier Garcia said reluctantly. It occurred to Javier Garcia that perhaps he was getting a little old for this. It was one thing to strike at one's enemy. It was quite another to play cat and mouse games with a phantom.

"If we strike at Sergei Ostrovsky," Esteban Martinez said, "who benefits?"

Javier Garcia sat back in his chair, frowning.

"The obvious answer," Martinez said, "is Alexei Rugov."

"Should we strike then at Rugov? Without evidence of any involvement? This seems…unwise."

Esteban Martinez said nothing. He waited. Finally, Javier Garcia's eyes snapped to his face. "No," Garcia said. "We will not take this bait. Not quite yet." His lips twitched upward. "Find out more."

"Of course," Esteban Martinez said.

The dead white guy, whose dismembered body now lay under the sands of the Chihuahua desert, had friends, most of whom had vanished into the wind. He also had a former girlfriend, who had not.

Rodrigo Diaz was annoyed. They had already done this. He resented being required to do it again. It was insulting to his own competence. Sebastian, however, was pleased. Sebastian truly loved his work and welcomed any opportunity to demonstrate his expertise.

The former girlfriend's name was Anita Lopez. She worked as a waitress at an all night diner outside of Las Cruces. She had been easy enough to snatch and now here they were, in the same shack with another victim strapped down to the same table. Anita Lopez did not try to resist, not even when they removed her clothing and tied her to the table. She had merely looked at them with wide, pleading eyes. She had sobbed a little when her legs were spread wide and her feet placed in restraints but she did not try to resist. Anita Lopez was far smarter than her former boyfriend.

Sebastian, Rodrigo Diaz could see, was frustrated with this situation. Sebastian much preferred it when they resisted, and this one was younger and more attractive than most, her breasts almost firm, her genitalia displayed like a succulent flower, ready for the plucking. Rodrigo toyed with the idea of letting Sebastian have his way with her, merely to satisfy the desires of a very valuable employee, but no…a certain level of discipline must be maintained. Sebastian needed to understand that the infliction of pain and humiliation had a purpose beyond his own gratification.

"I'll tell you everything!" Anita Lopez had said.

She did, of course, tell them everything. Unfortunately, she knew very little regarding her former boyfriend's work. She did, however, have a few names. "Brett Callender," she had said. "Jesse Montoya." And that was all.

"Please let me go," she had said. "Please!"

Rodrigo Diaz actually considered it. Anita Lopez had offered them no resistance and no offense. Then he sighed to himself and sadly shook his head. One never knew when a victim would be struck with a burst of conscience and a sudden urge to talk. Their task would be much easier if Brett Callender and Jesse Montoya were given no opportunity to flee.

He nodded to Sebastian, who smiled and selected a long thin dagger from his suitcase full of tools. Anita Lopez screamed as Sebastian placed the dagger against the left side of her chest and slipped it between two ribs and into her heart. She struggled for a bit, then her eyes glazed and she fell back, dead.

"Dispose of her," Rodrigo Diaz said, and walked out.

Brett Callender and Jesse Montoya…they should be easy enough to find.

"Albert Morelli is receiving anonymous deposits into his account on the fifteenth of every month," Jason Blair said. "In addition, of course, to any little envelopes he might receive."

"Anonymous," Barent said.

Blair nodded.

"Any way to trace them?" Barent said.

Blair shook his head. "Not a chance."

"How much are these anonymous deposits?"

"They vary. A couple have been for twenty thousand bucks. The smallest amount was twelve."

"Only on the fifteenth?"

"No." Blair grinned. "There have been three others, fairly recently." Blair glanced at Joe Danowski, who was sitting on a rickety looking chair in the corner. "The first was about six months ago, on February Fourth. The second was April Seventeen and the third was July Eleven. Danowski let his breath out in a slow sigh. Blair grinned at him. "Any significance to those particular dates, Joe?"

Danowski looked sick. "We had received information regarding what were supposed to be sizeable shipments of narcotics, two of them from Texas, one from Europe. When we arrived, there was nothing to find. Either our information was wrong or they had been tipped off that we were coming."

"My money," Barent said, "is on tipped off."

"Who was supposed to receive these shipments?" Moran asked.

"Alexei Rugov."

"We have received further information," Esteban Martinez said.

Javier Garcia looked up from his meal and favored Esteban Martinez with a smile.

"We have a description of the man who hired them. This man claimed to be acting on behalf of Sergei Ostrovsky."

"Go on," Javier Garcia said.

"He was white, tall, with broad shoulders. He wore a suit, despite the heat in the New Mexican desert. His hair was brown, his eyes were blue." Esteban Martinez paused.

Javier Garcia, who knew his old friend well, merely waited. Martinez grinned. "He had tattoos on his hands: the head of a snarling tiger on the left, a small eagle on the right. The letters, O-M-Y and T on the fingers of his right hand."

Javier Garcia sat back. "Russians," he said.

"These tattoos are distinctive. This man was undoubtedly Russian."

"And what do these distinctive tattoos signify?"

"The snarling tiger is a symbol for defiance of authority. The eagle is a mark of high rank in a criminal organization. The letters are an acronym. In Russian, they stand for the phrase, "None can escape me.""

"Excellent work," Javier Garcia said. "All that is left is to find out who among our Russian colleagues has such tattoos."

"I'm working on it," Esteban Martinez said.

Javier Garcia smiled. "I'm sure that you are."

"None of this makes any sense," Kurtz declared.

They were eating at Sarge's, one of New York's premier Jewish Delicatessens. Barent felt a particular loyalty to the place, since it was founded in 1964 by a retired police sergeant. Kurtz was always happy to go along. Moran had the day off. He was taking the kids to a Yankees game.

"No?" Barent looked at him, his disapproval plain.

"No. Andrew Fox and the Mexican guy who were murdered were peddling alpha-methyl fentanyl. Steven Hayward, and possibly his wife, were selling carfentanil. Yet both got whacked."

"This is true."

"I can understand one or the other, but why both?"

Moran looked up from his pastrami on rye. "Why not both?"

"Aren't the people selling China White competing with the people selling Serial Killer? Yet they both were murdered. This would imply two different killers."

Barent smiled. "So?"

"It seems unlikely."

Kurtz frowned down at his plate of Maatjes herring. He had never even heard of Maatjes herring before coming to New York. It was not a traditionally Jewish dish, having been invented by the Dutch, but somehow, as with most things herring, it had been happily adopted by New York's Jewish immigrants.

"You really like that stuff?" Barent asked. He peered down at Kurtz' plate and grimaced.

"Yes," Kurtz replied. "I do."

"You know how they make it?"

"Yes, I do, and I prefer not to think about it."

"They let it marinate in its own pancreatic enzymes before they pickle it in wine."

Kurtz winced. "You just had to say that, didn't you?"

"Yes, I did. I make it a point to steer clear of so-called food that marinates in its own pancreatic enzymes. It's a personal rule."

"Let's get back to the murders," Kurtz said. "A much more pleasant topic."

"Okay. Fine." Barent shrugged. "Drug gangs go after the competition all the time. It may have been two different gangs whacking each other."

Kurtz considered this, stolidly chewing on a piece of herring that had been marinated in its own pancreatic enzymes. Jackass. "If that was the case, I would have expected more killing by now. None of these guys are known for their restraint, or so you've always told me."

"Yeah, well, it may have been two different gangs playing tit-for-tat but it's just as likely to be one gang selling two different narcotics that's getting hit by a second gang. The clients don't care, and generally don't even know what particular drug they're putting in their bodies. They're just happy to get high."

"Huh," Kurtz said.

"But why assume a gang war? It could even be some Batman wannabe that's going after the bad guys, trying to keep Gotham safe from the forces of evil."

"That seems even more unlikely," Kurtz said.

"I'm just throwing it out there. It doesn't matter that it's unlikely." Barent shrugged. "One gang, two gangs, some lunatic crackpot…at this point, we just don't know."

"Lucky us," Kurtz said.

"Us?" Barent paused with his sandwich halfway to his mouth. "There is no '*us.*' This is not your investigation and it's none of your business. Remember?"

Kurtz cracked a smile. "How can I forget, when you keep reminding me?"

"Vasily Lukin was born in Russia, but so far as we are aware, he has not been back since coming to this country," Javier Garcia said. "He has most certainly never been incarcerated in a Russian prison. Where would he acquire such tattoos?"

"It seems that the American born members of the organization have adopted this custom," Esteban Martinez said. "There are many tattoo artists in New York City. These are, without doubt, Vasily Lukin's tattoos."

Javier Garcia puffed out his breath. "Alexei Rugov's principal lieutenant. This is disappointing."

"But not surprising. Rugov was not happy that we have ended our association."

Javier Garcia sipped his coffee, put down the cup and sighed. "And so it begins."

Esteban Martinez very diplomatically said nothing. Garcia smiled. "The prospect does not excite you?"

"We are both too old to pretend." Esteban Martinez drew a deep sigh. "No, the prospect of war does not excite me. We have much to lose and nothing at all to gain. At best, the status quo will be maintained. Unfortunately, war with Alexei Rugov has already begun. It began when he chose, for whatever reason, to attack us. Now, we must respond. It is the way of the world."

"Yes," Javier Garcia said. "Yes, it is."

Chapter 24

At the moment, Alexei Rugov had two favorite mistresses, one blonde, whose name was Irina, the other brunette, named Natasha. The two mistresses despised each other but existed in an uneasy and superficially cordial truce.

Alexei Rugov was smart, wily and tough. A survivor. He avoided using his own products. He utilized the equipment in his own private gym on a regular basis. A personal physician visited his compound every three months and conducted a thorough exam. Alexei Rugov expected discipline and efficiency, from his employees and from himself. Discipline and efficiency, however, did not require that he avoid life's simple pleasures.

Rank has its privileges, after all, and Alexei Rugov had worked very hard in order to achieve his current rank.

Czarina, the restaurant of Dimitri Petrovich, served excellent food. Every few months, Dimitri Petrovich offered what he called a "special dinner," a banquet consisting of a dozen small courses, each with its own carefully chosen wine or specialty vodka. The price for these dinners was high but well worth it. Alexei Rugov rarely missed one.

Dimitri Petrovich was well known in the Russian community, a man who had defied the Soviet authorities and escaped the prison that was the Soviet Union, a man who deserved respect. His establishment, as much a club as a restaurant, was considered neutral ground, a place where an enterprising member of the underworld could relax with a favorite mistress or two and be safe from challenge.

The limousine pulled into the spacious parking lot, preceded by one armored car and followed by another. Vasily Lukin emerged from the first car, inspected the lot and finding nothing suspicious, handed the keys to a valet. Three other men emerged and scattered to the corners of the lot, where they would remain throughout the evening. Vasily Lukin walked over to Alexei Rugov's limousine and opened the door. Irina emerged first, followed by Natasha and then Alexei Rugov.

The doors to the restaurant opened. Dimitri Petrovich emerged from the front entrance, smiling widely. He walked to the curb and bowed. "Welcome, welcome," he said. "Always a pleasure to see you again." His eyes flicked to Natasha and Irina, who ignored him.

"Thank you," Alexei Rugov said. "I am looking forward to a delightful evening. Please lead on."

"Impressive place," Kurtz said.

The Chef's Table, it turned out, was not simply a table. Kurtz and Lenore were seated in a smaller room next to the main dining room. The main dining room glittered. The lights were turned down. There were candles and white linen on every table. The seats were solid wood covered in leather.

This room was even more opulent, with crystal chandeliers dangling from the ceiling and oil paintings hanging on the walls. The paintings looked old, scenes of men on horseback, mostly, one of three women and two men sitting in a rose garden. Another depicted a Wedgewood vase in exquisite, shimmering detail, surrounded by a wine glass, an apple and a pear. Another was a portrait of an elderly man with white hair and sideburns wearing an Imperial Russian military uniform.

Two other tables were occupied, both by middle aged couples, the men in business suits, the women wearing dresses. A man, accompanied by two women, both very beautiful, one blonde, one brunette, walked into the room, preceded by Dimitri Petrovich.

These three were shown to a table near Kurtz and Lenore. Dimitri Petrovich gave Kurtz a nod and a smile, then bowed his way out. A waiter dressed in a tuxedo immediately walked up to the newcomers. He handed them all menus and said, "Wine, sir?"

The man scanned the menu. "Cristal will be served with the first course. We'll wait for that." He had an accent, probably Russian, Kurtz thought.

"Very good, sir," the waiter said.

Kurtz and Lenore had already finished with their first two courses: Osetra caviar with ice cold champagne, followed by cured herring with a type of vodka that Kurtz had never heard of. The food and champagne had been excellent. The vodka tasted like any other vodka, but Kurtz imagined that vodka lovers would be impressed.

"This herring is very good," Kurtz said, "but it's not as good as the Maatjes herring at Sarge's deli."

"Maatjes herring?" Lenore wrinkled her nose and delicately shuddered. "You know how that stuff is made? It's marinated in its own pancreatic enzymes."

Kurtz frowned at her. "Yes, I do know that," he said. "Let's not discuss it."

A young man appeared at Kurtz' side. He had coal black hair and brown eyes and looked vaguely Asian. Kurtz remembered what Harry Moran had said about Genghis Khan and the Mongol hordes raping their way across the steppes. The young man placed their third course in front of them, pheasant and wild mushrooms with a dill-cream sauce, wrapped in a blini, then poured the wine that accompanied the dish, a Louis Jadot Puligny-Montrachet.

So far, Kurtz estimated, the accumulated price of the first three courses on a normal restaurant menu would have been over three hundred bucks. Good that he wasn't paying for it.

The Asian looking waiter re-appeared a minute or so later with the first course for the nearby table. He placed the caviar in front of each diner, then displayed the label on the champagne to the male diner, who nodded. The waiter popped the cork and poured a small amount of sparkling wine into a fluted glass. He waited until the man sipped from the glass and indicated approval, then the waiter filled all three glasses. He placed the bottle in an ice bucket near the table and left the room. All three diners drained their glasses.

Approximately thirty seconds later, the male diner stood up. He appeared to be swaying. His eyes stared into space. The blonde said something to him. He ignored her. The brunette frowned. He took a step forward, clutched at the tablecloth, stumbled to his knees and crashed to the ground, knives, forks, plates and glassware clattering to the floor, the tablecloth fluttering around him.

"Oh, *fuck* me!" Kurtz said, and rose to his feet.

Kurtz knew the drill. He had been through it many times before. He pumped on the man's chest. The gorgeous brunette, who seemed to be proficient in CPR, gave mouth-to-mouth. Diners and waitstaff clustered around, murmuring. A tall guy who Kurtz vaguely recognized as Vasily Lukin hovered over them all.

"An ambulance is on its way," Dimitri Petrovich said.

Kurtz nodded, stopped pumping and felt for the carotid pulse. It was weak but palpable. "Stop for a second," Kurtz said. The brunette blinked at him, then stopped. The man's heart continued to beat but he still wasn't breathing. "Go ahead," Kurtz said. The brunette grimaced but did as she was told. Kurtz kept a finger on the pulse. Distant. The man's blood pressure was low but his heart at least was working.

The brunette, in the midst of exhaling through the victim's open mouth, suddenly raised her head. She squinted, blinked once, twice, then slid bonelessly to the floor, not breathing.

Kurtz stared. "Son of a bitch," he muttered.

Just then, the ambulance crew walked into the room. Two paramedics looked down at the scene, bewildered. "What is going on?" the head paramedic asked.

"Do you have intubation equipment?" Kurtz said.

The paramedic's eyes snapped toward Kurtz. "Of course," he said.

"Then intubate them," Kurtz said. "And don't touch them without gloves. They've both been poisoned."

"So, you prick, let's go over this again."

Bad luck that the lead cop was Bert Armstrong. Bert Amstrong did not like him.

"We've gone over it three times already," Kurtz said.

"And we're going to go over it as many times as I say. You understand that?"

"Why don't you go fuck yourself?" Kurtz said equably.

Bert Armstrong's face grew red. Armstrong's partner, a chubby little guy with short, black hair, named Jerry Conlon, looked worried. "Bert," he said.

Armstrong turned toward his partner, his breath coming faster, then he seemed to deflate. His fists clenched. He almost snarled. "Get out of here," he said to Kurtz.

Kurtz smiled. "Aren't you supposed to tell me not to leave town?"

They were sitting in a small private office, presumably belonging to Dimitri Petrovich or one of his staff. Armstrong turned on his heel and stalked out of the room. Jerry Conlon frowned. "He's not a bad cop. He's been under a lot of pressure, lately," he said. "His wife is divorcing him."

Kurtz shrugged. "Your problem. Not mine."

"Yeah." Conlon sighed. "Anyway, thanks for your help. Those two wouldn't have made it without you."

By now, the two patients had been trundled into ambulances and taken to the nearest hospital. Their hearts were beating but they still weren't breathing without assistance. The room had been closed off. The CSI boys and girls, dressed in hazmat suits, were working the scene. The Asian looking waiter, the one who had delivered the champagne to Alexei Rugov's table, had vanished. Kurtz had been stunned to discover the identity of his impromptu patient.

Vasily Lukin and the rest of Alexei Rugov's party had been sequestered in another room, reserved for private functions, no doubt being questioned. Kurtz knew that there was no chance whatsoever of his being allowed inside, and truthfully, all he wanted at this point was to get the hell out of here.

Lenore, along with Dimitri Petrovich, was waiting for him outside the office. "Never a dull moment, huh?" she said.

Kurtz looked at Dimitri Petrovich. "Alexei Rugov?" he said.

"He has been a valued customer for many years." Dimitri Petrovich looked grim. Not surprising. It did bad things to a restaurant's reputation when the customers wound up poisoned. Dimitri Petrovich reluctantly smiled. "I thank you most sincerely. This unfortunate incident could have been much, much worse. Please know that you will always be an honored guest in my establishment."

The place served great food in an opulent setting. Aside from the little unpleasantness they had all just experienced, it had been an excellent meal and would have been an enjoyable evening.

Dimitri nodded toward Lenore. "Mrs. Kurtz feels that you would prefer to go home. I understand completely. I have had the remainder of your meal packed up for you, along with a few additional items that you might enjoy."

At the moment, Kurtz was no longer hungry but this would no doubt change by the end of the evening. "That's great," he said. "Thanks."

Dimitri Petrovich gave a formal bow. "My pleasure."

The next afternoon, Lew Barent walked into Kurtz' office. Mrs. Schapiro, who by now knew Barent well, smiled at him. "He's with a patient," she said. "He should be free shortly."

"So," Barent said a few minutes later. "You just couldn't help yourself."

"I'm not the one who poisoned him," Kurtz said.

Barent cracked a smile. "Bert Armstrong seems unconvinced of that."

"Bert Armstrong is a flaming asshole."

"Yeah, well…" Barent shrugged. "I thought you might like to know the results of the tox screen on Alexei Rugov and the young lady. Her name is Natasha, by the way. Natasha Baranov. Russian. She's one of Alexei Rugov's favorite girlfriends."

"Who was the blonde?"

"Irina Zharkov, also one of Alexei Rugov's favorite girlfriends. Also, Russian."

"It's good to have friends. So, what were the results of the tox screen?"

Barent smiled. "Carfentanil, almost pure."

No surprise there. Kurtz clicked his tongue against his teeth. "What happened to the waiter?"

"Disappeared."

Also, no surprise. "So, who was he?"

"The papers that he filed with the restaurant list his name as Timur Beshimov, from Vladivostok, in Siberia. He came to the States five years ago. He's been working at the restaurant for three months." Barent shrugged. "The bottle of wine wasn't touched. The puddle of wine on the floor had enough carfentanil in it to kill a hundred men. The glasses were shattered and most of the pieces were sitting in the spilled wine, so it wasn't easy to tell, but most of the pieces outside of the puddle were clean. Some weren't."

"And neither Irina nor Natasha were drugged until Natasha gave Rugov mouth-to-mouth."

"Right. So, presumably, only Rugov's glass had the stuff in it."

"What does Irina have to say?"

"Nothing. She didn't see anything. She doesn't know anything." Barent smiled. "She's worried about Rugov. I don't think she likes Natasha."

Kurtz shrugged. "Vasily Lukin? Rugov's men?"

"Pissed off."

"So where is Timur Beshimov, now?"

"No idea."

Kurtz nodded. "Perhaps you should try to find him."

"Thank you, Sherlock," Barent said. "The forces of law and order will do their very best to carry out your suggestions."

Chapter 25

"The plan did not work as expected," Esteban Martinez said.

"No," said Ilya Sokolov. "It is unfortunate. Sergei will not be pleased."

Timur Beshimov, whose name was not actually Timur Beshimov, had been given a new identity and a large sum of money and been re-located to Calgary, far away from the New York authorities.

Timur Beshimov had done as requested. The plan's failure was no fault of his. It was simply bad luck. One did not punish good men for bad luck.

Ilya Sokolov cleared his throat. "So, what now?" he asked.

Esteban Martinez shook his head. "We had hoped that our conflict with Alexei Rugov could be resolved quickly, and with a minimum of bloodshed. Now...?" He held his hands out to the sides and let them fall. "More drastic measures will be required."

"And what of this man Kurtz? The surgeon?"

"A bystander," Esteban Martinez said. "Nothing more."

Ilya Sokolov sat back and considered this statement. "I am not so certain of this," he said. "Our sources within the department of police consider him to be dangerous."

Esteban Martinez shrugged. "Let me discuss the situation with Javier."

"Please do so, and please inform me before you take any action."

"Of course," Esteban Martinez said.

Albert Morelli was lazy but he wasn't stupid. The jig, as they say, was definitely up. Internal Affairs had sniffed around him before but this time...he sighed. Albert Morelli had made a conscious decision, years before, to take advantage of his opportunities. Albert Morelli was not the only dirty cop on the force. Far from it. None of that mattered. He was the one they had caught.

"I have nothing to say," Albert Morelli said.

His union rep, a hard eyed fellow cop named Alice Boyer, plus his lawyer, a thin guy in a dark gray suit, named Eric Cantrell, sat next to him. Across the table sat Jason Blair, two other officers from IA, Ted Weiss and Abby Blake.

Abby Blake's eyes flicked to Ted Weiss, who nodded. Abby Blake gave Eric Cantrell a truly evil little smile, the smile of a woman who knew that she held all of the cards. "So, let me summarize," Abby Blake said. "We have a total of 347,752 dollars deposited into your account over the past four years by a party or parties unknown. You were smart enough to pay taxes on that money. We will acknowledge that it is not illegal to receive funds from an un-named source; however, it is prima facie evidence of, at the least, corruption. This is certainly sufficient evidence for your separation from the force.

"We have also identified an account in the Bank of New York, registered to one Wanda Morelli, your wife, that contains an additional 222,472 dollars. It is unclear how that money was received. Neither you nor your wife have ever paid any taxes on that sum." Abby Blake peered at Eric Cantrell over the top of her glasses. "Tax evasion, as I'm sure you realize, is a felony.

"In addition, we have been recording your most recent phone calls. One call, made two days ago to a number that could not be traced, was rather cryptic, giving only a date three days hence, a specific time and a location at a residence in Brighton Beach. Another, again to a number that could not be traced, also gave a second date and time, and a location in Williamsburg, Brooklyn. Both of these dates and locations correspond to planned raids by the Narcotics Squad." Abby paused and squinted down at her notebook. "You might be interested to know that in both instances, the information that you transmitted was deliberately left for you to find. No actual raids were planned for those dates or at those locations."

Albert Morelli sighed. Alice Boyer, the Union rep, frowned and gave Morelli a disgusted look. Eric Cantrell shook his head.

"Okay," Albert Morelli said, "so what's the deal? Why are we even talking?"

"Cooperation plus evidence of sincere contrition might go a long way toward mitigating your sentence."

Morelli looked at his lawyer, who gave a rueful smile. "Cooperate how?" Cantrell said.

Morelli interrupted. "It doesn't matter how," he said. "If I talk, I'll wind up dead. Forget it."

"Forget it?" Abby Blake said. "You sure about that?"

Morelli shook his head sadly. "Yeah. Forget it."

Abby Blake shrugged. "Oh, well. It never hurts to try. Then I guess we'll see you in court."

"You're rather quiet this evening," Lenore said.

Kurtz blinked at her. "Huh?"

"Never mind," she said. "You're obviously thinking. Keep thinking." Lenore, sitting in an easy chair, went back to her book. She was reading the latest Harry Potter.

Frankly, none of this made any sense. There were too many players doing too many obscure and pointless things. Or so it seemed. Fictional detectives were fond of saying that they did not believe in coincidence, but in real life, coincidence happened all the time. Real life did not follow a convenient story arc. Real life often made no sense.

Still, whether it was fiction or real life, criminal masterminds were rarely in the habit, or so Kurtz imagined, of doing things that made no sense. Somewhere, somebody had an actual motive, a reason for doing whatever it was that they were doing.

Love and money, or so his police friends often said. In the end, those were the only real motives. There was revenge, of course, but revenge was spurred on by hatred and hatred was a perverted form of love. Political crimes? Terrorism? Maybe, Kurtz thought, but terrorism was caused by fidelity to a cause—love, in other words, in this case, love of an idea, love of a vision of what life could and supposedly should be like, if only the golden, glorious new way of organizing society could be made real.

Somehow, Kurtz doubted that Alexei Rugov and whoever had tried to kill him were motivated by such a vision. No, he remembered what Father Bob had said to him. Nobody in Russia had enjoyed living under Communism. Kurtz recalled a line he had once read, supposedly the ruminations of a Soviet worker: "They pretend to pay us and we pretend to work." Life in the Soviet Union had been a charade, a Potemkin village all the way down. It was every man for himself in the good old USSR.

Love or money? Mobsters, obviously, were in it for the money. And if love happened to be your thing, enough money could buy an awful lot of it.

Still, Kurtz thought, you couldn't discount love. It was too soon to discount anything.

A Russian mobster had tried to kill Arnie Figueroa. That was a fact. You had to start with the facts.

Albert Morelli had been in contact with a person or people who he refused to name, was in fact on their payroll. Probably, these were Russians. Arnie Figueroa had seen him with said probable Russians and since then, there had been two distinct attempts on Arnie's life.

Alexei Rugov, a Russian mobster, had been poisoned with carfentanil.

Mitchell Price, a stockbroker, had been drugged with heroin spiked with alpha-methylfentanil and then had his throat slit by his jealous girlfriend.

Steven Hayward and his wife, known drug dealers, had been murdered in a particularly violent and gruesome way.

Alejandro Gonzales, a Mexican drug dealer who had been dealing primarily heroin spiked with carfentanil, and Andrew Fox, a known associate of Steve Hayward, had been killed by professional hit men from out of town, who had also chosen to put bullets into the legs of a group of drug addicted suburbanites, supposedly sending a message to somebody, a message that may or may not have been received, but probably had been.

What else?

Oh, yeah…poor Steve Ryan and his sad, pathetic suicide, who had been married to Donna Ryan, who was employed by a corporation that was about to "merge" with the Rugov Corporation, which was owned by Alexei Rugov, who had been deliberately poisoned with carfentanil.

Then there were Iosif Kozlov and Sergei Ostrovsky…where did they fit in? From the outside, Rugov, Kozlov and Ostrovsky seemed much the same. Same gender, same nationality, similar background, not much to tell them apart. From Kurtz' point of view, which one was one on top and who was doing what to whom was a matter of complete indifference. So long as they stayed far away from Kurtz and the people he cared about, they could prey on each other all they wanted.

All pieces of a puzzle, but too many pieces were missing, and the pieces that they had didn't fit together.

His head was beginning to pound and he had a hernia and a gallbladder scheduled for the morning. He glanced at his watch. "I'm going to bed," he announced.

Lenore put down her book and stretched. "I'll join you," she said.

"Thank god," Kurtz said.

"This is probably bullshit," Barent said.

Kurtz looked at him. "You got anything better to do?"

Barent shrugged. "Not at the moment."

The sky was cloudy but the temperature was warm, steamy even. Summer in the city. It was Kurtz' favorite time of year. A little gust of wind swirled around their feet as they entered the lobby, walked over to the elevator and rose to the twenty-fourth floor.

Kurtz had briefly entertained the notion of coming here by himself, knowing that Barent would most likely think the whole idea absurd, but while Kurtz had very occasionally in the past acted without as much restraint as might be prudent, he was not going to step all over an actual police investigation…not that it was much of an investigation.

Still, having the imprimatur of the NYPD made it all so much more official. Richard Kurtz, MD and amateur detective could be ignored, or even laughed at. The police couldn't.

A secretary greeted them in the lobby, glanced at the appointment calendar on her computer screen, smiled and buzzed them in. "Second office on the left," she said.

The door was already open. A large man with short black hair going gray and sharp blue eyes stood up from behind a glass and metal desk as they walked in. "Officer Barent? Doctor Kurtz? I'm Jeremiah Phelps. Please sit down." They shook hands. Kurtz and Barent sat.

Jeremiah Phelps was the fourth generation of his family to run Hotchkiss and Phelps, his great-grandfather, Jonas Phelps having founded the company along with his best friend from the class of

1937 at Yale, Charles Hotchkiss. Jeremiah Phelps' father, Jeremy Phelps, had bought out the last heir of Charles Hotchkiss back in 1985.

"So, what can I do for you?" Phelps asked.

Barent smiled and glanced at Kurtz, who cleared his throat. No sense in beating around the bush. "Tell us about this merger, with the Rugov Corporation."

Phelps gave an abrupt nod. He sat back in his seat, glanced out the window and sighed. "You see that?" he said.

Kurtz blinked. "Not offhand. No."

Phelps' lips twitched briefly upward. He waved his hand out the window. "New York. Manhattan, the heart of the greatest city in the history of the world."

Tokyo and London and a few others might be able to dispute that claim. "So?" Kurtz asked.

"So, New York is expensive. Everybody wants to live here. Everybody wants to work here." Phelps gave them a tired grin. "*If you can make it here, you can make it anywhere.* Right?"

Kurtz cautiously nodded. Barent merely observed, a faint, interested smile plastered on his face.

"You don't get it?"

"You're implying, if I understand you correctly, that there's a lot of competition in the world of investment banking, and that maybe your finances are not what they used to be?"

Phelps cocked his head, stared out the window and sighed. "Exactly," he said. "There's always been a lot of competition in this business, but the recent economy has been difficult for us to negotiate. The country never really got over the last crash, and after a fairly tepid recovery, the GDP has been trailing off again for the last couple of years. The business environment is slow, not the worst that it's ever been, but slow. On top of that, some of the investments that the company made in the not so distant past have not paid off like we hoped."

Kurtz pondered this. "What investments might that be?"

Phelps rolled his eyes. "Ordinarily, we respect the confidentiality of our clients, but since the companies involved are already bankrupt, there isn't anything left to respect. First, there was a corporation called Underground Projects. They had a proprietary method for repairing underground pipe. Obviously, it's a lot cheaper to repair underground pipes than it is to dig them up and replace them."

"What happened?"

"Their process worked, but it turned out that the repairs broke down after about two years and needed to be done again. It wasn't cost effective. They went bankrupt and we lost our investment."

"Tough one," Kurtz said.

"I'll say." Phelps nodded. "And then there was Triangular Solutions. They had a test kit for diagnosing over fifty different conditions with a small sample of blood. It didn't work. They knew it didn't work, but they played us for fools. We lost a bundle. They've been indicted. Fraud, among other things. And finally, there was Enron."

Kurtz stared at him. Barent winced.

"You invested in Enron?" Kurtz said.

"Enron was named 'The Most Innovative Company in America' six years running by Fortune Magazine. We weren't the only ones who got scammed." Phelps sighed. "Not our finest moment."

"So, you're in trouble," Kurtz said.

"Yes," Phelps said simply, "we're in trouble."

"And where does Rugov fit in?"

Phelps shrugged. "We need money. Rugov has money."

Kurtz glanced at Barent, still listening with the same faint smile hovering over his face.

"Alexei Rugov is a criminal. You must know that."

"The Rugov Corporation may be involved in illegitimate business. I wouldn't know, but it's a legitimate corporation. Sometimes," Phelps said, "you don't have a lot of choices."

Jeremiah Phelps, and his father and his grandfather before him, had been doing this for a very long time. Not very well, apparently.

"What's the deal with you and Rugov? Specifically?"

"Pretty simple. They're buying us out. The terms are good. None of us are going to starve."

"But you'll no longer be associated with the company?"

Phelps grinned. "I will be, actually, in an advisory capacity, for which I will be paid a small, pro-forma salary. Rugov seems to feel that it will be good for the firm's image to keep somebody named Phelps on the payroll."

"You'll be a figurehead."

Phelps shrugged. "Yes."

"How do you feel about that?"

Phelps grinned. "Not as bad as you might think." He spread his hands to the side. "Look, I'm rich, and the buyout will make me richer. I've been thinking of retiring, anyway. Frankly, at this point? I'm tired of beating my head against a wall. I couldn't care less."

"What about the other partners? And the staff?"

Phelps hesitated. "Rugov is a holding company. Their business dovetails very nicely with ours, but there's a lot of redundancy. The employees have been apprised of the situation. About half have been told that their services will be retained, if they want to stay. About half of the remainder have already left. The rest of them are looking."

"And the partners?"

"As I said, bought out. A few have been offered shares in the new corporation, in lieu of money, the ones that Rugov wants to keep around."

Barent cleared his throat. "Which ones are those?"

"Ken Fischel, Dave Mahoney, Beverly Levinson and Donna Ryan. The young, smart ones."

"The ones who had nothing to do with Underground Projects, Triangular Solutions or Enron?" Kurtz said.

"Yeah. All four of them advised against all three investments. Donna in particular, was pretty vehement."

"What do you think of Donna Ryan?"

"Donna." Phelps smiled. "Donna is our star. She's brilliant."

"Lucky that she's staying then."

"Very lucky. We almost lost her, recently." Phelps shook his head, his expression troubled.

Kurtz blinked. "How so?" he said.

"She was negotiating with Halligan and Spence, in Scottsdale. Then her husband committed suicide."

Barent sat up straight in his chair. His look of vague disinterest suddenly vanished. "I don't understand," he said. "What does her husband's suicide have to do with Donna Ryan and Scottsdale?"

Phelps looked bewildered. "Didn't you know? Steve Ryan had accepted a position with a private plastic surgery group in Scottsdale, Arizona. It seems he had been having some problems at his current institution and wanted a clean start. Donna wasn't too thrilled about it but she wasn't willing to break up the family and she liked her husband. A lot of rich tourists in Scottsdale. Go away on what's been billed as a skiing vacation and come back a few weeks later with a new face." Phelps shrugged. "It was a good opportunity."

Kurtz drew a deep breath, his head spinning. Barent gave an almost inaudible chuckle.

Phelps looked back and forth between Barent and Kurtz. "You didn't know that?"

"No," Kurtz said, "we didn't."

"The plot sickens," Kurtz said.

A faint summer drizzle splattered against the windshield as Kurtz drove. The drizzle reflected his mood.

"Not exactly evidence," Barent said.

"A motive, though."

Barent nodded. "A motive isn't evidence. The body's been cremated. We can look at the note again. I doubt we'll find much."

"You've told me in the past that a lot more people than we think get away with murder. Isn't that so?"

Barent frowned at him. "About thirty percent of the murders that we know about are never solved. Then there are the ones that we only suspect, and the ones that we don't know about at all. Somebody dies and it's assumed to be an accident or natural causes." Barent shook his head. "Steve Ryan has just been moved from category three to category two. We have no evidence of anything, and at this point, I don't know how to get any."

"Great," Kurtz said. "That's just fucking great."

Chapter 26

"Ironic, is it not?" Alexei Rugov said.

Alexei Rugov, having been unconscious and on a ventilator for two days, had finally woken up and been released from the hospital, as had Natasha. Natasha, the would-be heroine of the moment, sat at his side. Irina, knowing better than to complain about her temporary reduction in status, sat across the table from them both.

Vasily Lukin appeared worried.

"Nothing to say?" Rugov shrugged. "This man Kurtz saved my life. It would hardly be fair to kill him now."

"Did he save your life? Or did he almost take it?"

A forkful of scrambled eggs paused halfway to Rugov's lips. He blinked. "You are suggesting that this was some sort of elaborate charade?"

"His presence there, a surgeon, a man trained to deal with medical emergencies, is certainly a coincidence, and the attempted murderer has vanished."

"You don't like Richard Kurtz," Rugov stated.

"My personal feelings are irrelevant. He's nosing about in things that are not his business."

"True," Rugov said. He swallowed his eggs and patted his lips with a napkin. "Very true, indeed."

"Make no sudden movements," the voice said.

Really? Did people really say that, outside of the movies or bad TV shows? Unfortunately, despite the absurdist nature of the situation, something hard was poking Kurtz in the center of his back.

Kurtz had already had a long day, having removed two gallbladders and an infected perirectal abscess, and then repaired two hernias. It was evening, the sun just beginning to set on the horizon and Kurtz had been trying hard to unwind, going for a little jog after work. Now this.

"Keep walking," the voice said, "straight ahead."

This was not the first time that Kurtz had been threatened. It wasn't even the first time he had been kidnapped. There were two of them, he could tell that much, the one holding a gun against his back and another one hovering at his side. Both of them were big. "Sure," Kurtz said. "Let's not do anything drastic."

The street was crowded with pedestrians. Random gunfire would not be a good idea.

"Turn left," the voice said.

Kurtz did so. They walked for another block before coming to a parked car, a Honda Odyssey. The door slid open. "Get in," the voice said.

Kurtz hesitated. A drop, a roll and a foot sweep might work. It might also get him killed…but getting into the car seemed like a really bad idea.

"You are thinking," the voice said. "This is not good. You should not think so much. Whatever you are thinking would not go well for you."

Inwardly, Kurtz shrugged. He got in the car. His assailant slid into the back next to him. The second man opened the left front door, sat in the driver's seat, started the engine and took off into the evening traffic.

Carefully, making no sudden movements, Kurtz turned his head. "You," he said.

The smiling face of Ilya Fedorov looked back at him. His brother, Dimitri, was driving.

"So," Kurtz said, "what's this all about?" He felt like an idiot even saying it, the bottom line being completely obvious. He was sitting in a car being driven somewhere he didn't want to go by two guys he didn't want to be with for a purpose that he would without any doubt whatsoever find unpleasant.

"You will see," Ilya Fedorov said.

No shit, Kurtz thought. "Don't want to tell me? Come on, you know you want to tell me. The bad guys always love to brag."

Ilya Fedorov smiled. "In a more perfect world, I might argue with your designation of us as 'bad guys,' but sadly, you are correct. My brother and I are both 'bad guys.' I could say that this outcome was inevitable, considering our upbringing and our circumstances, but who even knows if this is true? Would we be the same men, if our circumstances were different?" He shrugged. "Such might be the case. Or it might not. In the end, the question has no meaning.

207

Whether it is our circumstances, our nature or our destiny, we are what we are, and we will kill you without hesitation if we are required to do so. You should keep this in mind." Dimitri Fedorov said nothing but caught Kurtz' eye in the mirror and gave him a thin smile and a small nod of the head.

A philosophical bad guy, though, and hardly the idiot Kurtz had expected. Kurtz frowned. They hadn't killed him yet, so presumably they wanted something.

The empty black hole in the barrel of Ilya Fedorov's gun stared at him, unwavering. A Sig Sauer P220, 10 mm, not a cheap gun, the sort of gun that a man who cared about his work and took it seriously would carry. The car moved smoothly down the pavement. Inwardly, Kurtz shrugged and settled back into his seat. Sooner or later, he would know.

The trick was living through it.

They drove for almost an hour, crossing over the Manhattan Bridge into Brooklyn, then took Ocean all the way to the Belt Parkway. They turned off onto a small access road that led down to a small private marina on Sheepshead Bay and parked. Ilya Fedorov gave Kurtz a crooked smile and slid out of the car. "Get out," he said.

Ilya Fedorov kept an eye on his business, Kurtz noted. His gun never wavered from the center of Kurtz' chest. Somewhere in the back of his mind, Kurtz noted that the stars were shining brightly overhead, the breeze was warm, and the air held a faint salt tang. Not much else to focus on, aside from the gun.

He got out of the car. They stood across from a boardwalk, on the other side of which floated a small yacht, perhaps fifty feet. "Come," Ilya Fedorov said, and waved the gun barrel toward the boat. "You first."

Kurtz stepped down the ladder onto a teak deck. Ilya followed, then Dimitri, who opened a wood and glass door and stepped into the main cabin. "Inside," Ilya said. Kurtz went through the door, Ilya following close behind.

The cabin held a galley in one corner, with a table and benches set into an alcove nearby. A couch sat against one wall, under a long window, with two easy chairs under the opposite window.

Two women sat in the nook, both thin and average height, with black hair and dark brown eyes. They looked alike, probably related, Kurtz thought. They turned as the men came in. One of them looked at Kurtz and said, "This is him?"

"Yes," Ilya Fedorov said.

The second woman said something in Russian. The first woman answered. Ilya Fedorov frowned. "My mother," he said to Kurtz, "Nika Fedorov, and my Aunt, Olga Lukin," he said.

Lukin…somehow, barely a surprise. Kurtz cautiously nodded. Aunt Olga stared at him. She said something else and Ilya Fedorov answered, then shrugged.

"My aunt is the mother of Vasily and Arkady Lukin," he said. "She speaks little English." Ilya Fedorov gave Kurtz an apologetic smile. "She says that you have been asking too many questions. She wished to see you and to look into your eyes before we kill you."

Kurtz blinked. The boat's engine, he noted, had started up. He could see Dimitri outside on the deck, untying the lines that held the boat to the dock.

"So now she's seen me," Kurtz said. "Does this make her happy?"

Ilya sighed. "Please believe me when I tell you that I hold you no ill will. My aunt takes a simple approach to problems, and she has always been known for the fierceness of her temper."

Aunt Olga, who perhaps understood more English than she had let on, gave Kurtz a thin, cold smile.

"Sit down," Ilya said, and waved his gun toward the couch.

Kurtz sat. Ilya sat opposite him in one of the chairs.

"You should not have visited the offices of Hotchkiss and Phelps," Ilya said. "You should have stayed away from Donna Petrovich."

The gun was still pointed at Kurtz' chest. The gun was a problem. The last time he had been kidnapped and had a gun pointed at his chest, he had been fortunate enough to be wearing a bullet proof vest. Tonight, he was not so lucky. "So," Kurtz said, "if you're going to kill me anyway, you might as well satisfy my curiosity."

Ilya Fedorov glanced at his aunt, who stared back at him and shrugged.

"Tell me if I'm correct," Kurtz said. "I figure that one of you killed Steve Ryan. You waited for a family get-together, then slipped him a little cocktail spiked with Valium. Then somebody wrote a suicide note and forged his signature."

Nika Fedorov looked at her sister and frowned. None of them said a word.

"Why?" Kurtz said.

Ilya shook his head. Nika Fedorov set her lips and crossed her arms over her chest. Olga looked at her sister and rolled her eyes.

"My cousin," Ilya finally said, "Arkady. You know him?"

"Yes," Kurtz said.

"Arkady has always been…different." Ilya grimaced. "He had a difficult time growing up. When he was sixteen, he tried to commit suicide. It would not be too much to say that Donna Petrovich saved him." Ilya shrugged. "My aunt and her husband were perhaps not as sympathetic nor as accepting of Arkady's proclivities as they might have been. Donna was his friend. Donna understood him."

"You didn't want her to leave," Kurtz said.

Ilya nodded. "That is correct."

"You killed Steve Ryan so Donna would stay in New York, because you were afraid that Arkady Lukin would do what? Try to kill himself again?"

Ilya shrugged.

"And now this," Kurtz said. "This is amazingly stupid. You had gotten away with it. The police have their suspicions but they have no evidence. There's no way to prove anything. All you had to do was keep your mouths shut."

Ilya Fedorov sighed. "It is not the police who concern us. There are others who are much quicker to act than the police and who require no more than a suspicion before they do so."

Kurtz pondered this. "Alexei Rugov?"

Ilya Fedorov winced. "Among others."

"Sergei Ostrovsky? Iosif Kozlov?"

Nika Fedorov said something in Russian. Olga Lukin shook her head and scowled.

"I think that we have said quite enough." Ilya shook his head. "These are not names to mention lightly." He rose to his feet. "We have a long way to go before we reach our destination. The trip will take at least two hours. Get up."

Kurtz rose.

"This way," Ilya said. He pointed with the gun barrel toward a door opposite the deck, that opened onto a narrow corridor. They walked down the corridor, with Kurtz in front, and Ilya pushed open a door to a small cabin with a fold out bed, a desk and a chair. Another door led into a tiny bathroom. Ilya Fedorov grinned. "Make yourself comfortable," he said. "The door has been reinforced. You will not be able to open it." The door closed behind him. Kurtz could hear the lock click into place.

He released a breath he hadn't realized he had been holding, smiled, reached down to his ankle, pulled up the cuff of his pants and removed the gun from his ankle holster: a Glock 43, just a bit less than eighteen ounces, 9 mm ammo, seven rounds. Not quite the stopping power of his Sig Sauer but exceptional accuracy, especially considering the short length of the barrel. It felt good to have it in his hand. Comforting. Then he sat down to wait.

The room had one porthole but there was nothing to see except the water and the sky. The stars outside the porthole did not change, so presumably the boat was heading in a straight line. His captors hadn't said where they were going but it wasn't hard to guess: far enough from land so a dead body wouldn't float back to shore. Ilya Fedorov had said 'two hours.' Kurtz was not a boat person. He had no idea how fast these things could travel. Far enough, he figured.

Kurtz flicked off the light, sat on the edge of the bed and waited. For nearly two hours, a very long, tedious two hours, nothing happened. Then, as he had expected, the lock clicked. The door swung open. Ilya Fedorov stood in the doorway, his gun pointed before him. Kurtz could see Ilya, outlined by the lights in the hallway, but Ilya could not see Kurtz.

Kurtz didn't give Ilya a chance for his eyes to adjust. He shot him, once in the head. Twice in the chest. Blood sprayed back onto the wall and Ilya Fedorov dropped, already dead or dying, his gun clattering to the floor.

Kurtz picked up Ilya's gun and ran.

It took no more than three seconds to reach the main cabin. Apparently, Dimitri and the two women had been playing cards. All three sat at the small table. Dimitri was fumbling for a gun as Kurtz burst into the room, the women staring in bewilderment.

"Freeze!" Kurtz said.

Dimitri stared at him, his face white. His hand, seemingly on its own volition, continued to rise. The gun swung upward. Kurtz fired.

Dimitri screamed. The gun flew from his hand and he clutched his shoulder, his right arm hanging limp.

"I would prefer not to shoot you," Kurtz said to the two women, "but I will if you try anything stupid."

They stared at him. Kurtz stared back.

"Now," Kurtz said with a smile. "Where is the radio on this thing?"

The coast guard was used to dealing with emergency calls but a seemingly deranged person calling over a distress frequency claiming to be drifting somewhere in the Atlantic after having been kidnapped was not their usual sort of emergency. Still, they rallied quickly enough. Within an hour, a helicopter flew overhead, its searchlights shining down on the small yacht. An hour later, a 110-foot cutter hove to. Grapples were thrown. Sailors wearing life vests and carrying guns climbed down rope ladders to the deck.

Kurtz was ordered to give up his weapon and they were all taken into custody. Dimitri had lost a lot of blood but he was still, barely, alive. The two women did as they were told but said not a word.

Barent, Harry Moran and Lenore were waiting at the dock when they returned.

"It's always something with you, isn't it?" Barent said. Then he smiled weakly. "Good to see you're alive."

Kurtz hugged Lenore. She gripped him hard and breathed a long sigh.

"Let's get you home," Barent said. "Then you can tell us exactly what happened."

Half an hour later, they were sitting around the kitchen table in Kurtz' apartment. Barent and Moran had cups of coffee and a platter of cookies sitting in front of them. Lenore sipped a glass of white wine. Kurtz, who had missed dinner, had a roast beef sandwich, potato chips and a beer.

He told his story as he ate. All three listened intently, Barent or Moran asking a question now and then.

"Stupid of them not to search you," Moran said when he had finished.

"It's hot out. I wasn't even wearing a jacket. They could see I had nothing above the waist, and I'm a doctor. Why would a doctor be carrying concealed?"

Barent frowned. "Yeah," he said, "why *would* a doctor be carrying concealed?"

"What I don't understand," Lenore said, "is who exactly it is that they're afraid of? Why would Alexei Rugov, Sergei Ostrovsky or Iosif Kozlof care about Steve Ryan?"

"That is a question, isn't it?" said Barent. "Of course, you're the one who mentioned those names, not them."

"One mobster or another," Kurtz said. "Why should we give a damn?"

Moran shrugged. "In the abstract, we don't." He stared into space, as if weighing the odds. "Unfortunately, a backhanded confession is not going to go very far in the courtroom. They'll plead the fifth, or claim that you misunderstood them. You're the one who said that they did it. They didn't deny it but they didn't come out and admit it, either. Any competent attorney will know enough to blow smoke up the jury's ass. We're not going to get a conviction on murdering Steve Ryan, not without at least a little physical evidence."

"Kidnapping is a pretty good crime," Kurtz said. "And how about attempted murder?"

Barent frowned. "They didn't actually attempt to murder you. Presumably, they would have, but they hadn't gotten to that part yet."

"Ilya Fedorov stated that they intended to murder me. His mother wanted to look me in the eyes first."

Lenore grimaced. "Fucking bitch," she muttered.

Barent shrugged. "Your word against theirs. I don't think they're going to admit it."

"Kidnapping, then."

"Yeah," Moran said. "I think it's pretty safe to say that they'll spend a few years in jail for that one."

"Then all's well that ends well," Lenore said.

Barent shook his head. "We know who tried to kill Arnie, in general terms at least, and we know who killed Mitchell Price, and now we know who killed Steve Ryan. The connection between all of these crimes is tenuous, at best. And we still don't know who killed the Haywards."

"Russians," Kurtz said.

"Maybe," Moran said, "but maybe not. So, it hasn't ended," Moran said. "Not yet. Not really."

The next evening, a large young man knocked on Father Robert Kamenov's front door. He was admitted. The two men sat in Father Bob's study and spoke for a long time before the young man left.

Afterward, Father Bob finished his Scotch and rose to his feet. He stared at the phone for a long minute, thinking, then reluctantly shook his head. Some things were better said in person.

It was raining, a constant, steady drizzle. Father Bob sighed, grabbed his umbrella and kissed his wife. "I should be home soon," he said in Russian, and headed out the door.

Chapter 27

The next night was clear and cloudless. The streets were crowded. One by one, twenty five young men wandered into a neighborhood in Williamsburg, Brooklyn. They looked like every other young man intending to spend time in the nearby bars and clubs, neatly dressed in dark pants and black shirts, without visible scars or tattoos. There was nothing about any of them to arouse suspicion.

Fifteen of these young men gathered into five groups of three men each. Each group wandered into a different small building fronting on the street. Two of each three came out less than ten minutes later, each group leaving one man behind. Four of the ten men who emerged had small red stains on their clothing, unobtrusive against the dark material.

The five men who had been left behind ignored the dead bodies that were now piled in the corners of each room. Each man set up a stool by the window, opened a case and removed a Barrett M82 sniper rifle. The rifles were recently purchased and had never before been used. They were semi-automatic, designed for 50 caliber Browning Machine Gun cartridges. Each rifle had a suppressor attached. Each of the five men set up a tripod by the window, carefully aligned his rifle on the tripod, sat down on his stool and waited.

Across the street, five small groups wandered past five townhomes. The homes were constructed of red brick. They were well-kept, with stone walls separating them from the sidewalks, green lawns in front and walled gardens in the back. Each stone wall held an iron gate with a lock attached. Each gate led to a small brick walkway that ended at a flight of steps leading up to the front door. Beneath each flight of steps, an armed guard stood in a small alcove, on the other side of which stood a second door that opened into the basement of each building. The guards stared at every passerby on the street.

Each small group walked briskly along. They were animated, telling jokes in Spanish and English, embellishing their words with smiles, laughter and gestures. The guards noted them but quickly dismissed them.

Across the street, each of the five men sitting at their windows received a text message on his cellphone. Each leaned over his rifle, sited his scope on the chest of each armed guard and waited. Ten seconds later, each cell phone emitted a signal. Each of the five men then fired his weapon. Each of the five guards fell, the back of their chests exploding outward in a red spray.

On the street, each group of men pulled out handguns, shot the locks off each gate and charged inside. Two men crashed through into the basement. Two raced up the front steps, shot through the locked doors and ran inside.

Juan Moreno raised his head from the list of figures sitting on his desk. He was pleased. Business was good. Their profits were increasing, the narcotics supplied to his organization by the Russians, and supplied by his organization in turn to Javier Garcia, were making them all rich. He smiled. Very rich.

What was that? The smile vanished from his face. Juan Moreno did not like to be disturbed by extraneous sounds. The walls in this house were thick, almost soundproof, but the sounds of gunfire, sharp and immediate, from very close by, could not be concealed.

He reached into a drawer, pulled out a gun and rose to his feet, but he was already too late. The office door opened and four men charged inside. Juan Moreno raised the gun but before he could take aim, a hail of bullets took him in the chest. The last words that he heard were, "Javier Garcia and Sergei Ostrovsky send their regards."

Iosif Kozlov was pleased with himself. Iosif Kozlov knew that intricate plans did not always go as planned. Rarely did, in fact, and this plan was more intricate than most. Iosif Kozlov had risen to the rank of Colonel in the GRU. He knew that the love of intricate plans could be a weakness. Take advantage of your opportunities. Keep your objectives always in mind. Move with all deliberate speed, before the enemy has time to respond, or even prepare to respond, and most of all, do not allow yourself to be distracted. Iosif Kozlof smiled. As Napoleon had once said, "If you start to take Vienna, then take Vienna." This, of course, was some years before Napoleon attempted to take Moscow in the middle of the Russian Winter and suffered his worst defeat, losing over half a million of his men. Also, of course, the folly of one's old age did not negate the wisdom of one's youth.

There was a lesson in there, somewhere.

In October, 2002, a group of Chechen terrorists had taken a theater full of people hostage in Moscow. After three days of futile negotiation, the building had been filled with a gas composed primarily of carfentanil and then stormed by a Ministry of Internal Affairs SOBR Unit, accompanied by the Spetsnaz of the FSB. Medical personnel had been alerted and instructed to have narcotic antagonists available. The scope of the operation, however, had not been specified and the narcotic antagonists that had been brought to the scene proved to be entirely inadequate. The operation had been deemed a success, except that a quarter of the hostages, along with all of the terrorists had died. One of those hostages had been Iosif Kozlovs's sister.

Alexei Rugov had been second in command of the Spetsnaz Vega Group that had participated in the assault. It had been Alexei Rugov's responsibility to organize the medical response.

In Iosif Kozlov's opinion, Alexei Rugov had failed in his principal and most important responsibility.

And now, here they were, both leaders of their own organizations within the much larger organization of Russian oligarchs, spies and mobsters, whose tentacles stretched all the way around the world and into the Kremlin itself. Both of them living in the small Russian community known as Little Odessa, in Brighton Beach.

Brighton Beach, in Iosif Kozlov's opinion, was too small a place for both of them. Simply put, Iosif Kozlov had been planning his revenge on Alexei Rugov for a very long time. Alexei Rugov's continued existence offended him.

As for Sergei Ostrovsky, he had grown old and fat and sluggish. Sergei Ostrovsky was weak and easily duped. He could not be discounted, not exactly, but Sergei Ostrovsky could be removed from the board at almost any time. It had pleased Iosif Kozlov to use Ostrovsky as a distraction.

Iosif Kozlov looked up. The two foot soldiers stood at attention in front of his desk. They had patiently waited while he pondered on his strategy. Truthfully, Iosif Kozlov was not displeased with these men. They had proven to be efficient and reliable, despite their youth and their youthful mistakes. Nothing like losing a finger or two to point out the error of one's ways. "You wished to see me?" Iosif Kozlov said.

One of them looked at the other, who nodded. "Yes," the second man said.

Then both men did something unexpected, something that Iosif Kozlov had not foreseen. Each of them pulled a pistol from their holsters and pointed the pistols at Iosif Kozlov. He gaped at them.

The first man shook his head, a sad expression on his face. The second man sighed. "As you have said to us in the past, we must be dedicated, to ourselves and to our cause. We must be obedient to those who have been placed above us and we must be loyal to the organization of which we are a part. We must understand our environment and our world and the sacrifices that success requires. We must know of what we are capable, and we must know our limitations." The second man's lips quirked upward. "You underestimated the enemy and mis-judged your own position. Do you understand? You are not as valuable as you seem to think."

Both men smiled.

Iosif Kozlov's bullet riddled body was wrapped in a tarpaulin and carried down to the water, where it was transported onto a yacht. The yacht sailed to the Southeast for approximately twenty miles. The tarpaulin was wrapped tightly in steel chains and three fifty-pound weights were attached. The body was thrown overboard and quickly sank to the bottom of the sea.

It was announced that Iosif Kozlov had chosen to retire and had returned to his home city of Vladivostok. The operations of the Kozlov Corporation, whatever those operations happened to be, continued unchanged under the direction of Iosif Kozlov's second-in-command, Grigory Mazlov.

Both Alexei Rugov and Sergei Ostrovsky knew enough to know that they would never know exactly what had happened to Iosif Kozlov. They were both thankful that it had not happened to themselves.

A week later, Richard Kurtz called on Father Robert Kamenov. Father Bob smiled when he saw him. "I wasn't expecting you," he said.

"I brought you something," Kurtz said.

Father Bob's eyebrows rose when he saw the label. "Pappy Van Winkle? Where did you get that?"

"My father in law. He knows somebody."

Carefully, Father Bob took the bottle and eased out the cork. He took it over to the sideboard. "Join me?"

"Certainly," Kurtz said.

Father Bob poured a generous three fingers into each glass, hesitated, then added one very small ice cube to each one. "Cheers," he said.

They both sipped. "So," Father Bob said. "What brings you here?"

Kurtz nodded and peered at the light through his Bourbon. It really was excellent stuff, though still not worth the money. He sighed. "Did you ever get the feeling that things were happening all around you? Quiet things, big things, but things that you yourself could never quite figure out?"

Father Bob frowned. "Not exactly. No."

"I've been told that I have an active imagination," Kurtz said.

Father Bob looked at him. "And what is your active imagination imagining?"

"Something you said to me, the last time that I was here." Kurtz took another pensive sip of his Bourbon. "Something about a spider at the center of the web."

Father Bob blinked. "I don't remember saying that."

Somehow, seeing the guarded expression on the other man's face, Kurtz thought that he did. "We were talking about Alexei Rugov, Sergei Ostrovsky and Iosif Kozlov." Kurtz grinned and gave a small, almost silent chuckle. "Who I understand is no longer with us. You still don't remember?"

"No," Father Bob said. "No, I don't."

"It made me wonder," Kurtz said. "You told me that it's difficult to say where the mobsters end and the government begins. The Soviet Union had a lot of spies. Everybody knows that, or at least assumes it. What happened to those spies, when the Soviet Union ceased to exist? Did they lose all contact with the homeland? Were they left adrift? Their assumed lives suddenly the only life that they had left?" Kurtz paused.

Father Bob sipped his drink. "Excellent Bourbon," he said.

"Isn't it?" Kurtz grinned. "So, where was I? Oh, yes. So, we have all of these Soviet spies who are now cut off from their home agencies, because those agencies and the nation of which they were a part have vanished. Except that they didn't vanish, not really. They went dormant for a few years, and then Russia gathered the remnants together and re-constituted them. The KGB split into two branches, the Federal Security Service and the Foreign intelligence Service, the SVR. And what happened then?" Kurtz shrugged. "I have no idea. Maybe the CIA does, but I certainly don't. I wonder, though…the old records were presumably preserved. Somebody in the new agency must know who the spies were, and those spies have presumably been contacted and re-incorporated into the new organization."

"You use that word a lot, *presumed*," Father Bob said.

"Don't I? Like I said, I have an active imagination."

Father Bob leaned forward. "If what you are imagining is true, then talking about it could be dangerous for you. These people, these spies whose existence you presume, they would without doubt be dangerous men." Father Bob grinned. "And women as well. If they exist as you suppose, then they have kept their secrets for a very long time. I imagine that they would not wish those secrets to be exposed."

"No," Kurtz said, "I imagine that they wouldn't, but who are we kidding? If I can think of these things, then the FBI and the CIA and the NSA and God knows who else must also have thought of them a long time ago. I don't think that there is anything I can possibly imagine that the more paranoid factions of the United States government have not thought of first."

Father Bob scratched his head. "I suppose that's true."

"So…" Kurtz rose to his feet. "I have surgery in the morning. I'm not a cop and I'm certainly not a secret agent. I'm going to return to my normal, happy, hum-drum life, and hope that I never get involved with another murder."

"I think you are wise. A happy, peaceful life is something that all of us should wish for," Father Bob said. "Thank you for the Bourbon."

After Kurtz left, Father Bob sipped his drink until it was finished, then he drew a long sigh and picked up a phone. The number that he called was one that he knew by heart.

"Yes?" a voice said.

"You were correct about Dr. Kurtz," Father Bob said. "He is an intelligent and perceptive man."

"What does he know?"

"He knows nothing, but he surmises much."

"And what do you recommend that we do?"

"Nothing. Nothing at all. I am merely informing you. As Dr. Kurtz himself has said, the ravings of an overactive imagination do not present a threat."

Dimitri Petrovich chuckled. "I agree. Dr. Kurtz will live for another day. Who knows? Perhaps one day, he will prove useful."

The End

Information About the Author

I hope you enjoyed *Brighton Beach,* the fifth book in the Kurtz and Barent mystery series, which includes *Surgical Risk*, *The Anatomy Lesson*, *Seizure* and *The Chairmen.*

I graduated from Columbia College with a degree in English before attending Northwestern University Medical School. I've had a long career as an academic physician, which has resulted in over forty scientific publications. I began writing fiction many years ago, and in addition to the Kurtz and Barent mystery series, I am also the author of six science fiction novels to date: *Edward Maret: A Novel of the Future*, *The Cannibal's Feast* and The Chronicles of the Second Interstellar Empire of Mankind, which includes *The Game Players of Meridien*, *The City of Ashes*, *The Empire of Dust,* and *The*

Empire of Ruin. The fifth book in The Chronicles of the Second Interstellar Empire of Mankind, *The Well of Time*, is in progress.

For more information, please visit my website, http://www.robertikatz.com or Facebook page, https://www.facebook.com/Robertikatzofficial/. For continuing updates regarding new releases, author appearances and general information about my books and stories, sign up for my newsletter/email list at http://www.robertikatz.com/join and you will also receive two **free short stories.** The first is a science fiction story, entitled "Adam," about a scientist who uses a tailored retrovirus to implant the Fox P2 gene (sometimes called the language gene) into a cage full of rats and a mouse named Adam, and the unexpected consequences that result. The second is a prequel to the Kurtz and Barent mysteries, entitled "Something in the Blood," featuring Richard Kurtz as a young surgical resident on an elective rotation in the Arkansas mountains, solving a medical mystery that spans two tragic generations.

CPSIA information can be obtained
at www.ICGtesting.com
Printed in the USA
LVHW011344260420
654465LV00003B/576